CU01467079

Holly's Jolly Christmas

STEPHANIE ALVES

Copyright © 2024 by Stephanie Alves
All rights reserved.
No part of this book may be distributed or reproduced by any
means without the prior written consent of the author, with the
exception of quotes for a book review.
This book is a work of fiction. Any names, places, characters,
or incidents are a product of the author's imagination.
Any resemblance to actual persons, events, or locales is
entirely coincidental.

Editing: Cassidy Hudspeth
Cover designer: Stephanie Alves
Character art sketch: Ana P
Dog character: puppapillarart

ISBN: 978-1-917180-12-2

This book contains detailed sexual content, graphic language
and some other heavy topics.
You can see the full list of content warnings on my website
here: stephaniealvesauthor.com

Happy Reading!

Also by Stephanie Alves

Standalone

Love Me or Hate Me

Campus Games Series

Never Have I Ever (Book #1)
Spin The Bottle (Book #2)
Would You Rather (Book #3)
Truth Or Dare (Book #4)
The Final Game (Book 4.5)

For those who love their heroes grumpy with everyone else
but soft and sweet just for them.

Chapter One

— Holly —

Here lies Holly Everly. Age twenty-four. Died of embarrassment.

I can almost picture the words on my gravestone. They'd be hardly visible, seeing as they would be covered by dust and moss from the fact that no one would visit me since I'm going to die all alone.

Some might say I'm being overly dramatic, and others would blame my third drink of the night. I blame the fact that I've been sitting on this hard, wooden stool for over an hour, waiting for a guy I've never met, who still hasn't arrived.

Being stood up is bad enough, but being stood up by a blind date my best friend and her husband set up takes the cherry. There are three people now involved in my failure of a love life, four if you include the asshole who never showed, and somehow it becomes even more pathetic the more I think about it.

Laughter fills the bar when the door opens again, and I glance back for the umpteenth time tonight, locking eyes with a guy who just walked in. Dark brown hair, a seemingly attractive face, looks around my age. Hope builds in my chest as I smile at the man, but when his eyes flick away from me and I see who I assume is his girlfriend walking alongside him with their hands intertwined, I slump in my chair and turn back around to glance down at my glass that's as empty as my hope for this evening.

Fuck it. If I have to be here alone, I might as well get out of my mind wasted and have some fun.

"A refill, please," I say, sliding the empty glass toward the bartender.

"Another?" he asks, his deep, rumbly voice making me lift my head to look at him. It's the first time I'm really looking at him since I was a little preoccupied with my date who didn't show the whole night. My eyes rake over his face, taking in his scruffy beard, dark hair, and sunken eyes that soften as he glances down at my glass on the bar. "You've already had quite a few tonight."

I attempt to shake my head in denial, but in doing so, the whole room spins like a washing machine, and... crap. Did I take my clothes out of the washing machine today? Henry gets kind of annoyed when he has to take my clothes out. Apparently having to touch my thongs traumatizes him or whatever—such a big baby. I don't know what Olivia sees in him. If she wasn't my best friend, I'd—

"Are you okay?" The voice breaks me out of the thoughts rambling away in my head, and I look up to see the bartender's thick brows furrowing at me. "You spaced out for a minute there," he says. "Either that, or you're going to be sick." He shakes his head curtly, just two shakes before his brown eyes glare down at me. "I don't do sick. Not inside my bar."

Jeez. Ray of sunshine right here, I see. "I'm fine," I tell him. "Definitely not sick," I say, sliding my glass closer to him, tilting my head slightly, watching him. "I just need another drink."

"Are you sure that's a good idea?" he asks, eyeing me warily. "You're a tiny little thing, and you've had three drinks in the space of an hour."

I arch my brow at his comment and lift my shoulder in a shrug. "And yet I feel nothing. Are you even putting alcohol in there or skimping me out?"

His eyebrow raises, matching mine. "You might be able to handle more than I thought," he says before grabbing my glass. I keep my eyes on him and watch as he mixes the different alcohols before pouring the pink drink into my glass. I think I only just realized exactly what goes in a Cosmo, and there's a lot more alcohol than I expected it to be.

As soon as he places it down on the bar, I reach for it, bring it to my lips, and take a sip, feeling the sugary drink slip down my throat as the alcohol leaves its burn behind.

When I place my glass back onto the bar, the bartender is still looking at me, and our eyes lock. "Enough alcohol for you?" he asks, his face free from emotion. Does this guy ever smile? I highly doubt it.

"Much better," I say, though I didn't taste a difference between this and the other drinks I gulped down. "This will do the job."

His brows rise an inch. "Are you waiting on somebody or are you here alone?" he asks, his eyes drifting down to my glass again.

Drumming my fingers on the bar, I glance up at him. Do I really want to announce to the hot bartender that I've been stood up?

Wait a second. Did I just call him hot? Maybe I'm drunker than I thought.

"I'm waiting for someone," I admit, crimson painting my cheeks as I gulp down the embarrassment heating my body. "I don't think he's going to show, though."

He presses his lips together, his eyes flicking away from mine when he grabs a rag and begins wiping down the bar. "How long have you been waiting?"

"A little over an hour."

His gaze snaps back to me, and I blink at the expression on his face. It's the most movement I've seen from him yet, and my face screws up. "That's bad, isn't it?" I ask.

There's a chuckle beside me, making me turn my head to see an older guy, looking to be in his forties, shaking his head. "Honey, it ain't good," he says, his voice dripping with amusement.

My shoulders slump even further, and I wish for the ground to open up and swallow me whole. My eyes slide across the bar, seeing some other guys holding a beer in their hand, and their eyes on me.

The bar is pretty empty, with only a couple of people hanging around in the booths, but the stools are full with what I assume are regulars, and they all just heard that I've been stood up.

4

"Shouldn't you be heading home?" the bartender asks him, narrowing his eyes.

The guy beside me scoffs, downing his beer. "I'm under no one's thumb," he replies.

The bartender raises an eyebrow as he crosses his arms. "Are you sure your wife would agree with you?"

He lets out a low laugh and shakes his head. "Alright," he says, finishing off his beer before he places the empty glass on the bar and lifts himself off the stool with a groan. "You play dirty, Mark," he grumbles, pulling out a bill from his coat pocket and tapping on it twice before he leaves.

"Don't listen to him," the bartender—Mark—says, sliding the bill toward him. "He doesn't know what he's talking about."

"It's fine," I say with a low laugh, though my stomach twists into a million little knots. "I mean… he's not wrong."

"You never know," Mark says, swinging the rag over his shoulder. "He might still show up."

I shake my head, wincing when the room starts to spin again. "I doubt that." My face falls, a frown pulling at my lips.

Mark lets out a sigh and grabs another glass. "Where did you meet this guy?" he asks.

"Uh…" I scrunch my nose. "I technically haven't."

He pauses, glancing at me. "Blind date?" he guesses.

I nod, pressing my lips together as I shrug. "I guess. My friend set the whole thing up. He's her husband's friend."

A low noise of agreement leaves his throat, and he turns around, filling the glass. "Is there a reason your friend needs to set you up on a date?"

I chuckle a little, fluttering my eyelashes at him when he turns back around. "Are you flirting with me?"

Mark doesn't laugh, though. His face remains stone cold, a hint of a glare in his eyes as he places a full glass in front of me. "Drink this," he says. "You need it."

I tilt my head at the clear liquid. "What is this?"

"Water," he says dryly.

"Sounds boring."

His glare deepens. Boy, he's grumpy. I pick up the glass and sip on the water, finishing the whole thing in one. My throat was starting to feel pretty dry so it was actually kind of nice, but I screw up my face when I place the glass back on the table. "It was awful," I say. "Completely killed my buzz."

"Not enough it seems," the hot, grumpy bartender replies. "Why the hell did you agree to a blind date in the first place?" he asks. "Those are always awful."

I let out a deep sigh, my eyes dropping to my blue-painted fingernails I spent hours doing for this date. "I guess I have a hard time finding a decent guy who's actually looking for a relationship instead of just hooking up," I admit, looking up at his hard face, unwavering. He's like a robot or a statue. It's kind of scary. I should be scared.

But for some reason, I'm not.

"You're like twenty-five," he grumbles.

"Twenty-four, actually," I cut in.

"Even younger," he replies with a sigh. "You have plenty of time to find someone. This was just one shitty date."

"I guess," I mumble, not wanting to let him know this is the third date I've had this month alone that has gone wrong. This night has been embarrassing enough, and I don't want the hot, robot bartender to know how pathetic I am. "I just thought it would be nice if I had someone to spend the holidays with," I admit.

My brows shoot up when I hear a bunch of groans coming from the other men at this bar that I forgot were here. "Don't get Mark started on the holidays," one of them says while the others laugh and shake their heads.

I blink up at Mark, who's shooting the man a glare. "You don't like the holidays?" I ask slowly, unable to believe that's true.

"What's there to like?" he asks, sliding his gaze to me. "Consumerism? Crying, ungrateful children? Disgusting holiday drinks?"

My mouth drops open as I blink up at him. "Please tell me you don't actually believe that."

He shrugs. "Hate to displease, sweetheart, but it's the truth."

My mouth clamps shut at the sound of the nickname spilling from his lips, but I quickly shake it off when I remember he isn't human. "Maybe you *are* a robot, because what kind of person hates Christmas?"

He blinks. "A robot?"

"How can you not like Christmas?" I ask him, my words stumbling as I try to get them out.

7

"Maybe because I'm not a kid anymore," he says, stepping away from me to grab a glass.

"Neither am I," I reply. "But I still like Christmas."

His eyes fix on me when he swings his head over his shoulder. "Are you sure about that?" he asks. "Are you even old enough to drink?"

"Seeing as it was my twenty-fourth birthday a few weeks ago, yes, I'm sure."

Mark shakes his head and turns around, heading toward the end of the bar. I lift myself out of the stool and follow him. "I bet I could change your mind."

"Christ," he curses, glaring at me. "Quit following me."

I shake my head. "Not until you change your mind," I say, determined to make him admit there's at least *something* he enjoys about the holidays.

"That's never going to happen," he says dryly, walking to the back room. I step around the bar and follow him inside as he turns to glance at me. "Are you seriously going to keep following me?" he asks.

I lift my shoulder in a shrug. "My date didn't show up," I say. "I have nothing better to do."

"I'm starting to see why," he murmurs, lifting a crate of beer.

My brows dip. "I heard that."

I can tell he's trying to get rid of me, and normally, I'd just turn around and leave. But this guy hates Christmas, and that's just… blasphemy. There's no way I can just let this go. "There are so many amazing things around the holidays. The lights, the gifts, the snow—"

"I hate the cold."

8

I press my hand against my forehead and let out a deep breath. "Of course you do," I mumble to myself, starting to lose hope. "There has to be something you like about the holidays."

He places the crate on the ground, underneath the bar, and straightens, lifting his arm to wipe the sweat on his forehead, and holy hell, I only just realized how tall he is. My neck strains to look up at him as he shoots me a dry look. "When they're over."

I shake my head, feeling utterly heartbroken. "You poor little grinch."

He lifts a shoulder. "I actually agree with the guy," he says before glaring down at me. "Now get out from behind the bar."

My jaw drops. "Tell me you're kidding."

"I'm not," he replies. "Only staff can stay behind the bar."

"I mean about the Grinch," I say, screwing my face. "Tell me you're joking and you don't actually agree with him."

"I'm not joking," he confirms. "He knew it was all a sham."

"Oh god," I say, placing the back of my hand against my forehead, feeling lightheaded. "I'm going to need ten more drinks."

Chapter Two

— *Mark* —

This girl is a train wreck.

Beautiful, sure, but a train wreck nonetheless. Not only is she drunker than Old McLanahan when he gets into an argument with his wife, but she's actively trying to convince everyone here to dance with her.

And like a train wreck, I can't look away. I try to ignore the scene going on when I see her dancing with a guy who looks to be in his fifties. Try to clean the bar and do anything but look at her. But I can't. My eyes keep drifting toward her. Don't want it to. But it's impossible.

She looks like Bambi on ice out there, almost taking the poor fucker clung to her arm down when she almost trips. She quickly fixes herself and keeps on dancing like no one's watching. Everyone's watching though. Every eye in here is on her as she lets go and lets the alcohol do its job.

"Time out," he breathes out, clearly winded. "You're going to kill me if you keep that up."

"Oh, c'mon," she slurs, shit-faced drunk. *Jesus.* "One more dance."

The old man drops down into the booth and shakes his head. "I'm out."

I watch as she sighs, and then turns her eyes on the other men in here. They all shake their heads, turning away from her.

She sighs again, defeated and very, very drunk, and I almost feel sorry for her.

Almost.

Until I see her eyes lock on mine and a promising glint sparkles in them.

"Don't even think about it, Bambi," I tell her, narrowing my eyes down at her.

"Please?" She blinks those long eyelashes at me, and I turn around, avoiding eye contact. She probably has some kind of voodoo she does with her eyes that makes every guy do whatever she wants.

Ain't gonna let that happen.

No way in hell.

"Please?" she says again, popping out from behind me.

"What did I say about being back here?"

She just shrugs, smiling again when I meet her eyes. "I'll leave if you dance with me."

"No," I repeat for the umpteenth time.

She blows a raspberry. *Classy.* "You're boring."

"Fine by me," I reply with a grunt, reaching for the empty glasses on the bar.

"It's just one dance. C'mon, you grumpy old man," she says, tugging on my hand.

11

That makes me freeze, and I turn my head, arching a brow at her. "Old?"

"*So* old," she repeats again with a teasing smirk on her face.

I squint down at her tiny frame. "I am not old."

"Yeah?" she asks, turning around with that sweet smile of hers as she pulls me into the middle of the bar. "Prove it."

"I'm not dancing with you," I say as I let her pull me onto the dancefloor. "No fucking way, Bambi." She might have fooled the other guys here with her big brown eyes but it sure as fuck won't work on me. I don't *dance*.

She drops her eyes, frowns, and fuck, it tugs at my heart. *What the hell?*

"I'm working," I say, trying to get out of this ordeal without getting that frown back on her face.

She raises her eyebrow, looks around the bar, and giggles. *Giggles.* The girl fucking giggles. "There's no one here."

I rip my eyes away from her and look around, seeing that she's right. The place has emptied out, with the exception of two guys at the back. They seem busy though. They wouldn't need any drinks. I could just do this one—

No. Fuck. I'm not caving in. I don't care that she looked like an abandoned puppy when I said I wouldn't dance with her. I don't care that she got stood up by some fucking idiot. I don't care about how happy she looks right now.

I'm not fucking doing it.

But when she starts to wave her arms and move her hips, tugging on my hand, I don't push her away. I just let her.

Fuck.

"It's fun, right?" she says with a grin as she dances around me—not well, I might add—and dances to the music playing in the bar.

It's an old song Charles used to play around here, but Bambi doesn't seem to care. She spins in a circle, waving her arms, and bumps into a few glasses on the table, knocking them onto the ground.

"Ah!" she yells, shocked by the noise of glass breaking.

"Jesus," I mutter, pinching the bridge of my nose. Like I said. A train wreck.

She brings her hands up to her face, her eyes wide as she takes a step back. "I'm so sorry."

"It's fine. Why don't you come over here and sit down?" I shouldn't have served her those drinks. I found it a little weird that she was on her own and kept asking for drink after drink. Never seen her around here before, and a girl like her doesn't look like she drinks much. But once I knew about the blind date and saw how upset she was, I should have cut her off.

Now I have a drunk Bambi breaking my dishes on my hands.

The glass crunches under her heels as she steps over it and sits down on the chair I pulled out for her.

13

"Are you hurt?" I ask her, my eyes drifting down to her bare legs in a tiny black skirt she wore for some guy who never even bothered to show up.

She shakes her head, but I see a grin slowly spread across her face. "I knew I could get you to dance with me."

I blow out a breath. "You're a brat."

She shakes her head in an adorable manner I fucking hate. "I'm smart."

I tilt my head at her. "You've done some not-so-smart things today, Bambi."

"Why do you keep calling me Bambi?" she asks with furrowed brows. "My name's Holly."

Holly. *Of course.*

"Had to name you something," I say with a shrug.

Her brows dip. "And you chose Bambi?"

"You looked like Bambi on ice out there, sweetheart." Her forehead creases, looking like she's deep in thought. "Are you okay?" I ask her, wondering if she hurt herself on the glass.

She nods. "Mhmm. Just thinking."

"About?" I ask, lifting off my knee to sit down on the chair beside her.

"How I'm probably going to be alone for the rest of my life." Her face drops and the sight pulls at my chest.

"That won't happen," I assure her.

Her head lifts, and her glassy eyes meet mine. "How do you know?" Her eyes widen, lighting up as she lets out a loud gasp. "Are you my Christmas angel who'll help me find love?"

I lift a brow. "Excuse me?"

"You know." She grins. "Like in Hallmark movies."

"Never watched them."

"Of course you haven't. So, you're not my Christmas angel?"

Don't even know what that means. "Afraid not."

"Then you're my Christmas Grinch," Holly says, smiling up at me. "I'm here to make you believe in the magic of Christmas again."

I shake my head at that. "Don't think you can do that."

"I can," she says with conviction. "I got you to dance, didn't I?"

My jaw clenches. I can't even deny that, because… she did. "You're not going to be alone," I tell her instead.

"You have a lot of faith in me, dear old friend."

"Not your friend," I say with an arched brow. "Or old."

"It's been twenty-four years since I was born, and I've never had a boyfriend," she tells me with a laugh I can tell is strained. "How sad is that?"

"You're still young," I assure her. "You'll find somebody."

She laughs, shaking her head. "This was the third date I've been on this month, and I got stood up," she admits, making me freeze.

Shit.

Her eyes find mine, and vulnerability shines in them. I could be honest and tell her that the odds aren't great.

15

That having three failed dates in less than a month seems bad, but I hate the thought of being the reason for that sad look on her face.

"He's an idiot," I choose to say because it's the fucking truth.

"He is?" she asks, looking up with hope in her eyes.

"Well… based on tonight, maybe he saved himself," I joke. She laughs along, looking up at me, waiting for me to continue. "But yeah, he's an idiot. You're pretty funny, Bambi."

Her eyebrows lift. "I am?"

I narrow my eyes. "Are you going to ask that after everything I say?"

She laughs a little until it settles down, and she looks deep in thought. "How about you?" her small voice asks. "Have you ever had a girlfriend?"

My jaw tightens.

"Oh," she says, widening her eyes. "I'll take that as a yes?"

Don't want to talk about her. "Weren't we talking about your tragic love life?"

She sighs. "Distract me? Please."

"Yes," I tell her. "I've had a girlfriend."

"And?"

"Didn't end well," I confirm with a shrug, not wanting to get into it.

She nods, sympathetically. "Well, at least you've had one. You have me beat."

"You'll get there," I reassure her.

The girl is fucking beautiful. A little crazy, loud, and a handful, sure, but beautiful. There are millions of guys who'd love to be with someone like her.

"You really believe that?" she asks, glancing at me from the side.

"Yeah," I confirm with a nod. "I do."

She furrows her brows and looks up at me. "But you don't even know me."

I press my lips together. That's true. Hardly know the girl. Up until a few minutes ago, I didn't even know her name. But… "Don't need to."

"You're that confident?" she asks, sounding hopeful. Almost like the idea of someone wanting to date her is preposterous.

"Very," I tell her, staring right into those chocolate-brown eyes.

She shifts in her chair, facing me with an excited expression on her face. "Then maybe you can teach me."

My eyebrows raise. Don't like the sound of that. "Teach you?" I ask her, wondering what the hell she means.

"Yes," she confirms, nodding. "You can teach me how to date. I'm hopeless."

My brows lift. "And what makes you think I'm an expert?"

She lifts her painted fingertip and circles it in the air, pointing it at me. "You've been in a relationship before."

I let out a deep sigh. The alcohol definitely hasn't worn off. "Were you not listening when I said it ended badly?"

17

"I don't know anyone else that could help me," she admits with a frown. "My best friend has been married since she was five—"

"A little concerning."

"And whatever it is I'm doing clearly isn't working," she continues, locking her big brown eyes on me. "So…"

Nope. Not a chance in hell. I don't even know what she wants me to do, but the words 'teach me' do not sound good. "Maybe if you didn't ambush people into dancing…" I joke, but she drops her head onto my shoulder. My body tightens and I try to move her. "C'mon. You need to go home."

"Why?" she asks, glancing up at me with droopy eyes, looking like she's less than a minute from falling asleep.

"Because the sun is starting to rise," I say dryly.

She lets out a soft laugh and slaps me on the chest lightly. "You're funny," she says, chuckling.

"You're drunk," I point out, trying to ignore the way I like the sound of her laugh. "Anything is funny to you when you're this inebriated."

She shakes her head, screwing her face up before she opens her eyes. "I'd think you were funny if I was sober too."

My lips twitch. Kinda like that. A sigh leaves my lips, and I hold out my hand. "Give me your phone," I tell her.

Holly's lips curl into a smile. "If you wanted to take me on a date, all you had to do was ask."

I shoot her a glare. "Do you have anyone I can call to come pick you up?"

She shakes her head, lifting her shoulder in a shrug. "I was just going to get a cab," she says, which makes me freeze.

"Yeah, that's definitely not happening." She's drunk as hell and friendly as fuck. There's no way she's getting in some stranger's car this late at night.

"You're so serious," she says, pinching my cheeks. "You should smile more."

I move her freezing-cold hands from my face and place them on her lap. "I'm good."

"Have you *ever* smiled?" she asks, arching her perfectly shaped brow at me.

"Didn't you say you had a best friend? Can she come pick you up?"

"I bet I could make you smile," she continues, clearly ignoring me.

I glance back at the drunk girl in my bar. "What's your friend's name, Bambi?"

"Funnel Cakes."

I blink, trying to figure out if I heard her correctly. "Huh?"

"Funnel Cakes," she says again. "That's her name."

She's fucking with me... right? "Her birth name?"

"Of course not." She blinks. "It's a nickname."

"Ok..." My brows furrow. "Why Funnel Cakes?"

"Well..." Oh boy. Why the hell did I ask? Holly crosses her legs, my eyes drifting to them without thought. I tear my eyes away and look up at her instead.

19

"I met her at a carnival when we were ten, and she was getting a funnel cake, and it just… stuck."

"And how long have you known her?" I ask.

"Fourteen years," she replies, tilting her head. "Why?"

I shake my head. "You never thought to change her contact name after all these years?"

"What?" She lets out a laugh, shaking her head. "No. How would I know it's her?"

Is she… serious? "Maybe by using her name?"

Holly screws her face up. "No, that would just confuse me."

What the fuck am I doing arguing with her. I glance down at her phone and scroll until I see 'Funnel Cakes' and press call.

"Hey, are you on your way back home?" her friend asks when she answers.

"Not Holly," I clarify. "My name is Mark, and Holly here drank a little too much, so I think it's best for someone to come and pick her up."

"Oh my god. Honey, wake up."

I hear a male voice groan. "Huh?"

"Wake up," Funnel Cakes repeats.

"Is the house on fire?"

"No."

"Then let me sleep, woman."

I hear the bed sheets ruffle. "Wake up. We need to go pick up Holly."

"What?" he groans. "What time is it?"

"Two AM," her friend tells him. Fuck. It's two AM already? I look down at Holly, seeing her start to drift off.

"What the hell is she still doing there at two AM?" he asks. "The date was at nine."

"Hate to interrupt," I say, clearing my throat. "But her date never showed up, so she just stayed here and drank, and now, she's halfway to sleep."

"I knew it," her friend says. "I should have known your friend was an asshole."

"He's not an asshole to me."

Funnel Cakes groans. "Why the hell did I marry you?"

"For the money," her husband replies dryly.

Jesus Christ. I think Holly might actually be the normal one between her friends.

"Mark, was it?" Funnel Cakes asks.

"Yep," I affirm, pinching my nose when I see Holly slobbering on the table, fast asleep.

"Okay, great. We'll be there in ten."

She hangs up the phone, and I place Holly's phone on the table, moving her soft brown hair out of her face.

"Holly," I say, softly, hearing her groan as her eyes flicker open. "Wake up. Funnel Cakes is coming."

"The snack?" she asks, delirious.

"The friend," I clarify, this whole thing sounding ridiculous.

"Oh." She lifts her head and looks around at the empty bar. "I'm so sorry I stayed so late. You probably wanted to close earlier than this."

21

"It's fine," I assure her.

Her pink lips lift into a smile as she watches me for a beat. "You're a softie, aren't you?"

"No."

She shakes her head softly, her eyes on mine. "I think you are," she sings, a bright smile on her face.

"It's the lack of sleep," I tell her dryly. "And the alcohol."

Her shoulders relax. "I had fun tonight." She smiles, subtly fixing her hair that's a little crazy since she was falling asleep on a hard wooden table. "Even if I did get stood up."

I narrow my eyes. "I repeat, an idiot."

A light chuckle leaves her lips. "I can't wait for you to be my dating coach."

"I don't even know what that is, and I never agreed to that."

She laughs again, a smirk on her lips. "But you will."

"I won't."

She doesn't reply, just smiles and lifts her shoulder in a shrug.

"We might not see each other again," I tell her, even though the thought of that actually happening brings a strange feeling to my stomach.

"Then give me your number," she demands, handing me her phone.

I blink down at her, her phone heavy in my hand. "You want to see me again?"

She tilts her head. "Of course. How else am I going to get in touch with my dating coach?"

"I'm not…" I drift off, not finishing the sentence. Fuck me, she's going to convince me to be her dating coach, isn't she? "Fuck it," I say, typing out my number in her phone. "Any special nickname you want?"

Her face brightens up with a smile as she mutters, "Grinch."

"Of course," I mutter as I type out the name.

The door opens, and I snap my head up, feeling the cold breeze. "Oh, thank god you're not dead," a woman, who I assume is Funnel Cakes, says, standing at the door. My eyes drift to her very pregnant belly as she walks toward me and Holly. "Thank you for taking care of her," she says. I nod as she lifts Holly out of the chair and interlinks their arms. "Come on," she tells Holly. "Henry's in the car, and he's pissed I woke him up."

"My date sucked," Holly tells her friend.

"I know," she replies, smoothing down her hair. "I already gave Henry an ear full for setting you up with that asshole."

"He didn't even show," Holly continues. "I wore my sexy panties and everything."

"Oh Jesus," I mutter under my breath, pinching my nose.

"His loss," her friend says.

"And then I met Mark," Holly says, turning to look at me behind her shoulder.

"I see that," her friend says, glancing back at me.

"And he was so nice to me," she says, turning away from me.

Her friend, however, keeps her eyes on me as she furrows her brows, and I shake my head. "She's exaggerating."

"He's *soooooo* sweet," Holly says.

Funnel Cakes narrows her eyes. "He doesn't look sweet."

"I'm not," I affirm.

"He is," Holly says, nodding. "He's such a big softie, you wouldn't believe."

Funnel Cakes' eyebrows shoot up, unconvinced, as she turns around, facing Holly. "Is he?"

"No," I interrupt.

Holly nods, clearly not listening to me. "Yep. And he's going to help me get a date."

"Really?" her friend asks, sneaking a glance back at me.

"Again," I say dryly with a shake of my head. "No."

"Mhmm," Holly continues, smiling up at her friend. "I can't wait."

Her friend lets out an unconvinced laugh, and turns her around, heading toward the door. "Okay, let's get you into bed. You can tell me all about it tomorrow."

"Okay," she says. "Bye, Mark!" Holly shouts before she walks outside and the door closes behind her, leaving the place completely empty.

"Bye, Holly."

Chapter Three

— *Holly* —

I wake up in the middle of being attacked.

"Get up," I hear Olivia say as a pillow hits my face.

I shake my head, groaning at her deafening voice. "Let me sleep," I beg, twisting away from her on the bed. "I feel like I'm dying."

"You look like it, too," she says with a snicker. *My best friend, ladies and gentlemen.* "Come on, get up. You desperately need a shower. You stink."

Olivia pulls the sheets off, and I start to plan her murder in my mind. "You're evil," I cry out, feeling the freezing New York air hit my skin. "Why are you waking me up at this ungodly hour?" My eyes blink open, squinting at the light coming in through the window.

"It's two in the afternoon."

"What?" I sit up so fast, the aftermath of last night catches up to me and I groan when my head starts to pound. "Oh, god," I cry out, holding my head in my hands. "I think I'm going to be sick."

"Not on my mattress," my best friend says, her voice rising two hundred octaves.

"I had work today," I groan.

"I know," Olivia says, sitting on the edge of the bed. "I called in sick for you." I groan again, and she shakes her head at me. "How much did you drink last night?"

"Way. Too. Much."

"Yeah." She places the back of her hand on my forehead. "I can see that. Do you even remember anything from last night?"

I squeeze my eyes closed, trying to recall the events of last night. What the hell happened? "I remember... being stood up." I lift my head, frowning at Olivia. "Do you think he came in, saw me, and walked out?"

"What?" My best friend slaps at me.

"Ow. Why are you—"

"Don't be ridiculous. You're gorgeous."

I slap her hand away, narrowing my eyes at her. "I don't see why I'm being assaulted for my beauty, then." I let out a sigh, dropping my head onto her lap. "I was so excited for this date," I tell her. "I even painted my nails."

"I know, darling," she says, petting my hair.

"I would have been a good date," I murmur.

Her hand stops moving on my hair. "That's debatable."

"Hey," I say, lifting my head off her lap to scowl at her.

"You've been on three shitty dates this month alone," she says with an arched brow. "It probably wouldn't have been amazing. And honestly, you suck at small talk."

"God," I groan. "I hate small talk. How do you just talk to someone you don't know?" I ask her. "How did we even become friends?"

"I don't know," she says with a shrug. "I just met you and then you never left."

A grin spreads across my face. "And I never will."

She smiles back and then snaps her fingers. "What about Mark?"

I blink. "Mark?" I repeat the foreign name.

"Yes. Mark." She shakes her head at me. "The bartender? The guy who called me to come pick you up."

"Oh my god," I gasp. "Mark. Of course." How could I forget?

"You seemed to be able to talk to him," my best friend says.

"Yeah," I muse, chuckling as last night's memories come back to me. "He danced with me."

"He did?" she asks, an amused look on her face. "He doesn't look like the type of guy who likes dancing."

I nod, letting out a soft laugh. "He didn't want to," I confirm. "But I made him. Granted, he barely moved, and then I broke one of his glasses."

"Oh boy."

"But you're right. I somehow managed to talk to him." *Huh*. "Maybe it was because there was no pressure," I tell her. "I wasn't on a date with him. He just served me drinks."

"I guess," she replies with a nod. "You're always best when you're you."

My lips curl into a smirk. "Henry," I call out to my best friend's husband. "Your wife is flirting with me."

"We're married," he calls back.

Olivia smiles. "I don't remember that."

"My wallet sure fucking does."

Olivia lets out a snort. "He's so salty about that. Like, come on." She rolls her eyes. "It's been three years."

"It was an expensive wedding, though."

She lifts her shoulder. "He knew what he was getting involved with when he proposed. Besides, it wasn't *that* expensive."

I shoot her a look. "You had five ice sculptures."

She waves me off. "They matched the crystal chandeliers."

A laugh bubbles out of me. My best friend is ridiculous. I love her. "My point, exactly."

"So…" She wiggles her eyebrows. "Mark?"

I tilt my head at her in amusement. "What's with the eyebrow dance?"

"He was hot, right?"

"You're married," I remind her with a laugh. "Your husband is like…" I gesture toward the door. "Right there."

Her eyes roll as she nudges me in the arm. "I meant for you."

"Oh…" I furrow my brows, thinking about it. I did call him hot last night. But was that just the alcohol? "I guess."

Olivia nods, a smirk curling her lips. "He was like a real burly man, you know?"

"I thought so, too," I say with a chuckle. "Until he called me, Bambi."

"He did?" she asks with a laugh. "Like on Ice?"

I nod, feeling my face heat up. "He didn't know my name, and I guess I tripped a few times, and it just… stuck." I shake my head. "Alcohol and balance do not go hand in hand."

"Bambi," Olivia muses, chuckling at the name. "I can totally see that."

"No." My eyes widen. "Oh, god, no. Please don't make that a thing."

"Babe," she calls out to Henry. "We're calling Holly Bambi from now on."

"Okay."

Olivia turns back to face me with a grin.

"I hate you," I tell her.

"I love you, too," she says, blowing me a kiss as she lifts herself off the bed. "Do you want some food?"

"No," I say, shaking my head, disgusted at the idea. I just need to sleep for three business days, and I should be better.

"It'll help your hangover," she says, tilting her head at me. Being a personal chef, she's used to feeding people being her remedy for everything.

I'm willing to try anything to get rid of this feeling. I'm never drinking that much ever again. "What do you have?"

"Food," she says with a shrug.

"Wow." I let out a scoff. "So specific."

"Whatever you want, we probably have it."

I furrow my brows in concentration. "Duck."

My best friend blinks. "Duck?"

"Yes. I want duck," I confirm with a nod.

She pauses, her eyes locked on mine. "But… we don't have duck."

"Ah. Ah." I hold my finger up. "You said you had everything."

"Yes, but—"

"Is duck not a food?"

"It is, but—"

"Then I want duck."

Her mouth gapes open. "But…" She stomps her foot. "We don't have duck."

My head tips back as I let out a laugh. I love fucking with her. "I'm joking," I say between laughs. "I want a cinnamon roll."

She lets out a breath, smiling a little. "That, I can do."

She walks out of the room and I fall back on the bed with a smile on my face. Thoughts of last night come back into my head, and I feel my smile widen when I remember how I ended up having a good time, even if my date didn't show up.

Reaching over to my nightstand, I grab my phone and scroll through my contacts, pausing when I see 'Grinch'. A laugh bubbles out of me, and before I can think about it, I press call and bring my phone to my ear.

The line rings for a few seconds before he picks up. "Uh… hi?"

I smile at the sound of his voice. "Hi, Grinch."

"Bambi."

My smile widens as I settle onto my side. "The one and only."

"Well." He clears his throat. "There's the actual deer, for one."

"Sure. But how many girls do you call Bambi?" I reply.

"Only you."

"Only me," I repeat with a smile.

"I'm actually kind of busy here. Is there a reason you're calling? You get home okay?"

"Yes. Thank you for that." I sit up, swinging my feet over the edge of the bed. "I was actually seeing if you're still up for what we agreed on last night?"

"Uh…" I hear him moving, and I feel a little guilty that I called him while he was at work. "Remind me what that was again?" he asks.

"Being my dating coach."

A heavy breath leaves him. "Okay, well, I definitely didn't agree to that."

"Come on," I plead. "You're good."

"I'm… good?" he repeats.

"Yes," I tell him. "You can like…" I wave my hands in the air. "Talk."

"And what you're doing right now isn't talking?"

I blow out a breath. "You know what I mean."

I hear him grunt on the other end. "Holly, I don't think I'm what you're looking for."

"No." I shake my head. "You're exactly what I'm looking for."

"I…" He pauses, clearing his throat. "I am?"

"Yes," I confirm, rolling onto my stomach. "You were so easy to talk to last night," I tell him. "I had so much fun with you."

"Alcohol will do that for you," he replies.

31

I groan. Convincing him is harder than I thought. "Come on, Grinchy."

"I don't—"

"Do this for me," I ask him again. "Please?"

"I don't think—"

"What do you want in return?" I ambush him before he can reject me. "Do you want me to set you up on a date?"

A breath leaves his lips. "I highly doubt you'd be able to do that, Bambi."

A loud gasp escapes me as I place my hand on my chest. "You're doubting my skills?"

"Since you're asking *me* for dating advice, yes."

"You know…" I swing my legs back and forth. "My friend thinks you're hot."

"Funnel Cakes?" he asks, unconvinced. "Isn't she married… and pregnant?"

"She'd be up for it," I say instead. She won't. She's stinkingly in love with her husband, but he doesn't need to know that.

"Where the hell did you come from?" he says with a voice that sounds almost like amusement. *One step closer to making him smile.* "You're the most fascinating woman I've ever met."

"So you'll do it?" I ask, hope lingering in my chest.

"Jesus fuck."

My eyes widen, a grin forming on my lips. "That's a yes."

"That's not a yes," he replies, and I can almost picture him scowling.

I smirk, because… it's a yes. "You're not saying no," I point out.

Mark doesn't reply, and with every second of silence passing through us, the hope builds.

"It's a yes," I say when he doesn't say anything.

"You're impossible. Fine, yes. I'll be your… whatever the hell it is."

"Dating coach," I finish for him.

"Yeah. That."

I do a little happy dance, pumping my fist in the air. "And you're sure you don't want anything in return?" I ask him.

"I don't think there's much you can give me."

"Well…" I tap my chin. "I could make you a sweater?"

"You knit?"

"No." I frown. "But I could learn."

"I'm good," he replies.

"A hat?"

A light scoff escapes him. "Do you think I need new clothes or something?"

I smirk. "Well…"

"Bye, Holly."

I let out a laugh. "Wait. Where do you want to meet?"

"You can just come over to the bar."

Oh, god no. My face twists, wincing. "If I smell alcohol for the next year, I think it will be too soon."

"Your hangover's that bad, huh?" Mark asks.

"Horrendous," I affirm.

"Okay." He lets out a breath. "Then, just pick a place. Text it to me."

"Do you even know how to text, old man?" I tease.

"Didn't anyone tell you to respect your elders?"

"Ha." I laugh. "You just called yourself old."

"Bye, Bambi."

"Bye, Mark."

I hang up the phone, my eyes drifting to my mirror, where I see the huge smile on my face.

I have a very good feeling about this.

My nose twitches when I smell my favorite smell in the world.

"I smell cinnamon," I call out, jumping out of bed before heading into the kitchen.

Chapter Four

— Mark —

"**W**ho was that?"

I shoot McLanahan a scowl as I hang up the call and stuff it back into my pocket. "No one," I tell the nosy fucker.

"Come on," he groans, tapping on the bar. "Tell us. We're old."

I pause cleaning the bar to arch a brow at him. "And this is going to make you young all of a sudden?"

"Hell yeah," Johnson says, agreeing with the old fart. "We need to live vicariously through you. We're old and married. Our life is over. You're still young."

I almost scoff at the 'our life is over' comment. That's what marriage does to you, I guess. I wouldn't know since I was smart enough not to go through with it. Or dumb enough to get cheated on. Jury's still out on that one.

"I'm thirty-four," I point out, returning to cleaning up the table. While these guys might consider that to be young, seeing as they're well into their fifties, there's a certain someone who would call me old. My mind drifts to her immediately, and I guess I can kind of see why she'd think that. I'm ten years older than her. She wasn't even alive when my favorite movie was in the theatres.

Christ.

"It was the girl from last night, wasn't it?" McLanahan asks with a laugh as he shakes his head. "I swear I called it the moment I saw you talking to her."

I keep my damn mouth shut, not wanting to give him the satisfaction.

"Wait. What girl?" Johnson asks, his curiosity peaking as he glances at me for information. "He met a girl?"

"I didn't," I cut in. No one fucking listens to me, apparently, because McLanahan nods.

"He sure did. Cute young thing. Danced with her and everything."

That gets Johnson going, a smirk spreading across his face as his eyes twist to me. "You *danced* with her?" he asks as if I'm allergic to the word.

"She's twenty-four." I glare at them both. "Have some respect." McLanahan lets out a low laugh, gulping down his beer. "And I didn't *meet* a girl. She was a customer. Came to get a drink. She was drunk, and sad, and…" I breathe out a sigh. I'm never going to live this down. Am I?

"I'm drunk and sad all the time," McLanahan says with an amused look on his face. "I don't see you dancing with me."

I shoot him a glare, pulling his glass away. "I'm cutting you off, old man."

"Fuck no." He grabs the glass, pulling it back toward him. "This is my only happiness right now," he says before letting out an aggravated exhale. "Maurine wants to adopt another cat."

"Lord have fucking mercy," Johnson joins in, shaking his head. "How many do you have now?"

"Five." The poor fucker shakes his head. "I swear I have a furball permanently lodged in my throat."

"Meow for me," Johnson replies.

McLanahan flips him off. "Fuck off."

I shake my head. "You two are like ten-year-olds."

"And you're deflecting," he says, lifting his beer at me.

I glance at the door when it swings open, and shoot him a glare. "I'm working," I say, turning around to grab a clean glass.

McLanahan nods, letting out a low hum. "You know you can work and talk at the same time, Mark. It's the beauty of being human."

I cast a sideways glance at them, a crease forming on my forehead. Fuck it. They'll never shut up otherwise, and it's not like I have anyone else I can tell this shit to. Well, there's always Murray, but all he does is bark, eat and sleep.

I place the empty glass on the table. "She wants me to help her get a date."

McLanahan whistles.

"Oh, boy," Johnson says.

"What?" My face falls into a frown. "You don't think I can do it?" I mean, I didn't think I could do it, but now these guys are *agreeing* with me, and I don't fucking like that at all.

"Your last girlfriend was five years ago," McLanahan points out, stating the fucking obvious.

"And it went horribly wrong," Johnson adds.

"You know damn well that wasn't because of me," I reply, my brows dipping. Everyone here knew what happened with Sasha, and honestly, it was a fucking kick in the nuts to have my life spread out for everyone to see like that.

"True." Johnson taps his glass. "But what the hell do you know about dating?"

"Have you even dated anyone after Sasha?" McLanahan asks.

My teeth grind against each other. The answer to that question is a big *fuck no*. They're right. I know they are. I'm not even close to being the right person for what she's looking for. But Bambi doesn't fucking give up, and it's impossible to say no to her.

"I told her that." I lift my shoulder in a defeated shrug. "She just won't listen."

"Hell." McLanahan laughs. "I'd be better than you. At least I'm married."

"Do you know why she wants you to help her?" Johnson asks.

"She said she can talk to me. Whatever the hell that means." I've only met her once, but I doubt she has a hard time talking. Both times I've talked to her, the girl doesn't seem like she has the capability to shut up.

"Maybe she's lonely," McLanahan points out. "She did get dumped."

"She wasn't dumped. He just didn't show." And it fucked with her head. I could tell when she was downing drink after drink, and spilling her guts about how she was going to end up alone.

I know what it's like, being alone. And while I might prefer having my own space, and living in peace and quiet, that shit gets lonely sometimes. Someone like Holly doesn't deserve to live like that.

"So, what did you say?" he asks.

"I said yes," I admit.

"Really?" Johnson asks with a laugh. "You said yes?"

"It was hard to say no, okay?" Like *really* fucking hard. It was a challenge last night when she asked me with those big, sad eyes, but hearing her the next morning telling me I was exactly what she needed…

She might regret asking me later on, but if she wants my help, then I'll fucking do whatever I need to help her.

"How hard can it be?" I say. "Any guy on the street would fall face first at a chance to be with her." There are worse women out there. That girl can't have this much trouble getting a date. "I doubt it will take me long."

"Good luck," McLanahan says with a laugh.

"With what?"

"If she doesn't end up killing you by the end of this, I'll be surprised," he says, shaking his head.

"She won't kill me," I say dryly. "She's a short little thing."

"With a big personality," the old man points out. "She'll drive you nuts. Trust me on that."

He might be right about that. I'm used to peace, and quiet, and Holly is anything but. "It won't be for long," I assure them. "I'm sure this whole thing will end in a week, tops, and then she'll be out of my life."

"Oh shit," McLanahan says, glancing behind me. "Heads up, bud."

Twisting my neck, I glance up and my stomach churns when I see Mia climbing down the stairs. "Fuck."

I race out from behind the bar, and rush toward her, grabbing onto her frail arm on the railing. "What are you doing here?" I ask her, my heart pounding out of my chest. "I told you if you wanted something, to call me."

"Oh." She pats my cheek. "You worry too much." *For good reason.* "I was looking for Charles." I squeeze my eyes closed. *Shit.* "Do you know where he is? He hasn't been up for his tea yet," she says, looking around the bar.

She was having such a good fucking week, and now we're back to square one. I gulp as I glance back at the guys, whose face has dropped. I fucking hate them seeing her like this. I glance down at her nightgown. "He's…" *Dead.* "He went to get some food," I say instead. "He'll be right back."

"Oh." The wrinkles on her forehead deepen as she frowns. "That's good. I'm starting to get a little peckish."

"I can make you some food." My throat constricts as I try my fucking hardest to let some air into it. "What would you like?"

"I'd love some tomato soup."

"Okay." I nod, forcing my lips to twist into a soft smile. "And a grilled cheese with that, right?"

She smiles. Breaks my fucking heart. "That would be lovely. You know, Charles made me a grilled cheese on our first date."

"Yeah." Can't fucking breathe. I swallow hard. "I know. Why don't I take you back upstairs, and I'll make you some food. Okay?"

Her frail hand reaches up, tapping my cheek. "Such a lovely man," she says. "I wish we had a kid like you."

My fucking throat still won't move as I nod, blinking away the stinging feeling in my nose. They never had a kid of their own. It just wasn't in the cards for them. So they took me in like I was theirs.

"Why don't I take you upstairs, Mrs. Benson?" Johnson asks, lifting off his chair.

I swallow, glancing at him. "Are you sure?"

"Yeah." He shoots me a sympathetic smile. "C'mon," he tells her, wrapping her arm around his while he helps her climb the stairs.

"She isn't doing better?" McLanahan asks.

I shake my head. "Some days are better than others, but..." Eventually, they're all shit.

"You ever thought of putting her up somewhere?"

"Fuck no." I glare at him. "That's not even an option." I would never put her in the hands of someone who doesn't even fucking care about her. She took care of me when she didn't need to. So I sure as fuck am going to take care of her.

"Sorry man," he says, raising his arms. "I was just throwing ideas out there."

I shake my head to tell him it's fine when my phone rings again. No one fucking calls me, which means there's only person it could be.

I'm in a shit fucking mood but I reach for my phone anyway and read her text, seeing a dropped pin location.

Holly:

> I know old people wake up at like 4am. But I don't function before 9am and a bucket of coffee.

I press my lips together, amusement flashing in my eyes. I doubt she needs any more energy.

McLanahan clears his throat, making my head lift, seeing him smirk. "Are your cheeks… red?"

I lower my phone and glare at him. "Drink your damn beer."

Chapter Five

Holly

"Wait," I say, tugging on the sleeve of Mark's leather jacket. I never would have thought he was the kind of guy to wear a leather jacket. Sure, it has a fur trim and is more of a coat than a jacket, but it's still cool. And if I'm honest, it looks really good on him.

"What's wrong now, Bambi?" he asks with a grunt. "You have your coffee."

"That one looks better," I say, pointing toward the large promotional poster.

Mark, however, doesn't seem to share my sentiment since he arches a brow. "Aren't they the same thing?"

"Of course not. I ordered a cinnamon latte, and that one's a gingerbread latte." I let out a groan. "Damn it. I should have picked that one."

His thick brows dip as he furrows them, glancing from my cup to the poster. "They both have cinnamon," he says as if I'm crazy.

I glance back at the poster, see the cinnamon swirl at the top, and then glance back at my coffee. "I guess you're right," I say. "Never mind. I'm just being stupid." I tug on his sleeve again, ready to drag him toward an empty table, but he doesn't budge, so I turn around seeing him still staring down at me.

Mark lets out a heavy breath, closes his eyes for a second, and pulls his wallet out of his jacket, heading toward the counter. My eyes follow him as he reaches the counter, and points at the poster.

My brows lift. He didn't just buy me a new drink... did he?

My question is answered when the server places a hot drink on the counter, and Mark picks it up, heading toward me. Oh my god, he did.

"Here," he says, holding out the gingerbread latte like it's a bomb. My smile widens as I reach out and grab it from him. He tilts his head, with a hint of a scowl still on his face, as he watches me take a sip. "How is it?" he asks.

The hot drink engulfs my mouth, and I swallow it down, letting out a hum. "*Mmmm*. So much better."

He watches me for a second, his face free from any emotion, before he arches a brow. "It tastes the same, doesn't it?"

"No," I lie, shaking my head before I take another sip of the coffee. "It tastes *so* different."

Honestly, I can't even tell a difference from the normal cinnamon latte I usually get, but there's no way I'm going to admit that to him after he bought me the damn thing.

Even with my amazing acting, Mark doesn't seem all that convinced, shaking his head as he grabs my cinnamon latte from me. Since I'm not going to drink it, I figure he'll just throw it out, but he does the last thing I expect and brings it to his lips, taking a sip. His face screws up as he swallows the drink and shoots me a glare. "How the hell can you drink this?" he asks. "It's pure sugar."

"Well then maybe it'll sweeten you up," I tell him with a chuckle, lightly patting his cheek. The big grump narrows his eyes down at me, and I can't help but laugh. "You didn't have to buy me a new drink, you know?" I say, with a smile. "But I definitely like you more now that you have."

His brow lifts an inch. "You didn't like me before?"

"I did," I confirm with a nod. "But I like you more *now*," I clarify with a grin.

He furrows his brows at that, watching me. "You hardly know me, Bambi."

Pursing my lips, I shake my head. "That's not true."

"No?" he asks, lifting his brows with curiosity.

I shake my head again. "I know a lot about you. For example, I know that you're secretly a softie."

Mark shoots me a glare. "You live in your own world, don't you?"

"And that you love to dance," I continue with a smile.

"Do not."

I wave him off. "And that you hate Christmas for some bizarre out-of-this-world reason."

"Oh look," he says, dryly. "Finally hit one on the head."

"See?" I say, shooting him a wink before I take a sip of my coffee. "I know you so well."

He blinks. "That's the complete opposite of what just happened."

45

"Okay, fine," I sigh, pulling out a chair from the nearest table before I sit down. "Tell me something about you then."

He watches me for a minute. "We're not here for me."

"C'mon," I say, gesturing toward the empty chair in front of me. "I want a friend."

"You want a *friend*?" he asks, like the concept is foreign to him.

"Yes. A friend." I pat the table, gesturing for him to sit down. "And I have a feeling that we could be great friends."

I have a bad feeling that I could get Mark to do just about anything, and I'm slowly proving that theory when he pulls out the chair and takes a seat in front of me, letting out a grunt. "Fine."

I break out into a smile, trying to hide it as I take a sip of my coffee, the sweet taste coating my tastebuds. "So… tell me about yourself."

"This is so fucking stupid," he mutters, shaking his head, but a second later his hard eyes land on mine. "I'm thirty-four."

My eyes widen. I knew he was older than me, but hearing how old he actually is catches me off guard. *He's ten years older than me.* "Woah." I wince when he narrows his eyes, and I let out a soft laugh. "Sorry. Continue."

"I grew up in New York my whole life, and I work in a bar."

I wait for him to continue, but when he doesn't, I blink up at him in confusion. "That's it?"

He lifts his shoulder. "Yeah."

"That can't be it," I say, widening my eyes. "You're thirty-four. There has to be more than that. I mean, that's practically when the dinosaurs were roaming around."

His dark brown eyes narrow down at me. "Don't push it, Bambi."

"C'mon. There's definitely more that you're not telling me. How did you get the bar? Did you go to college? What did you study? And what about that girl you dated? I remember you telling me about her."

Mark grunts. "You ask a lot of questions."

"I guess that's true, but…" I lift my shoulder in a shrug. "Isn't that what a date is?" I ask, bringing my cup to my lips.

"I guess," he says, reaching up to stroke his beard. "Probably why I haven't been on one in five years."

I nearly choke on my drink, sputtering and coughing uncontrollably as I manage to choke out, "Five years?"

"Yeah," he says with furrowed brows as he watches me cough. "I haven't been interested in dating."

"Because of your ex?" I ask, finally able to breathe properly.

Mark lets out a hard sigh, tilting his head. "You told me you have a problem with talking, but I don't think you do. You seem to be doing a lot of it right now, actually."

My lips pull into a smirk, acknowledging how he's deflecting the question. He's so secretive and broody, and for some reason, it makes me want to know more. "I know," I agree with a nod. "It's because of you."

He blinks. "Me?"

"Yes," I confirm. "For an inexplicable reason, I can talk to you just fine. But when it comes to anyone else… I freeze."

His eyes narrow. "Was that a Christmas pun?"

I let out a laugh. It actually wasn't, but the fact that it bothers him so much makes me question why. "Why *do* you hate Christmas so much?" I ask, curious to know more about him. I mean, who the hell hates Christmas?

He grunts, leaning back in the chair. "Trust me, Bambi. You don't want to know. We'd be here all day."

"I do," I affirm, placing my drink on the table. "I'm genuinely curious as to why you seem to hate the holiday so much. There has to be a reason."

He grunts again. "Drink your gingerbread, Bambi."

"You want to try it?" I ask, holding my drink up to him. "It's delicious."

"I'm good," he says, shooting me a dry look. "I'd rather not risk catching any of your germs."

My jaw drops in disbelief. "Hey. I don't have germs."

He scowls, crossing his arms. "Everyone has germs."

I huff out a breath. "Well, mine aren't *bad* germs."

Mark glances at me, shaking his head, and I notice the corner of his lips twitching into something kind of resembling an inkling of a smile. But not quite.

I'll get there. One day, I'll get Mark to smile for real. "You really are a fascinating creature," he says.

"Creature?" I gasp, placing my hand on my chest. "I'm a woman."

"A fascinating *woman*," he corrects, dryly.

"Thanks," I reply with a grin. "I got it all from my mom."

"Yeah?" He takes another sip of my cinnamon drink, his face screwing up a second later. "Is she as crazy about Christmas as you?"

I swallow hard, my smile slipping as I nod. "Yeah," I say with a strained laugh. "She was."

"Fuck." Mark places the coffee on the table, and I look up, seeing his features have softened. "I'm sorry, Holly. I didn't—"

"It's fine," I cut him off. "She was an amazing mom, the best I could ever have," I tell him with a smile, remembering her. "And to answer your question, yes, she loved Christmas, even more than I did."

He arches a brow, seeming shocked by my answer. "I wouldn't have thought that was a possibility."

A laugh bubbles out of me. "No, seriously. It was her favorite holiday. Halloween and Thanksgiving didn't exist for her. My mom would start decorating the house for Christmas in September. We'd listen to Christmas music in the months leading up to it, and bake cookies, and brownies and every delicious treat there was." I glance down at my coffee, blinking away the tears building up in my eyes. "She was so fun, and kind," I say, my throat getting clogged with emotion. "Both of my parents were."

It's been so long since my last Christmas with them, and I'm about to spend one more without them. Without anyone.

"Where do you want to start?" Mark asks, making me lift my head to meet his eyes.

"Huh?" I blink up at him.

"With the dating thing," he clarifies. "What exactly are you looking to get out of this whole thing?"

I lift my shoulders into a small shrug. "I guess I just want someone to share the holidays with. I want someone to cuddle with by the fireplace, to bake cookies with, to open presents with. I want what my mom and dad had. What Henry and Olivia have."

"Henry and Olivia?" Mark asks, his brows dipping.

"Funnel Cakes and her husband," I clarify.

"Oh. Right." He reaches up, running his hand over his beard. "How long has it been since you were last on a date?"

"Well, two days ago—"

"Aside from the asshole who stood you up," he cuts in, arching a brow.

I didn't want to admit that I've had more failed dates than there have been days that snowed this month, but I guess he can't help me if he doesn't know where I stand with the whole dating thing. "A little over a week ago."

He hums, his eyes examining me. "And how did it go?"

I blink. "Great. We're happily married, and I'm pregnant." I tilt my head. "You want to meet my child?"

He squints, not appreciating my humor. "Not great, then?"

I groan, shaking my head. "It was awful. He was so boring and watched game shows—"

"I watch game shows," Mark interrupts with a hard look.

I blink. Blink again. "You watch game shows?" He shrugs as a response and I place the back of my hand on my forehead. "Oh, sweet baby Jesus."

"Moving on," he says, narrowing his eyes at me. "Anything else went wrong, or was it just the fact that he watched game shows?"

I wince at the reminder of that date and let out a sigh. "He flirted with our waitress right in front of me."

"Okay," he grunts. "I think I'm starting to see the problem."

"I just don't know if the reason all my dates are failing is because there's something wrong with me, or if I just choose the most awful guys."

His expression is serious as he meets my eyes. "I think it might be a bit of both."

My eyebrows knit together. "Hey."

"We're going to do a little practice date," Mark says, taking a quick glance behind my head. "There's a guy who's been looking over here for the past ten minutes."

"What?" I snap my head backward, scanning the coffee shop. "Where?"

"Jesus," Mark grunts. "You couldn't have been more obvious if you tried." I turn back around, seeing him wipe a hand down his face. "He's by the counter," Mark continues. "And by the way he's looking at me, he probably thinks you're here with me."

"Well, I'm not," I say louder than I need to. "I'm *definitely* not with you."

"Okay, you don't need to say it like that," he says with a glare. "Just get up and go talk to him."

I blink, the word sounding foreign. "Talk?"

"Yes," he says dryly. "Exactly what you're doing right now."

"But…" I furrow my brows. "What do I say?"

"Anything," Mark says with a shrug.

I shake my head. Nope. Not ready for that yet. "Maybe we should practice first."

"That's the point," he says, his brows dipping together in confusion. "This is a practice date."

"No. You and me," I clarify, gesturing with a wave of my finger between us both. "Tell me what he'll say, and then I'll think of something."

Mark looks at me like I've grown two heads. "I don't know what he's going to say."

"Can't you guess?" I ask him, confused. "Aren't all guys like… the same?"

"No."

"Dammit." I chew on my bottom lip. "What do you think he's going to say?"

"Hey."

"Hey?" I repeat, blinking at him. "That's it?" I let out a groan. "Why are guys so mysterious?"

"We're actually pretty simple," he says with a shrug. "He keeps looking over here, so he obviously thinks you're attractive. Just go up to him, smile, flirt and ask him out for coffee."

"Okay," I say warily as I lift myself off the chair and turn around, spotting the guy standing at the counter, whose eyes lock on mine. He's cute. Looks around my age, or maybe a couple of years older. Clean, fresh haircut, and nice style.

"Hey," I say when I approach him.

He blinks. "Hi?"

What next? I smile at him. "I um… I'm single." His brows furrow. "And we're not—" I point at Mark. "He's not—" I lift my hand, tapping on my empty ring finger. "See?"

"Um…"

God, this is not going well. "Want to grab a coffee?"

He lifts his cup in the air. "I have coffee."

"Yeah." I blow out a breath. "I meant tomorrow or another day, maybe?"

"Uh…" His eyebrows lift a little. "I'm gay."

"Oh." I lift my head, realization sinking in. "*Ohhhh*." I wince, embarrassment flooding through me. "So, no coffee?"

"No. I'm sorry."

"That's fine," I say with a nervous laugh, wanting the ground to swallow me up. "No hard feelings." When I turn around, I see Mark covering his mouth with his hand, shaking his head at me. "You failed me," I say when I sit back down.

"Jesus," he grunts. "I totally underestimated how bad you'd be at this."

"He's gay, Mark," I say with a glare. "It's not exactly my fault. I have *nothing* he'd like," I say, gesturing down my body.

He tilts his head. "You showed him your ring finger?"

"I wanted him to know I was single," I mutter, realizing how dumb that sounds. "Turns how he was looking at you, not me." I shake my head. "How the hell did you get someone's attention, and I don't?"

"My charming personality," he says dryly.

I lean back into the chair. "Well then maybe I should just become more like you, then."

"Don't." I look up at him, and his hardened eyes lock on mine. "I don't want you to be like me. I like your... free spirit."

I blink, a smile curling up my face. Did Mark just compliment me? "I thought you hated my personality."

"I never said that," he says with a hint of a glare. "Just because we're different doesn't mean I hate it."

"So you'll still help me?" I ask, a little bit of the hope I had earlier today gone after that whole interaction. I wouldn't blame Mark if he wanted to call this whole thing off. I'm probably a lost cause at this point.

"Yeah, Bambi," he says with a nod. "I'll still help you. I'll get you your Christmas boyfriend."

Chapter Six

—— *Mark* ——

"**G**o fish," Johnson mutters, shaking his head as he looks at his cards.

I usually stay out of their silly games and pointless banter, but I can't help arching an eyebrow when Mclanahan's jaw practically hits the floor.

"We're playing poker," McLanahan says.

Johnson scrunches his face in confusion. "What's the difference again?"

McLanahan lets out a frustrated groan, tossing his cards onto the bar. "I give up," he says before turning to me. "I'll buy this round. Just get me a beer. Actually, make it two."

I let out a scoff. It's hard to believe I'm the youngest one here with the way they act. It's been like this ever since I first met them. The first time John McLanahan and Andrew Johnson came into this bar, I was only sixteen, and they were arguing about who'd buy the next round. And eighteen years later, nothing has changed.

I grab a glass, fill it with beer, and slide it over to McLanahan.

He takes a hearty gulp, then looks up at me. "What are you doing here on a Sunday, anyway?" he asks, taking another drink.

"Indulging your drinking habits," I reply, busying myself with cleaning the bar, though it's pretty quiet today.

McLanahan chuckles, shaking his head. "Do you ever take a day off?"

"I don't think he does," Johnson adds with a scoff. "The kid does nothing but work."

"Not a kid," I shoot back, narrowing my eyes at them. "And I do take time off."

McLanahan raises an eyebrow. "You do? When? Because the only day I've ever seen you take off is—"

"Don't," I cut him off before he can finish his sentence. My jaw clenches, and my hand tightens around the cloth I'm holding, squeezing it as if it might somehow dissolve the tension building in my chest.

"Shit. I'm sorry, kid. I didn't—"

"It's fine," I reply, forcing the words out as my throat feels like it's closing up. "Just drop it."

"Sure," he says, nodding. "It's dropped."

The silence in the bar is heavy, almost suffocating, until Johnson clears his throat.

"McLanahan's an idiot, but he's not wrong," he says. "You should get out more. Have some fun, meet people. Don't just stand behind this bar all your life."

Jesus, that sounds fucking bleak.

"I'm good," I reply, though his words linger in my mind. Is that what I'm doing? Wasting my life behind this bar?

"What about your girl?" he asks.

I grunt. "She's not my girl."

A low chuckle escapes him. "Then how did you know who I was talking about?"

I shoot him a glare. "I'll ban you for life," I threaten.

He scoffs. "I'd like to see you try," he says, nudging McLanahan's shoulder. "We're the reason this place is still up and running."

"By drinking?" I raise an eyebrow.

"By keeping you in business," he counters.

I grunt in response.

"You know I'm right," he says with a smirk that makes me want to wipe it off his face.

I shake my head. "You're an idiot."

His laughter dies down, and McLanahan gives me a meaningful look. "Jokes aside, when was the last time you went out?" he asks. I open my mouth to answer, but he holds up his hand. "And I'm not talking about grocery shopping, or walking Murray, or taking Mia to her doctor's appointments. I mean *out*. For real."

I hesitate, searching for a response, but the silence that follows says it all.

"My point exactly," he says. "You need to have some fun, kid. You deserve to be happy."

"Not a kid," I repeat, but the words feel hollow. "And I'm fine. I don't need your old ass worrying about me."

"Fine isn't the same as happy," he points out, taking another gulp of his beer.

His words sink in. When was the last time I felt genuinely happy? I think back to my time with Sasha, trying to recall any moments of real joy, but they're buried beneath a cloud of painful memories. Every good moment seems tainted, mixed in with the worst times of my life.

"I'm just saying," he says with a shrug. "There's a reason you have wrinkles."

"Because I'm thirty-four?" I reply dryly.

He shakes his head. "Because you've got nothing to smile about. You need a release, kid. You need to do something for yourself. You need to meet people who aren't just your customers."

I watch him, my jaw tightening as he keeps talking. Why haven't I kicked him out yet?

He raises his glass, smirking. "You know I'm right," he says before finishing off his beer in one final gulp.

I want to argue, to tell him he's wrong and that I'm perfectly content with my life as it is. But deep down, I can't deny the nagging doubt he's planted.

"I have a bar to run," I say instead. "A dog to feed and Mia to take care of. I don't need anything else distracting me."

"Not even that girl?" he asks, raising an eyebrow.

A flash of a short brunette, always smiling, pops into my head.

My lips twitch. The time I spent at the coffee shop with Holly was probably the most fun I've had in a long while. Watching her make a fool of herself was entertaining, sure, but it was more than that. Hearing about her parents and seeing her so full of life despite her loneliness—it resonated with me. She's everything I'm not, but I get her. I understand the emptiness she feels inside.

She's a distraction, that's for sure. But it's a distraction I don't mind. I welcome it. Want it. I'd never admit that to these guys, though. They'd never let me hear the end of it.

My thoughts are interrupted when the door swings open, and in walks Daniel with his trolley, loaded with the alcohol I'd sent him out for.

"Where do you want me to put this, boss?" he grunts, struggling to lift a crate of alcohol in his arms.

"Set it down right here," I say, gesturing to the stock room behind the bar.

He takes a step forward with the crate still in his arms. I open my mouth to tell him to put it back on the trolley and wheel it here like a sane person, but before I can say anything, he drops the crate. Bottles shatter and alcohol spills everywhere.

"Jesus," I mutter, pinching the bridge of my nose. He's lucky it's a slow night.

"Fuck. I'm so sorry, boss," Daniel says, kneeling to pick up the broken glass.

I let out a heavy sigh and move toward him. "It's fine. Just move over."

He swallows, nodding as he gets up, and makes room for me to start sweeping up the shards.

"I really am sorry," he says. "It was just heavy and—"

"It's fine," I say again. It's not like this is the first time a bottle's been knocked over in this bar.

My mind drifts back to the night Holly came in, drunk and clumsy, knocking over a bottle. I shake my head with a scoff, remembering her disastrous practice date last week. I thought she was exaggerating about not

59

being able to talk to men, but I definitely underestimated how bad she would be.

I glance over at Daniel, who's staring at his phone, seemingly oblivious. Daniel's been working for me for a couple of years now. He might be a bit aloof and easily distracted, but I think he might be a good match for Holly. Besides, she did want someone who shares her love for Christmas, and this guy comes to work dressed as an elf during the holidays. Almost fired him for that costume.

"Hey, Daniel."

He looks up, quickly stuffing his phone into his pocket as if he's caught doing something wrong. "Yeah, boss?"

"Are you single?"

His eyes widen, and he chokes. "Uh… I'm not…" He clears his throat again and shakes his head. "I'm flattered, but I'm not—"

"Didn't know you swung that way, kid," McLanahan interjects, making me narrow my eyes at him.

"No, Jesus." I pinch the bridge of my nose. "It's not for me," I clarify, wanting to make it clear that I'm not hitting on him.

"Oh." Daniel's brows furrow. "Then, yeah. I'm single."

I nod, relieved. "I have a friend."

Snickers erupt behind me, and I fight the urge to turn around and face their smug faces. "A friend, huh?" Johnson says, trying to stifle his laughter.

"It's a girl, right?" Daniel asks, his tone turning concerned.

"Yes," I say dryly. "She's… looking for a date, and I think you guys would hit it off. Would you be interested?"

"You're really doing this?"

This time I do turn around, my brows knitting as I look between Johnson and McLanahan as they share a look I don't quite know what to make of. "She asked for my help," I tell them with a shrug.

"Yeah, but Daniel?" McLanahan says with a scoff.

"What's wrong with him?"

"Yeah," Daniel adds. "What's wrong with me?"

McLanahan shakes his head slightly. "You think he's up for dating her?"

I turn back to Daniel. "What do you think?" I ask. "Are you up for it?"

Daniel purses his lips, deep in thought. "Is she hot?"

Christ. Is that all that guys care about? "Sure."

"Okay," he says, nodding. "Cool. Then yeah, maybe… she's not crazy or anything, right?"

I blink. *Define crazy.* "She's very hot," I say instead.

That seems to please him because he smiles. "Alright. Yeah. I'm down."

I nod. "Good. I'll set it up."

"Cool," he says with a grin.

I finish sweeping up the glass, and my shoulders slump when I catch McLanahan and Johnson's expressions. "What?" I ask, wondering what's got them so amused.

"You set her up on a date," McLanahan says.

"Of course I did. That's what she asked me to do."

61

He hums in agreement, nodding slowly. My shoulders relax, thinking the topic is done, but then he speaks again. "And you're completely fine with that?"

"What are you getting at?"

He shrugs. "She's cute."

My eyes narrow involuntarily, my spine straightening at McLanahan's words. "She's young," I remind him.

He scoffs. "She's not that young."

"She's ten years younger than me," I point out, the realization hitting me like a blaring alarm.

Both McLanahan and Johnson raise their eyebrows. "Damn."

Yeah. "And I'm not looking for anything even remotely close to what you're insinuating," I tell them as I finish making sure the room is clear of glass.

McLanahan snickers and glances at Johnson. "How long has it been?" he asks. "Since… you know."

My jaw tightens, and I head out to sweep up the rest of the glass on the floor. I know exactly what he's asking, and I'm not going to dignify it with a response.

"Okay, I get it," he says as I work, his voice slightly muffled. "I'll get out of your hair."

"About time," I mutter under my breath.

He laughs, giving me a light pat on the shoulder, making me look up at him. "Think about what I said," he says, tossing me a wink before he and Johnson head for the door.

"I'd rather not," I reply, hearing him laugh as the door swings open and shuts behind them.

The old man has clearly lost his mind. What was he even thinking, bringing that up? Holly is only in my life because she needs my help finding someone who's perfect for her—someone who shares her love for cheesy movies and Christmas. That's not me, and it never will be. Hopefully, this all works out, and she finds exactly what she's looking for with someone who can truly make her happy.

Chapter Seven

— Holly —

"**I** got you a date."

Given the fact that I've just walked through the door a few minutes ago, I'm caught by surprise when Mark calls me out of the blue to tell me he's somehow found me a date. It's the last thing I expected, especially after the fiasco of our recent practice date at the coffee shop.

"Jesus?" I joke, a smirk playing on my lips as I swing my legs over the edge of the bed and push myself up.

"Funny," he deadpans, and I can almost picture the frown on his face. I can't help but wonder if the muscles in his face ever get sore from all that frowning.

I let out a low chuckle, shaking my head. "I thought so."

A heavy sigh leaves him. "Did you even hear what I said?"

"That you did the impossible?" I say, pulling the curtains closed. "Yeah. I heard you."

"It wasn't impossible," Mark says dismissively. "It wasn't even hard."

I arch a brow, suspicion taking over. I find that a little hard to believe, considering the last time Mark tried to get me a date, I ended up practically throwing myself at a guy who was checking *him* out.

"Did you at least vet this person, or did you just grab a random stranger off the street?"

"He's vetted," he replies.

My brows knit together. "And you're sure he's not gay this time?"

"I'm sure."

"Cute?"

There's a pause on the other end. "Are you seriously going to make me answer that, Bambi?" he asks.

"How else am I supposed to know what to expect?" I ask, wedging my phone between my ear and shoulder as I rummage through my wardrobe for my sweats. "What if he's really old and on his deathbed?"

"Then you'd gain an inheritance," he deadpans.

My face breaks out into a grin, chuckling as I unzip my skirt and step out of it. "Now you're talking."

"Why are you panting?" he asks. "What the hell are you doing?"

"Getting changed into my sweats," I tell him as I start unbuttoning my shirt.

"Now?" he asks, his voice tinged with surprise.

"Yeah," I reply with a shrug as I pull off my shirt. "I just got home."

"Jesus," he curses under his breath. "And you couldn't have waited until after I called you?"

I gasp in mock horror. "Of course not. What kind of monster lounges in their work clothes after they get home?"

Mark groans deeply, and I can almost feel the frustration radiating through the phone. "You're killing me."

"Like I'm going to kill the old guy you set me up with?" I joke, letting my hair fall down from the bun I put it in this morning.

He sighs. "He's not old, Holly."

"So he *is* cute?" I press with a smirk.

"Jesus Christ," he murmurs, breathing hard. "Fine. Yes, he's… cute."

"Well, damn, okay." I breathe out a laugh. "Don't steal my date."

Mark lets out a groan. "You're impossible."

I smile as I pull on my sweats. "I'll take that as a compliment."

"It wasn't one."

"I beg to differ," I say, climbing back into bed and leaning back against the headboard. "So, how did you do it?"

"Do what?" he asks.

"Get him to date me," I clarify.

A low grunt leaves him. "Like I said, it wasn't hard. I asked him if he wanted to go on a date with you, and he said yes."

My brows tug together. "That's it?"

"What else could I have done?" he asks. "Not all of us can be as eloquent as showing our empty ring finger."

I'm never going to live that one down, am I? "I don't know," I admit. "You could have at least talked me up a little. Did you even say anything about me?"

"I said you were hot."

My eyes widen, and I feel the warmth in my body flooding to my cheeks. Mark thinks I'm hot? "Stop flirting with me," I joke.

He lets out a heavy breath. "I wouldn't dream of it, Bambi."

Of course he wouldn't. Mark doesn't date, and even if he did, he'd never even think twice about dating me. I guess that's why I'm so comfortable around him. I don't have to try and make myself attractive, or desirable. I can just be myself.

"Did you say anything else about me?" I ask him.

"No."

I blink, waiting for more, but it never follows. "No?" I repeat, my brows tugging together. "That's it? All you said was I'm hot?"

"Yes," the big grump says. "He seemed quite pleased by that."

I shake my head. "Well, did you at least show him a picture of me?"

"I don't exactly carry around a picture of you in my wallet, Bambi."

"Oh my god," I cry out, slamming my hand over my face. "This is what I get for getting a guy to do this."

"What's wrong, now?" he grunts.

A nervous laugh leaves me. "Are you kidding me? Everything." I groan. "What if he thinks I look like a Victoria's Secret model, and then when he shows up, he gets disappointed when he finally sees me?"

"That won't happen," he assures me.

"How do you know that?" I ask, a rush of nerves flooding my chest. "What's his definition of 'hot,' anyway? What if I'm not it?" I let out a loud gasp. "Oh god, what if he's going to stand me up too?"

"He won't."

"He will. I know it," I continue, groaning as I tilt my head back against my headboard. "It will be just like the last time. He'll walk inside, take one look at me, and run out the door."

"He's not going to do that," Mark says firmly. "Stop flailing around and calm down, Bambi. There is no way anyone could be disappointed by going on a date with you." My eyes widen slightly at that statement. "And if he does stand you up, you come and tell me, and I'll beat some sense into him."

My jaw drops, and I blink in surprise. "I thought he was your friend."

"Not if he ends up hurting you."

A smile tugs at my lips, and I let out a teasing chuckle. "You'd fight someone for me? Mark, you big softie."

"I'm not a softie," he says in that deep voice of his that lets me know he's serious.

"Of course not," I joke, pulling my bottom lip between my teeth. "You're a big grump. Always mean, always scowling, never smiling… secretly a softie."

He groans in frustration. "You kill me, Bambi."

"Make sure I'm credited on your headstone," I tease, still smiling.

He grunts. "Well, this has been an effective call. I just called to let you know I got you a date. And now you know. Bye, Bambi."

The call hangs up and I let out an exhale, hoping this date goes well.

Chapter Eight

— *Holly* —

"**I**'m nervous," I admit, exhaling slowly as I clutch my phone tightly against my ear.

"Don't be."

I roll my eyes, letting out a scoff as I tap my fingers on the table, staring at the empty chair in front of me. "Wow. What great advice. Has anyone ever told you that you should be a motivational speaker?"

He pauses, and I can immediately picture the expression on his face. His dark eyebrows would furrow, and his lips—the ones that have never felt the hint of a smile—would curve into a frown. I almost wish he was here with me. I feel less nervous when he's here. Even though we're in the café of failed dates past.

"Daniel's a great guy. Just be yourself. I think you two will hit it off."

My brows knit together. *Be yourself.* "Who am I, though?"

He exhales deeply. "You're a mystery, Bambi. Even to me."

"Well, that's not exactly helpful. Aren't you supposed to be my dating coach? Give me something to work with here."

"I'm no such thing," he retorts. "Besides, I already did my job by getting you this date. Just relax, have fun, and be your funny self. He'll love you."

"Wow," I snicker, raising my eyebrows. "Love on the first date? You must think very highly of your dating coach skills, Mark."

"Jesus," he grumbles. "Why the hell did I ever agree to this?"

"Because you had nothing better to do?" I tease.

He grunts again. "Something like that."

A smile tugs at my lips. "Also, did you just call me funny?"

"I'm hanging up now."

A laugh escapes me as Mark abruptly ends the call, and I tuck my phone into my pocket, pulling my coat tighter around me.

"Holly?"

I glance to the side and see a guy looking down at me with a smile. My heart picks up, nerves surrounding me. Is this Daniel?

"Hi, that's me," I say, laughing lightly. "Are you Daniel?"

He nods, his head shaking slightly as he takes me in with a quick once-over. "Wow. When Mark said you were hot, he wasn't lying," he says with a laugh that makes my cheeks flush at the reminder of Mark calling me hot.

I'm sure he just said that as a throwaway comment to get this guy to date me, but I'm glad it worked. I let my eyes fall to the length of him. He looks to be around my age, or maybe even a little younger, but he's actually pretty cute.

"And when he said you were cute, he wasn't lying either."

My date frowns, his smile faltering. "He said I was cute?"

I nod, my lips lifting into a teasing smirk. "Yeah. He even threatened to steal you away and everything," I joke, letting out a small laugh, but his frown deepens, letting me know he doesn't appreciate my humor. "Just kidding," I say, my cheeks flushing with embarrassment. "Do you want to grab a coffee?"

His face settles as he shrugs off his coat and takes a seat in front of me. "Sure," he says with a shrug. "I'd love an espresso."

I blink, caught a little off guard. My brows knit in confusion when he doesn't make any attempt to move. Since this a small café, there aren't any waitresses coming to the table, and seeing as he's made himself comfortable, it doesn't look like he's heading to the counter anytime soon. Does he expect me to order for him?

"Um… sure," I manage, lifting myself out of the chair before heading to the counter to order our drinks. The barista gives me a sympathetic smile as I fumble with my purse.

When I return with our drinks, Daniel's already scrolling through his phone. He doesn't even look up as I set his espresso down in front of him.

"Thanks," he says absentmindedly.

"You're welcome," I reply, forcing a smile as I take a sip of my drink. "So, you work with Mark?" I ask, hoping to make some conversation.

"Yeah," he says, lifting his head to grab his espresso and taking a sip. "I'm a vendor. I bring in the liquor for Mark."

"Oh." My eyebrows lift in intrigue. "That's interesting. How did you get into that?"

He shrugs, taking another sip. "Just did, I guess."

I blink, trying to hide my disappointment. Not exactly a talker, then.

"That's… fun. I'm actually a social worker," I say. "I work with foster kids."

He arches his brow slightly. "Oh. That's cool… I guess."

I blink at his dismissive tone. "You guess?" I repeat.

"I mean…" He shrugs. "I don't like kids all that much, so working with them seems like a nightmare."

"Oh." My smile falters as I process his words. I've always pictured having kids of my own someday, but if Daniel doesn't like children, could there even be a future between us? Could I seriously give up on something so important for a guy I barely know?

I glance out the window, my mood lifting slightly as I watch snowflakes softly landing on the glass. "Oh hey, It's snowing," I say, my lips lifting into my first genuine smile since Daniel sat down.

He turns to look out the window and grins. "Fuck yeah. I love when it snows."

My smile widens, and for a moment, I think there might be hope after all. "You do?"

"Yeah," he says, laughing as he shakes his head. "People always trip on the ice. It's hilarious."

"Oh." I lean back in my chair, my smile fading. The silence between us grows heavy, and I find myself at a loss for words.

We sit in silence for a while as I try to think of something to say that might salvage this date, but nothing comes to mind. I glance up at Daniel, who seems perfectly content to sip his espresso, and occasionally glance down at his phone as if looking for something more interesting to occupy his attention.

"So," I say, clearing my throat to turn his attention back to me. "What do you like to do in your free time?"

He shrugs, not bothering to look up from his drink. "Not much," he says. "I hit the gym sometimes. Go out with the guys. You know, typical stuff."

I nod, feeling the conversation slipping away again. "Do you have any hobbies?"

"Not really," he replies, his tone flat. "I guess I watch a lot of sports. And I like cars."

"Oh, that's cool," I say, grasping at any straws I can. "Do you have a favorite team?"

"Not really," he repeats, and I can feel my patience starting to wear thin. "I just watch whatever's on."

"Right," I murmur, taking another sip of my drink. The warmth of the coffee does little to ease the chill between us.

The cafe door swings open, and a gust of cold air rushes in as a couple walks inside, laughing together as they shake the snow from their coats. They seem so happy, completely absorbed in each other, and I feel a hint of envy settle within me. This is what a date should feel like—effortless, enjoyable, fun. Instead, I'm sitting across from a guy who barely seems to care whether I'm here or not.

Daniel's eyes flicker towards the couple, and I catch him smirking at the woman's ass when she turns around. It's subtle, but I see it, and my heart sinks a little further.

"Listen, Daniel," I start, clearing my throat slightly. He looks up at me, his eyes widening slightly as if he's been caught. "I don't think this is going to work out."

"Why not?" he asks, genuinely surprised.

I can't believe he's serious. Did he think this was going well? "We have nothing in common," I tell him. "And I just caught you checking someone else out while you're on a date with me."

He lifts his shoulder in a shrug. "We're not together, though."

My brows lift of their own accord. Wow. "No, we're not," I agree. "But I think I deserve a little respect if you're on a date with me."

He watches me for a second, the lines between his brows creasing before he shakes his head. "I don't get what the big deal is," he says.

Of course, he doesn't.

I lift off the chair, his eyes immediately dropping to my cleavage that I wish was covered right now. I quickly zip up my coat and grab my bag. "I think it's best if I go," I tell him.

"Alright, I guess," he says with an irritated sigh. "Do you want me to tell Mark it didn't work out between us?"

I shake my head. "No, I'll tell him myself."

That is if I don't kill him first.

I step outside, the cold air hitting me immediately. I pull my coat tighter, my breath puffing out in front of me as I hurry down the street. The snow is falling faster now, covering the sidewalks in a thin layer of white.

A gasp leaves my lips when I almost slip on a patch of ice, and a bitter laugh escapes me. How fitting.

I reach into my purse, grabbing my phone as I scroll through my contacts. I can barely feel the tips of my fingers as they hover over the screen, searching for Mark's name. My heart pounds with disappointment.

Is this seriously what he thinks I want? What I deserve?

The thought makes my stomach churn. I know I deserve better. I deserve someone who cares about the things I care about, who respects me, and who actually wants to get to know me.

And I'm going to make sure Mark knows that.

Chapter Nine

It's snowing.

Charles loved the snow. He used to keep the windows and doors wide open just to watch it fall. But I can't fucking stand it.

The cold seeps into my bones as I stand by the window, arms crossed tightly against my chest, watching as Murray rolls around in the fresh snow, wagging his tail. I can't help but feel my lips lift a little seeing how happy he is, but then the cold hits my skin again, and I've had enough.

"Okay, time to come inside," I tell him. He stops rolling in the snow, trotting inside as I push the door wider to let him in. The moment he's inside, he shakes vigorously, sending snow flying in every direction, covering the floor.

Good thing the bar is closed today. I shake my head as I close the door, locking it before I head upstairs, the stairs creaking under my feet, a sound I've gotten familiar with over the years as Murray follows behind me.

I knock a couple of times on Mia's door, then push it open. Murray sniffs the floor, his nose following an invisible trail, while I step into the living room. Mia is on the couch, wrapped in a thick blanket, watching some old Christmas movie on TV.

"Hey. Are you hungry?" I ask her.

She glances up at me, offering me a small smile, one that doesn't quite reach her eyes. "Oh, I'm fine," she says, but my jaw tightens. She's lost weight. Her cheekbones are more pronounced than they used to be.

She hasn't been eating much lately, and I can't stand to see her like this. "I'll make some soup," I say, heading toward the kitchen without waiting for her reply. I open the fridge, my eyes flicking to the discolored magnets she's had forever.

"Don't worry about me," she says. "What about the bar? Aren't you opening up today?"

My footsteps halt, my heart aching as I keep my eyes on the fridge, and I shake my head. "No. Not today."

"Why not?" she asks.

My stomach drops, and I wince inwardly. *She doesn't remember.* "Just didn't feel like it," I reply, trying to keep my voice steady. I open the fridge and pull out some vegetables and a half-full carton of broth in the back. I start chopping the vegetables, trying to keep my mind occupied

She sighs, making me look over my shoulder at her, seeing her looking around her apartment. "You know, it's almost Christmas," she points out softly, her voice carrying a sadness that's too deep for me to address right now.

"I know," I murmur, barely loud enough for her to hear as I turn back around and drop the vegetables into a pot and turn on the stove.

"Charles loved decorating the bar for Christmas." I stop what I'm doing and look over my shoulder at her, a frown tugging at my lips.

Loved. She said loved. She knows he's gone.

But she doesn't remember what day it is today.

"I like keeping it simple," I tell her, though the memory of the bar covered in decorations flashes in my mind. Every year, Charles would string up lights and deck the place out. The jukebox would play Christmas songs all day long. That feels like a lifetime ago now.

She lets out another sigh, sinking deeper into the couch and pulling the blanket tighter around herself. "I sure do miss decorating the place with Charles."

I narrow my eyes at her. "Are you trying to make me feel guilty?"

She lifts her head, meeting my gaze with a sparkle in her eye. "Is it working?"

"No," I lie. What is it with the women in my life thinking they can bend me to their will… and why are they right?

"A little mistletoe never hurt anyone," she says with a smile. "You never know who might walk underneath it."

I let out a breath, leaning against the counter as the water in the pot begins to heat. She never gave up on the idea of me settling down and getting married. After Sasha, she always held out hope that I'd find someone again, and when I didn't, it made her a little sad. But the truth is, I don't want a relationship. I don't want to go through the pain of losing someone again. I'd rather keep to myself, even if it means being alone.

And seeing how hard dating is for Holly, I'm kind of glad I'm not in the middle of it all. It looks like hell.

"I don't think the usual guys who come here would love the idea of kissing each other," I tell her, trying to change the subject.

She waves me off dismissively. "You never know. There might be a cute girl who's lost and wants a drink."

My mind immediately flicks to Holly. "I doubt that," I say instead because if Mia knew there'd been a girl near me, she'd jump at the opportunity to play matchmaker.

"I met Charles at this bar, you know," she says.

I arch a brow, surprised. "He told me you two met in college."

"We did, but I first saw him here," she says. "My friends and I came to have a drink one night, and Charles was here. He was hanging out with his friends, laughing, drinking, and I thought he was the cutest guy ever."

My chest warms, and I feel my lips twitch. "Charles? Cute?" I raise a brow, teasing her a little. "Seriously?"

She tuts, a small smile on her lips. "He was a hottie in those days," she says, a twinkle in her eye. "You remind me so much of him."

I blink, taken aback. "I do?"

She nods, her expression softening as she looks at me with a hint of sadness. "Brown hair, kind eyes, grumpy."

"Grumpy?" I ask, surprised. "Charles was not grumpy."

She chuckles, shaking her head. "Oh, he was, until he met me."

I raise my eyebrows, genuinely surprised. I knew the man for over a decade, and I never saw a frown on his face, never heard him complain about anything. He was the epitome of joy, always smiling, and always making others feel at ease.

"Some people can change a person," she says, her eyes softening as the memories course through her. "And I changed him."

I like the sound of that. It makes me wonder if someone could change me, too. If I'd even let them.

She blinks up at me, a flicker of confusion crossing her features. "Do you know when he's coming back?" she asks.

My smile slips, and I swallow hard, my chest tightening with the weight of her question. "Soon," I whisper, turning back to the stove. Can't look at her when I lie to her. "Soon, Mia."

❄

"This is your last one," I tell Murray firmly, holding a treat up, waiting for him to sit before tossing it in his direction. He catches it mid-air, his jaw snapping shut with a crunch before he sits down again, waiting for another.

"You're relentless, you know that?" I say, handing him another treat. He chomps down on it, his tail wagging slightly, and I force the box closed before he can gilt-trip me into feeding him the whole damn thing.

Dropping down on the couch, I flick through the channels, trying to find something—anything—to take my mind off this shitty day. But nothing holds my attention. Murray jumps up beside me and lies down, resting his head on my lap as I stroke his fur.

"I miss him too, buddy," I murmur, the words barely a whisper as they catch in my throat.

God. Today sucks. I just want to go to bed and forget this day, forget the sadness, forget everything. But when my phone rings, my eyes flutter closed. I can't do that.

I glance at the screen, see Holly's name flashing, and my brows knit together. She's supposed to be on a date with Daniel right now. What's going on?

I press the button and bring the phone to my ear, but before I can say a word, her voice comes through. "Where are you?"

"Why?" I ask, my concern growing.

"I'm at the bar, and you're not here," she snaps, making my brows rise. I've never heard her sound like this before.

"Are you okay?" I ask, sitting up straighter.

"I'm fine, I just… ugh, where are you?" she asks again.

"I'm upstairs," I reply, confused. "Why are you at the bar?"

"Upstairs?" Her voice softens slightly. "You live upstairs?"

"Yes."

"Why isn't the bar open?" she asks.

The muscles in my jaw tighten. "Just isn't," I say, not wanting to get into the details.

"Can I come up?" she asks.

I sigh, rubbing my face with my free hand. "Will you leave if I say no?"

"No," she admits, and I can hear the faint smile in her voice.

"Then sure, come on up," I say, giving in. "The key's under the mat."

"You're telling me where the key is?" she asks slowly. "What if I rob the place?"

"Will you?" I counter, my brow lifting, knowing she couldn't be capable of hurting a fly, never mind robbing a bar.

"No," she admits.

"Then come upstairs, Bambi," I reply, hanging up the phone.

I blow out a breath as I stand, putting the beer I was nursing back in the fridge and rub my face, trying to shake off the weariness that's been clinging to me all day. It's a good thing Mia doesn't remember much, or else she'd be a wreck today.

"Behave," I tell Murray when a knock hits the door, and he starts to bark.

I make my way to the door, swinging the door open, and I'm met with the sight of Holly standing there, her eyes narrowed and slightly puffy.

"What's wrong?" I ask, my voice soft, concerned.

"You're horrible at this," she says, brushing past me into the apartment.

"At opening the door?" I ask, closing it behind her.

"At setting me up on dates," she snaps, throwing herself onto the couch, looking utterly defeated.

Fuck.

Murray jumps up beside her, and she lets out a yelp. He pants, his tail wagging as he stares up at her, and I pinch my nose.

"Murray. I told you to behave," I tell him, but the dog doesn't pay attention to me, completely enraptured by Holly. "Get down from there. You're scaring her."

"No, don't," she says, her hand resting against his golden fur. Her lips tip up into a smile. "I was just a little shocked, that's all." She smiles down at him. "Hi, buddy."

I watch Holly play with my dog, rubbing his chin as she baby-talks to him.

She laughs when he licks her face and then glances at me, wiping the slobber Murray left on her cheek. "You have a dog," she says, a little surprised.

"Yeah."

She eyes me, her lips twitching. "His name is Murray?"

I nod, my brows dipping, wondering why she's acting like that.

She lets out a chuckle. "As in... *Murray* Christmas?"

My face drops. "I'm changing his name immediately."

She tips her head back, laughing, and my chest warms. It's such a difference from when she walked in here that I'm reminded of the fact that she left her date early.

"What did Daniel do?" I ask her, dropping down on the couch beside her.

She sighs, her hand coming to a stop playing with Murray's fur, and she shakes her head. "It doesn't matter. I don't even care anymore. This little guy made it all go away," she says as she scratches Murray's head.

My frown deepens. "Tell me."

She closes her eyes for a second. "It was awful," she admits, her shoulders slumping. "I was trying hard to be funny and just be myself like you told me to, but he was giving me nothing. He completely disregarded me the whole time, and then…" She looks up at me, pressing her lips together as if to stop her from saying anything else.

"What?" I ask, my voice hardening.

"I don't want to say."

"Why not?" My voice drops, and my chest pounds harder with each second.

"He's your friend. And he works for you."

"Not if he hurt you," I tell her, already picturing firing his ass. If he hurt her—

She shakes her head slightly. "He didn't hurt me, he just…" She sighs. "It's stupid."

"I don't care," I say. "Tell me anyway."

She chews on her bottom lip for a few seconds. "He checked out a girl's ass right in front of me."

Again? What is it with these assholes being able to look at anyone else when she's right there?

"Is my ass not good enough?"

Jesus.

"I mean, I squat," she says with a huff. "Not often, but I do. I even do those donkey kicks and everything. Is my ass that bad?"

Is she seriously asking me this question right now? I swallow hard, my throat tight. "I don't know. I've never looked."

Liar.

I tell my brain to shut up, wanting to keep those thoughts buried deep. Now is not the fucking time.

"Oh great," she mutters, slumping back against the couch. "It's not even good enough to look at."

I breathe out a sigh, pinching my nose. "You're not going to make me say it, are you?"

She furrows her brows, glancing at me with confusion. "Say what?"

"Sweetheart, you're gorgeous," I tell her, noting the way her eyebrows lift in surprise. I can't lie and say I've never looked at her. She's a beautiful girl, of course I have. "You have a great body, ass included, a beautiful face, and any guy should be willing to kill to be with you."

The silence between us stretches, and for a second, I'm worried I've crossed a boundary, but then a smile curls her lips. "Wow," she says with a light scoff. "Mark has a crush on me."

"I do not," I say with a glare.

"Don't lie," she teases. "You just confessed your love for me."

"I did no such thing," I grumble, looking away. I don't want her to get the wrong impression. Yes, she's beautiful, but I can't be what she wants. I run my hand through my hair. "Holly, I don't—"

"Don't worry. I know you were just being nice," she says, cutting me off with a smile. "I know you're not interested in me."

I'm not?

The fuck was that? I shake the thought away, watching as she glances around my apartment. "So… this is your place?" she asks, as if suddenly remembering she's never been here before. Granted, I forgot, too. Holly has a way of making it seem like she belongs in a place, no matter where it is.

"Yeah," I say, watching her closely as she looks around.

"It's empty," she remarks, her brow furrowing slightly.

My brow lifts. "And you're sitting on air?" I reply.

She shakes her head, a heavy sigh leaving her lips. "Sure, you have basic furniture, but where are the decorations?" she asks. "Not a plant in sight, or a bookshelf, or a coffee table to put your knick-knacks."

I blink at her. "I don't have knick-knacks, or books for the matter, and who the hell wants a plant to take care of, anyway? They're just more work."

Holly sighs, closing her eyes in despair. "You poor creature," she mutters, glancing down at Murray, who pants up at her. "You're living in a house of torture. Not even a bauble or tinsel in sight," she says with a shake of her head.

I give her a dry look, unimpressed with her dramatics. "I bet you've already decorated your whole house by now," I say, imagining the sight. I have no doubt she'd be one of the people who love colored lights instead of the warm white ones.

She shakes her head, her brows pulling together. "Olivia does all the decorating since it's her place," she explains. "She also does all of the holiday baking since she's a chef and a very good one at that." The corner of her lips drops slightly. "I haven't baked in such a long time," she admits quietly. "I miss it."

My own face drops, feeling a hint of sadness for her, but then she lifts her head, her eyes sparkling as she bats her eyelashes. I already know what she's going to ask before she even opens her mouth.

"No," I say firmly.

"Please?" she asks, her voice soft, pleading, and fuck, why the hell am I thinking about it?

"No," I repeat again, shaking my head. "I don't partake in Christmas traditions."

She rolls her eyes. "Don't be a Grinch. It's just a few cookies. I promise I won't ever ask you for anything else ever again."

I give her a dry look. "That's a lie."

She lets out a breath. "Okay, fine, it is, but come on," she pleads, leaning closer to me. "I promise you'll love them."

I try to avoid her eyes, not wanting to get sucked into them, but when I turn my head and see the expression on my face, it caves my chest in. Jesus fuck. What is it about this girl that gets me to do anything she wants?

Her face breaks out into a grin as she leans in. Everything happens so fast that I don't even get the chance to acknowledge that she just pressed her lips to my cheek until she hops off the couch. "I'll get the ingredients ready," she says, heading toward my kitchen before I can even say anything.

I still feel the burn of her lips against my face, and I glance down at Murray, letting out a low groan. "I don't know what I did to deserve this," I mutter before following her into the kitchen.

Chapter Ten

Mark

"I'm not sure if I have the ingredients," I warn her, already dreading the mess this is going to create.

She's already opening cabinets and peering inside. "I can work with what you have," she says, pulling out a bunch of stuff I didn't even know I had.

"Can you grab the bowl?" she asks, and I lift my brows.

"I'm included in this now?"

She turns her head and bats her eyelashes, and I let out a hard breath, completely and utter putty in her hands. "Fine," I grumble, grabbing the large mixing bowl and handing it to her.

Lifting my hand, I rub at my chin, watching as she starts to mix the ingredients together, folding the batter carefully, but I note that she isn't following a recipe. "You ever do this before, Bambi?"

"Yeah," she says with a light laugh that eases something in me. "All the time," she says, squinting at the bowl as she pours the sugar in without using a scale. "Why? Do you think they'll be bad?" she asks, giving me a look.

I lift my shoulder. "I mean, the fact that you didn't even think of looking for a recipe kind of scares me," I admit.

She shakes her head, her lips pressed together in an amused smile. "Oh, Mark, you live too much by the rules," she teases, nudging me with her elbow.

"They're there for a reason."

"To break them," she replies.

"Definitely not," I retort, shaking my head.

She chuckles, turning her attention back to the bowl. "I beg to differ," she says, and I watch as she mixes the ingredients together, glancing at me for a second. "I memorized the recipe," she admits.

That relaxes me a little, knowing she isn't just throwing ingredients in at random. "You make them that often?" I ask.

"Not really," she admits, with a curt shake of her head. "I don't get the chance to bake living at Olivia's. But my mom used to make them a lot," she says, her voice softening.

"Oh?" I ask, glancing at the side of her face where I can see her expression fall.

"We used to make them every year," she says, staring at the bowl, her gaze distant as if she's lost in the memory.

I feel a tug at my chest and clear my throat. "And you're sure you memorized it correctly?" I tease, wanting the smile back on her face. "It's looking... interesting."

She snaps out of it, her lips curling into a warm smile as she lets out a soft chuckle. "Trust me, Mark. You'll be begging me to make them again," she says confidently.

A low grunt leaves my lips. "I wouldn't be so sure about that," I reply, though as the smell of the vanilla and butter enters my nostrils, I start to think she might be right.

"You're going to eat your words," she teases, her grin stretching from ear to ear.

"I'm going to eat something. Not sure if it'll be edible."

She starts to pour the flour into the bowl with a laugh, and starts to mix together the dough. "I used to make cookies all the time when I was in foster care," she admits, her voice low, catching me off guard.

My brows shoot up in surprise, and I swallow down the rock lodged in my throat. "You were in care?" I ask, my voice softening.

"Yeah," she says with a soft smile that doesn't quite reach her eyes. "Funnel Cakes was in there with me actually, but um… she got adopted," Holly says, her voice trailing off as she focuses on the mixing bowl in front of her.

"And you?" I ask, dreading the answer.

My eyes dip to her slender throat as she swallows hard. "I aged out," she says.

I gulp, feeling a deep, gnawing sadness for her. "I'm so fucking sorry, Bambi."

"It's okay," she says with a smile I can tell is forced. "I'm so happy Olivia found a family, and we kept in touch throughout the years. We even went to college together, where she met her husband, and now is having a child." She lets out a hard breath, her eyes fluttering closed for a second. "I'm so happy for her. I am, it's just…"

"You wish you would have had the same." I finish for her, the sadness swimming in her eyes, breaking my heart.

She nods slowly, her voice catching as she continues. "My parents were amazing, and it wasn't my fault that they died. But no one seemed to want me," she says with a slight croak in her throat. "I went from home to home, with nothing but a pink Barbie backpack that I got the Christmas they died." She shakes her head, and I notice a tear dripping down her cheek. "I lost everything," she says. "Even the backpack years later."

How could anyone not want her? The thought claws at my insides, and I try to swallow down the anger, but it's impossible. The thought of her never having a family again makes me fucking angry. Why did I get one? She would have deserved it so much more than me. I was a waste. But she is… Holly is…

I'm sprung out of my thoughts when I feel something land on my face, and I slowly blink down at Holly, who's grinning up at me with her hand full of flour.

I slowly wipe the flour off my face and narrow my eyes down at her. "You're dead."

She yelps, grabbing the bowl as protection and attempts to move away from me. I reach into the flour bag and grab a handful of flour, ready to throw it right back at her.

"Not the cookies," she begs, laughing as she dodges out of the way.

"You started this," I warn her, throwing more flour at her, feeling the corner of my lips tug when it lands on her hair, earning another yelp from her.

"Fine. Fine, I'll stop," she concedes, holding the bowl in front of her face. She pokes her head out, seeing if it's safe, and when she sees I'm standing with my arms crossed, she puts the bowl back onto the counter and lets out a hard breath. "You're evil."

I arch a brow, grabbing a tea towel before making my way over to her. "Says the woman who invaded my kitchen and threw flour at my head," I say, slowly wiping away the flour covering her hair.

I can't help but admit how much I enjoyed it. This day is usually one of the worst ones in the year, but somehow, Holly came and made me forget. She brightened up the day and stopped me from sinking into the darkness of my thoughts.

I stare down at her, seeing those big, brown eyes locked on mine, and I feel something tug at my chest. Holly brings the light with her, and I don't know what I'm going to do once she finds the love of her life and leaves.

I realize my hand is frozen on her hair when she clears her throat and takes a step back. "The cookies," she says, gesturing toward the bowl. "We need to bake them."

"Right," I reply curtly.

I roll my sleeves up and copy her movements, grabbing some dough and rolling it into a ball before placing it on a baking tray, trying my fucking hardest to avoid looking at her. I don't know what the fuck I was thinking even being as near to her as I was.

I just… I forgot. I forgot what it was like to enjoy the presence of a woman, to feel this lightness in my chest. I forgot, and Holly is a constant reminder of it.

Once the cookies are in the oven, I busy myself with washing up the dishes until the oven dings a few minutes later.

Holly grabs an oven glove and takes the cookies out, the smell of warm, sweet chocolate filling my kitchen. Jesus. I haven't smelled something like that in a long time around here.

Turning the faucet off, I place the tea towel back on the rack and turn to see the cookies. "Fuck, they look good," I admit, eyeing them with surprise as I reach out to grab one.

But Holly slaps my hand away before I can do just that. "Not yet," she says.

My eyes thin. "You promised me a cookie," I remind her.

She laughs, bright and light, and I love the sound of it way too much. "They're too hot right now," she says. "You need to have some patience."

"I don't have any of that," I grumble.

"Well, you're going to have to learn to, Mark," she says, her voice soft as she takes off her oven gloves.

My jaw tightens. I have a feeling I'd do anything she asked me to. Even if I didn't like it.

After an eternity, Holly finally deems them cool enough and I grab one, taking a large bite. I might have doubted her skills for a second there, but she proved me so wrong. The taste is perfect. Just the right amount of sweetness, and it's still chewy in the middle. "Fuck, these are good," I admit, my mouth full as I take another bite.

"I told you," she says, a smug smile on her lips.

Murray comes trotting into the kitchen, and Holly kneels down to his level.

"Hi, buddy," she says. "You want a cookie?"

"He can't have chocolate," I remind her, but Holly offers me a smile.

"I made him one without any chocolate," she says, grabbing a tiny cookie the size of a dime before she drops back down and hands him the cookie, letting out soft little laughs as she rubs his stomach and kisses the tops of his head.

And for the first time in fucking forever, I feel a hint of a smile caress my lips.

"You see?" she says, looking at me with those big, hopeful eyes. "Christmas isn't so bad."

Yeah. Maybe not.

Chapter Eleven

Holly

"Another one?" I laugh as Mark reaches for yet another one of my cookies. "I told you they were good. You're never going to survive without them now."

A puff of air leaves his nose as he shakes his head. "Yeah. I guess I was wrong."

"How many times do I need to remind you, Mark?" I say, dropping onto the couch. Murray, his adorable dog, immediately hops up beside me. "I'm always right."

He sinks into the couch next to me as I tuck my legs up, feeling comfortable in a way I only do when I'm around him. I came over to rant about my terrible date and how it was entirely his fault, but now I'm just happy to be here. There's something about Mark's place that feels so cozy, especially with Murray around.

"Feel like watching a movie?" I ask, glancing over at him.

He raises an eyebrow. "So, you're staying over?"

I hesitate, not wanting to overstep. "I mean, I wanted to hang out with you," I admit, trying to keep my tone casual. "But I can leave if you need your space." I hope he doesn't want me to go. As much as I enjoy teasing Mark, I really like spending time with him.

"You can stay," he replies almost too quickly, and I relax, slowly petting Murray as he curls up on my lap. "I have nothing else to do anyway. I was thinking of crashing early since I didn't open the bar today."

"You were going to sleep?" I ask with widened eyes. "It's the middle of the day."

He shrugs and lets out a tired grunt. "I'm just not feeling it today."

My brows knit together as I watch him point the remote at the TV. "Why didn't you open the bar today, anyway?"

He hesitates, his eyes closing for a moment. When he opens them again, I can see the effort it takes to speak. "My parents got divorced when I was young," he begins.

I frown in confusion. "What does that have to do with—"

"I'm trying to open up here, woman," he interrupts, shooting me a glare.

"Right, sorry," I say with a nervous laugh, pulling the throw blanket over me and Murray, trying to settle in. "Keep going."

He leans back against the couch, his eyes fixed on the TV. "It was hell. They fought about everything—who would do the dishes, who would take me to school, every little thing. When they finally split, I thought things might get better, but it just got worse."

I stay quiet, sensing he needs to get this out.

"My dad moved to the city, and my mom stayed in our old house, so I bounced between them. It was painfully clear that neither of them wanted me around. And then, one day, my mom never came to pick me up. I haven't seen her since," he admits, the muscle in his jaw ticking. "My dad was furious. But not because he was furious for me. I think he hated that he never thought of leaving me behind like she did."

He finally turns to face me, and my eyes dip to his thick Adam's apple as he swallows harshly. "When I was sixteen, I'd had enough. I couldn't stand hearing how much of a burden I was anymore, so I just… ran away. I didn't know where to go, but I knew anywhere was better than staying in a place where I wasn't wanted. I wandered the streets for hours, and when it started to rain, I ran into a random bar nearby."

He pauses as if remembering that moment. "I expected to get kicked out since I was a scrawny sixteen-year-old in a bar, but instead, the owner, Charles, just asked me if I was okay. And I broke down right there, in front of everyone. I couldn't remember the last time someone asked me that or the last time someone *cared*."

My heart clenches, knowing exactly what it feels like to be alone like that.

"His wife, Mia, made me a grilled cheese, gave me one of Charles' coats, and told me to come back if I ever needed anything. And I did. Going home was the worst part of my day, so every day after school, I'd go straight to the bar. My dad didn't even notice I was gone. That's how little he gave a shit about me."

He looks around his apartment, his lips pressed together in a thin line. "Charles eventually closed off a section of his own house and made me this place. He gave me a home when I didn't have one."

Mark's voice grows quieter. "He died five years ago today."

My brows shoot up. No wonder he didn't open the bar today.

"He left me this bar and this apartment in his will. He wrote me a letter saying I was the son he never had. I guess he wanted someone to carry on what he built all those years ago, and I was his first choice." He shakes his head, running a hand through his hair. "I don't even remember the last time I heard my own dad say anything remotely close to that… I don't even know if he's *alive*."

He swallows hard, his jaw tightening. "Mia was devastated when Charles died. She had lost the love of her life and was all alone. She completely broke apart. And then, about a year later, she was diagnosed with dementia."

My heart aches for him.

"She doesn't even remember what day it is today," he says, letting out a hard breath. "And maybe that's a good thing. I don't want her to feel the pain I'm feeling, but… I fucking hate seeing her like this. I hate having to lie to her and hear her questions about where Charles is and when he's coming back because he's *not*. He's not coming back, and I don't have the heart to tell her that."

Hard, heavy breaths leave his lips as he squeezes his eyes closed, and there's nothing I can do in this moment that will make this better. I know how much it hurt for me to lose my parents. I know how much he's hurting.

I reach over and place my hand over his clenched fists, and Mark lifts his head, keeping his eyes on our joined hands.

"I'm so sorry," I say, my voice low as Mark turns his head to look at me.

He studies me for a moment, his eyes scanning my features. "You... you didn't speak," he points out, the tension slowly leaving his body.

I shrug. "You didn't need me to. You just needed me to listen."

He holds my gaze for a second, and a million different expressions cross his face before he dips his chin. "Thank you."

I shake my head. "You don't have to thank me. I'm your friend, Mark. I'm here for you." I try to lighten the mood with a teasing grin. "Even if you are sick of hearing me talk."

I expect him to agree with me with a grunt or a groan, but he just shakes his head instead, placing his other hand on top of mine. "I like hearing you talk."

I blink, feeling warmth spread through me, and my heart skips a beat. I quickly pull my hand away and playfully shove his arm. "Stop flirting with me."

The grump I know, and slowly am getting used, to rolls his eyes as he grabs the remote. "Are we going to watch a movie or what?"

"Absolutely," I say, snatching the remote from him with a laugh. I start scrolling through the options until my eyes land on *The Holiday*. My face lights up as I turn to him with my best pleading look.

He groans, pinching the bridge of his nose. "I'm gonna lose this argument, aren't I?"

"You could always say no," I remind him, though I'm hoping he won't. "But it's such a good movie."

"I've never seen it," he admits, rubbing his beard.

"Really?" I ask, genuinely surprised. I suppose I shouldn't be, given how little joy Mark seems to indulge in.

"I don't watch much TV," he says with a shrug.

I tilt my head. "So, what do you do for fun? Do you have any hobbies?" I ask him.

"No."

"No?" I repeat, blinking in surprise. "How is that possible? I have SO many. I love to bake and read, and shop and dance—"

"Dance?" he asks, cutting me off with an arched brow.

"Not well," I add. "But I still love to do it. You need hobbies in life."

He shrugs. "Don't know what to tell you, Bambi."

My brows furrow. "Then what do you do?"

"I work," he says simply.

I wait for more, but it never comes. "And when you're off work?" I ask.

"Sleep."

A heavy sigh escapes me. "You sad little man."

He glances at me with slightly narrowed eyes. "Sweetheart, there's nothing little about me."

The heat in my body floods to my cheeks and I glance at the TV, clicking play on the movie.

"Did I embarrass you?" I hear Mark say, his low voice sending shivers down my spine.

"No," I lie, feeling my face burning hot as I pull the blanket up, tucking it under my chin. "Of course not." The movie starts to play and all the warm memories come rushing back to me as the familiar music starts to play and I glance around the room, wishing there were some decorations. "You seriously need a Christmas tree in here," I tell him.

"I'm good."

I glance at him, letting out a laugh. "It'll liven up the place."

He meets my eyes and arches a brow. "And the other eleven months?" he asks. "It's dead?"

My lips twitch. "Well…"

"Watch the damn movie, Bambi," he says, with a glare before turning his attention back to the screen.

As the movie plays, a thought nags at me. "What if I end up like that?" I blurt out.

"Like what?" Mark asks, his eyes still on the screen.

"Single, depressed, alone at Christmas," I say, my voice tinged with worry as I watch what could possibly be my future on the small screen.

"You won't," Mark says. "I made you a promise that I'd help you find the perfect guy for you, and I intend to keep it."

"But what if you can't?" I ask, turning my head to look at him, and he turns his head and meets my eyes. "What if I never find someone? I've been single for twenty-four years, Mark. I've never even had a boyfriend."

103

He shakes his head. "That doesn't mean it won't happen. I won't let you end up like that."

I let out a sigh, not convinced he'll be able to make that happen. "Can you promise me something?" I ask.

"Depends on what it is," he says with a lift of his shoulder.

"If I end up alone, can I come celebrate Christmas with you?"

He watches me for a second. "I don't celebrate Christmas."

"Please?" I beg, my lips falling at the thought of being all alone during the happiest time of the year. "I'm going to need to move out at some point. Olivia and Henry are starting a family and I already feel like a huge burden on them," I admit. "And I hate the thought of spending Christmas alone with no one to laugh with, or bake cookies with, or to open presents with." I shake my head. "Please promise me you can be that person."

He blinks. Blinks again. "Yes, Holly," he finally says. "I promise if you're alone, you can always come infest my house with your holiday cheer." I smile a little, thankful to have found Mark. "But I have faith you won't need to. You won't be alone."

I shake my head. "Don't hold your breath there, Mark. Your dating coach skills aren't exactly paying off."

He narrows his eyes at me but then his face settles and he lets out a breath. "You just need to work on your flirting a little, and maybe stay away from assholes who check other women out," he suggests.

I let out a laugh, too enraptured with Mark to even pay attention one of my favorite movies. "Are you saying my flirting is bad?" I ask him.

He gives me a dry look. "Sweetheart, I saw you that day in the café," he says, the nickname making my cheeks burn with heat. "I know it's bad."

I let out a laugh. "I got you to fall for me, didn't I?" I tease.

He shoots me a glare. "Do you want me to help you or not?"

"Okay, fine," I say, straightening my shoulders. I did ask him for help, so I should start taking his suggestions into consideration. "What should I do?" I ask. "Flutter my eyelashes?" I blink, my lashes fluttering against my cheek.

"Dear God, stop that," he says, making me snap my eyes open. "Forever." I let out a laugh and he shakes his head, a low grunt leaving his throat. "Do that, and you'll scare away every guy on the East Coast."

"You're still here," I point out, a smile curving my lips.

"God, help me," he groans. "I don't know why."

"Because you love me, Mark," I tease, shooting him a wink.

His eyes slowly blink down at me before he lets out a sigh. "Pass me the damn cookies."

Chapter Twelve

— Holly —

Shopping for Christmas presents is hands down my favorite thing ever.

There's just something so special about searching for the perfect gift for someone, to know that they'll feel cared about and thought of. There's nothing like it. And it's why I'm struggling down the crowded street with too many shopping bags hanging off every possible limb, barely able to see where I'm going.

Totally worth it, though.

The cold air nips at my cheeks as I make my way through the crowds, trying to avoid bumping into anyone or slipping on the patches of ice that seem to be everywhere. I can't stop the memory of Christmas mornings with my parents. Back then, I'd wake up to a living room filled with gifts, and it felt like pure magic.

After they passed, those moments stopped existing, but I try my hardest to keep the magic alive. Every single present I received in one of my foster homes, I've kept tucked away in a box under my bed. It's not always the best reminder, but it's a token of my past. It's a part of me.

I yelp when my phone rings, jolting me out of my thoughts, and I try to juggle the bags, nearly losing my balance as I dig around in my purse. After what feels like an eternity, I manage to grab my phone and bring it to my ear.

"Hello?" I answer, a little out of breath.

"Where the hell are you?" Olivia's voice comes through. "And why do you sound like you've just been mobbed?"

"I'm present shopping," I reply, trying to balance the bags on my arms when one of them attempts to slip.

"Alone?" she says, her voice raising ten million octaves. I wince when her voice practically deafens me. "Oh, great. Henry, she's gone shopping alone." I can practically see her frantically moving back and forth. "Are you out of your mind? With the way you shop, I wouldn't be surprised if you end up falling and breaking a hip."

I let out a scoff. "I'm twenty-four, not eighty," I tell her, rolling my eyes even though she can't see me. "How would I break a hip?"

"By carrying your body weight in presents and slipping on the ice, obviously," she says as if it's the most logical thing in the world.

"You're so dramatic. That won't happen," I assure her, sidestepping a particular sketchy-looking patch of ice. "Is there a reason why you called or did you just want to scold me?"

"I wanted to know if you're staying home tonight," she says. "I'm cooking and I wasn't sure if you'd want some or if you have any plans elsewhere."

The reminder of last week when I spent the day watching movies with Mark and baking cookies comes to mind. I kind of want to go to his place again, but I also don't want to invade his personal space and have him annoyed by me.

"Yep, I have no plans," I tell her. "I'm heading home after this. I'm exhausted and I need a bubble bath and a big plate of your lasagna."

"I was actually going to make a salad, but lasagna sounds so much better. Oooh, I can try out my new garlic bread recipe, too."

My stomach starts to growl. "Don't tempt me. I have another fifteen gifts to check off my list."

She lets out a laugh. "Okay, I'll let you go. Don't forget to bring wine."

"Wait, how am I going to carry—"

She hangs up before I can finish, and I quickly shove my phone back into my purse. I'll find a way. She probably thinks I won't find a way to carry all of these bags, and that I'll be stupid enough to slip on some—

"Ahhh!" I let out a yelp as my feet slide out from under me and I go down, bags flying in every direction.

"Woah," I hear someone say when I feel a hand grab my arm. "Are you okay?"

I let out a heavy breath, wanting the ground to swallow me up. "I'm definitely not going to tell her this happened," I mumble to myself.

"You're not telling who?"

I lift my head, glancing up at the guy crouching down next to me, concern written all over his face as his hand is still wrapped around my arm.

The corner of his lips lift a little. "Are you okay?"

"Yeah, I think so," I say, a little flustered. "Thank you."

"No problem," he says, bending down to pick up my fallen bags. "Looks like you're carrying half the store with you."

I let out a laugh as I try to help him gather the bags. "It's a bit much, I know. But I just couldn't help myself. I love gift shopping."

He grins, handing me the bags he's picked up. "I get it. Shopping for presents is kind of addictive."

"It is," I agree, taking the bags from him. "But it's probably a sign I should call it a day before I actually break a hip."

He laughs, a warm, genuine sound that makes me smile. "That might be wise. I'm Ryan, by the way."

"Holly," I reply, finally meeting his gaze, seeing his brown eyes soften as he smiles. The subtle lines around his eyes let me know he's a little older than me. That, and his designer business attire.

"Nice to meet you, Holly," he says, still holding onto one of my bags.

I glance at the bag, then back at him. "You're not planning to run off with that, are you?"

He chuckles, holding up his hands in mock surrender. "Nope, just trying to help."

"Well, I appreciate it," I say, taking the last bag from him. "I'd shake your hand, but…" I gesture to the mountain of presents I'm holding.

"How about your number instead?" he asks, tilting his head.

I blink, caught off guard. "Huh?"

"Your number," he repeats, still smiling. "I hope I don't scare you away, since we only just met, but it's not every day I bump into someone as beautiful as you."

"You want my number?" I ask, feeling a blush creep up my cheeks at him calling me beautiful.

"I mean…" He shrugs. "As much as I'd wish fate would intervene and I could telepathically communicate with you, I'm thinking a text would be better," he says with a teasing smile.

I can't help but smile at his playful attitude. "You're smooth, aren't you?"

"Only when I'm trying really hard," he admits with a wink. "So, what do you say? Can I get your number? I'd love to take you out sometime."

I hesitate for a moment, thinking about my last date and how awkward it was. But there's something about Ryan. Something that intrigues me. I glance back at him, seeing him look at me expectantly.

"Did I bore you?" he teases.

"Yes." My eyes widen at the realization of what just came out of my mouth. "No, I mean, no!" I say, closing my eyes in frustration. "I'm very bad at this."

He chuckles softly. "Nah, you're doing great."

I take a deep breath. "Let me try this again. No, you didn't bore me. And yes, I'd love to go out with you."

"Great," he replies with a grin. "I just need your number."

"Right. Of course," I say, trying to shift the bags so I can reach my phone. But it's impossible with everything I'm holding.

Ryan notices my struggle and holds out his hand. "Want me to grab it for you?"

I hesitate, then nod. "Sure, but if you run off with my purse, I'm calling the cops."

He grins, reaching into my purse with exaggerated caution. "I promise I'm not a thief. But I have to say, if I was, you'd never know."

"Good point," I say, watching as he pulls out my phone. He quickly taps in his number and places it back in my bag.

"There you go," he says, handing the phone back with a grin. "The ball is in your corner. Just text me whenever you're ready. I'll be waiting," he says, flashing a smile before walking away.

I keep my eyes on him as he walks away, and a small smile tugs at the corners of my lips. Did that seriously just happen?

But before I can fully wrap my head around it, my phone rings again, dragging me back to reality and I groan glancing down at the million and one bags hanging off my arms.

Chapter Thirteen

— *Mark* —

I've never thought about having kids.

Sasha wanted them, but it was never something I was interested in.

Maybe that's why our relationship ended.

And yet, five years later, I have a fully grown forty-three-year-old child sitting in front of me, sighing loudly to try and garner my attention.

When McLanahan lets out another dramatic sigh, I roll my eyes, finally fed up. "What?" I ask, wondering why he's acting like a five-year-old.

He shrugs, running his finger over the rim of the glass. "I miss Johnson," he murmurs, making me narrow my eyes down at him. "Why the hell couldn't he come have a drink with me, anyway?"

Seriously? That's what's got him sighing and sulking all day?

"Because he's at his daughter's school Christmas musical," I remind him. "You know this."

He shrugs again, pouting down at his empty glass. "I guess. I just wish he invited me along."

I arch a brow. "You want to go to a school musical?" I personally couldn't think of anything worse than having to listen to out-of-tune children attempt to sing Christmas carols.

He sighs again. "I just want to be *included*, Mark. Keep up."

I shake my head, not able to handle him. "You two are like a married couple, I swear."

McLanahan lets out a gasp. "Don't you dare insult my Maurine like that. She's the apple of my eye, the peanut to my butter, the beer to my belly." I arch a brow. "I just wanted to be thought of for a change. I invited him and his wife to our Christmas Eve potluck, but did I get an invite back? *No*. Of course not." He rolls his eyes. "Not even a bleeding ticket to the school musical."

"Jesus," I mutter, pinching my nose. "I just… I don't… you know what? I give up." I throw my hands up, shaking my head. "Next time he comes in, you can argue all you want about your invitations and potlucks. I'm out."

"*Ahhh*," he says, dipping his chin. "Jealous, are you?"

"Of course I'm not," I say with an eye roll.

His shoulders shake with a laugh. "I think you're a big fat liar."

I shouldn't even entertain him, but I arch my brow anyway. "What would I be jealous of, exactly?"

"You don't have any plans for Christmas, do you?" he says, a teasing smirk plastered on his stupid, smug face.

I cross my arms, my brows dipping. "I'm working."

"On Christmas day?" he asks, his eyebrows arching in surprise.

"People still drink," I say with a shrug. McLanahan blinks slowly, unmoving as he stares at me. My frown deepens. "Quit doing that. It's creepy."

"You can't be serious," he says, incredulous.

I shrug again. "It's not like I have anything else to do, like you pointed out," I tell him, the muscle in my jaw ticking.

"Aw, come on. I was only kidding." His mouth twists. "You could always come over to our house," he suggests with a grin. "Johnson and his wife and children will be there—though the jury's still out on whether I should uninvite him or not," he says with a bitter scoff.

I shudder at the thought of being in another person's house, surrounded by screaming children. Besides, I'm not coming along just because he feels guilty. I don't need anyone's pity. "I'm good," I tell him, polishing off a glass. "I have to stay here and take care of Mia, anyway."

"Bring her along. C'mon it'll be fun." he says, his brows dipping as he meets my eyes. "It's Christmas. You have to take a day off sometime."

My body tightens at the reminder of last week. The one day I take off every year, and how this year it was completely different. Holly made that day more than just a crappy reminder that everything in life is shit. She made that day… fun. She made it special, warm and—

Before I can finish my thought, the door swings open with a jingle of the bell hanging above the door, and my head jerks up seeing Holly burst inside, her cheeks flushed and her hair wild from the wind.

"Jesus, Bambi," I say, noting the million and one bags hiding her small frame. "You look like you've been running."

"I have," she says, letting out an exhausted breath as she drops all of her bags down onto the ground before she takes a seat at the bar.

"And why's that?" I ask her, grabbing a glass to make a drink for her without thinking about it. Don't know if she even wants a drink right now, but it kind of looks like she needs one.

"I went present shopping," she says.

I raise an eyebrow. "And that's an activity that requires running?" I ask, a little amused.

Holly laughs, a bright infectious sound that makes my chest jump. "You haven't been present shopping with me before," she says with a smirk. "It's practically a sport."

I slide a Cosmo across the bar to her. "I think you'd have me dead before we even made it out of the store," I joke, although… is it really a joke?

She lets out a relieved breath and gives me a sheepish smile. "Thanks," she says, grabbing the glass before drinking half the contents in one large gulp. "Usually Olivia comes shopping with me, but she's pregnant and can't run or fight, so I thought it would be better to go alone."

I blink. "Fight?" I repeat, hoping—praying I heard the wrong word.

She shakes her head, a soft laugh leaving her. "Oh, Mark. You have no idea how vicious women are when there's a good sale."

I shake my head, not even wanting to know in case I accidentally become an accessory to murder. "Did you get any good presents?" I ask.

"Lots," she replies, her eyes lighting up. "I even got you one."

My brows shoot up in surprise. "You did?"

"Of course," she replies with a playful grin. "You're my friend now, Mark."

Her words elicit some weird fucking fluttering feeling in my stomach. And I don't like it. Don't like it at all. "How the hell did I get roped into this?" I ask, her previous words repeating themselves in my head over and over again.

She chuckles, lifting her shoulders. "You were kind to me," she says.

I give her a dry look. "Sweetheart, you need to raise the bar a little higher than simply being *kind*," I tease her.

I hear a scoff come from McLanahan who I somehow forgot was still here and I turn my head to see what's got him so bothered, but his expression is filled with a teasing smirk, which makes my jaw tighten.

She tilts her head, her smile growing wider. "Maybe. But you were kind to me and I like you. So, I'm going to keep you."

"Keep me?" I repeat, blinking down at her.

"Yep," she confirms, her eyes twinkling. "You're stuck with me now."

I glance over at McLanahan, who's observing us with an amused look. "You hear that, Mark? She's said she's going to keep you," he says with a wink.

I shoot McLanahan a scowl, but the bastard just laughs, clearly enjoying this. I just know he's going to gossip all about this when Johnson comes in.

"But that's not even the best part," Holly says, a wide grin on her slightly red lips, tinted from the cold.

"It's not?"

"Nope. Guess what happened today?" she asks, her eyes practically glowing with excitement.

I raise an eyebrow. "I have a feeling you're going to tell me anyway."

"You're right about that," she says with a chuckle. "I met someone."

"You…" Her words finally dawn on me and my jaw clenches involuntarily, my shoulders tensing. "You met someone?"

"Mhmm," she says with a nod. "It was the weirdest thing ever. I was juggling a million shopping bags when Olivia called, and then I slipped on ice and dropped everything." My ears perk up at 'slipped on ice' and I do a quick glance down her body, making sure she's alright.

"And then this guy helped me up," she says.

"Okay…" I try to keep my voice steady, but the tightening in my chest is hard to ignore. The fuck is this, anyway? I need an Advil or something.

"And then he asked for my number and said he'd love to take me out," Holly continues with a smile on her face.

"Just likc that," I say, my voicc cdgcd with something I don't want to acknowledge.

"Just like that," she confirms, nodding enthusiastically.

My hand reaches up as I stroke my beard. "And you're going to go," I say, though I don't know why. Of course she is. This is what she's been looking for. This is the whole reason she's in my life in the first place, and now that she's managed to get a date all on her own, she doesn't need me. She never did. But I somehow let myself believe that I was finally good for something, finally needed in someone's life. But after this, there's no reason for us to communicate anymore.

"Of course," she says.

McLanahan laughs, shaking his head, but I barely register it. My attention is solely on Holly, and the way her eyes light up as she talks about this guy.

"Right," I mutter, more to myself than to anyone else. I don't even try to mask the gruffness in my voice.

Holly's smile fades slightly as she picks up on my expression. "What's wrong?" she asks, her brows knitting together.

"Nothing," I say quickly, trying to ease the tension in my shoulders as I clear my throat. "So, what's this guy's name?"

"Ryan," Holly says, a hint of a smile gracing her lips. "He was kind and tall and very handsome," she says, eyes locking on mine. "And he had a beard. Actually, he kind of looked like you. But in a formal, businessman way."

I blink. "You think I'm handsome?" I ask. Don't know why. It wouldn't change anything whether she thought I was handsome or not. I don't need to know. Actually, I don't want to know. But before I can open my mouth to tell her just that, she answers.

"Of course I think you're handsome," she says, her eyes softening as my chest does the fluttering thing again. Jesus. What the hell is that?

She lets out a content sigh. "I have a very good feeling about this date."

And the gnawing in my stomach is back.

"When is this date, anyway?" I ask her, ripping my eyes away from her as I grab a rag and pick up an already clean glass, giving it an unnecessary polish.

"I don't know yet," she says, chewing on her bottom lip. "He gave me his number and told me to text him, so I guess we'll see."

I lift my head to look at her and press my lips together, nodding slowly. "That's… great, Bambi. I'm really happy for you."

Well, what do you know? Mclanahan was right. Turns out I *am* a big fat liar.

"Will you help me figure out what to wear?" she asks, flashing that sweet grin at me that somehow gets me to do whatever the fuck she wants.

My brows shoot up. "I have absolutely no clue how I could help you with that, Bambi. I'm not exactly a fashion guy." When she frowns slightly, I grunt, hating that look on her face. "Can't you ask Funnel Cakes for help?"

She groans, shaking her head. "She's gone to visit Santa."

I blink. "In the north pole?"

"Yeah. She went on his sleigh and everything," she says dryly, rolling her eyes. "Of course not. She went to the mall."

119

My brows dip. "She has a kid?" Don't remember Holly telling me about that.

"No, not yet," she says. "But she's practicing."

"Practicing…" I repeat slowly.

"Yeah," Holly replies with a shrug. "She wants to know exactly what to do when the baby arrives."

"Jesus," I grumble, shaking my head at how ridiculous that is. "You need to hang out with normal people."

She chuckles. "That's why I have you, Mark," she says, flashing me a smile. "And that's also why I *really* need your help."

Christ. Why am I considering this? I don't know shit about clothes or what the hell someone wears on a date, given that I haven't been on one in years. "Can't you wait for her to come back?"

"There's no time," she says with a huff. "I don't know when he'll call, and then what if you're busy and I have no one to help me and—"

"Fine," I say, wanting to put a stop to her rambling. "I'll help you, Bambi."

She pauses, her smile widening. "You will?"

Fuck me. This is a bad idea. Don't need to be spending more time with her alone when I'm starting to get confusing as fuck feelings running through my body. But I can't say no. Don't know what this woman did to me, but I just *can't* say no to her.

"Yes," I say. "Send me your location and I'll come over."

She lets out a yelp, bouncing in her seat as she breaks out into a grin. "This is why I like you."

"Because I do whatever you want?" I ask her, arching my brow.

She chuckles, a teasing smirk pulling at her lips. "Exactly." Leaning down, she grabs all of the million shopping bags, balancing them in her arms. "Thank you, Mark," she says, glancing back at me. "I'm so happy I met you."

She flashes me one more smile before heading out of the bar, and I keep my eyes on the door long after it closes behind her until Mclanahan's scoff pulls me out of it.

"You're fucked, man," he says, shaking his head.

Can't even argue with the guy.

I am fucked.

Chapter Fourteen

— Mark —

Holly is deceptively strong. At 5'5" with a petite frame, you'd never guess it, but the moment I arrive at the location she sent me, I'm yanked inside by this girl with an iron grip.

"Come on," she pants, tugging me along. "This is an emergency."

"Jesus," I grunt, nearly tripping as she drags me through the door that slams shut behind us. "Don't rip my arm off."

She whirls around, her cheeks tinged with pink, and abruptly drops her hand. "Sorry," she says, looking flustered. "I'm just a little nervous. I don't have any time to prepare, and I want this to go well."

"Bambi," I narrow my eyes at her. "You told me the date is next week."

"Exactly," she says, throwing her hands up. "No time at all."

I shake my head, a scoff escaping me, and she freezes, her wide eyes locking onto mine.

"What?" I ask, confused by the way she's staring at me as if I've suddenly grown two heads.

Her head tilts slightly, and she blinks. "Did you just… laugh?"

"What?" I frown. "No."

"I think you did."

"You heard wrong."

"I didn't," she insists, a grin spreading across her face. "I definitely heard you laugh all sputtery and weird."

Sputtery and weird? Seriously, where the hell did this girl come from? I shove my hands into my pockets, my jaw tight. "I didn't laugh. I merely scoffed."

"Aha!" she shouts, pointing an accusatory finger at me. "A scoff is a type of laugh."

"It's not," I mutter, but doubt creeps in. *Is it*?

"It is," she affirms with a smirk. "You just laughed."

Jesus. I let out a long sigh. "I did no such thing. I simply exhaled."

Her shoulders slump, and her expression softens as she shakes her head. "One day, Mark," she murmurs. "One day I'm going to make you laugh."

"I doubt it, Bambi," I say, though I can't help but feel the corners of my lips twitch whenever she says something completely outrageous.

Finally, I glance around the room she dragged me into, only now taking in my surroundings. "Is this where you live?"

"No," she replies, hopping onto the arm of the couch and swinging her legs playfully. "I broke in earlier today," she deadpans, before a sly smile forms on her face. "This is Olivia and Henry's place. I'm just staying here with them until I can afford to move out."

Her smile fades slightly, and before I can ask what's on her mind, she hops off the couch and starts walking away.

"Let's go," she calls over her shoulder, not bothering to look back.

I curse under my breath. What the hell have I gotten myself into?

Reluctantly, I follow her into her bedroom, where she gestures toward her bed, covered in a bunch of small pillows. "Sit."

I raise an eyebrow. "Do you expect me to bark too?"

She chuckles, turning around to flip through a million hangers.

"Jesus, Bambi," I mutter, my eyes widening at the sight as I drop down onto the edge of her bed. "How many clothes do you have?"

"Not a lot," she says while rifling through endless options. "Ooh, I love this one." She pulls out a long black fabric and holds it against her body, studying herself in the mirror. She spins around, nearly whipping me with the dress, a smirk on her lips. "What do you think of this?"

I rub my jaw, unsure what I'm looking at. "Nice?"

Her brows knit together. "Nice?" she echoes, clearly unimpressed. "What kind of compliment is that?"

I shake my head. "I don't know anything about fashion, Bambi. To me, it just looks like a big sack."

She bites her lip, contemplating my words. "Maybe it's better if I try it on," she says, pulling her sweatshirt over her head.

"What the hell?" I gawk, quickly averting my eyes.

Fuck.

My fist clenches as I wrestle with the surge of emotions I'd rather not acknowledge. I shouldn't be ogling her. I hate myself for even thinking it, but…

Holly is gorgeous. It's hard not to notice how beautiful she is—long brown hair, caramel eyes, peachy skin, and a slender frame that would fit perfectly in my hands. *And way too fucking young for you, asshole*, I try to remind myself.

I blame McLanahan for putting the idea in my mind. I hate to admit it, but the old guy is right. It's been a long time since I've talked to a woman like I do her and an even longer time since I've *been* with a woman.

"Don't worry," she says with an amused tone. "I'm wearing a tank underneath." I glance over, confirming she's right. Except the tank is thin and white, and I can clearly see the outline of her nipples pressed against the fabric.

Jesus.

I scrub a hand down my face, trying to regain some composure.

When I lift my head, I see Holly's pink lips tipped up in a smirk. "Don't worry. I don't strip when I'm not working at the club."

My eyes widen in shock.

"Kidding," she says, her own expression mirroring mine. "Jeez, you'd think I told you I kill people for a living."

I let out a heavy breath. "Honestly, Bambi. That wouldn't even surprise me at this point."

She laughs, shaking her head, and pulls the dress over her head, shedding her sweats once the dress is on. The dress fits her perfectly, hugging her slender frame in all the right places. The black fabric drapes down to just below her knees, with ruffled edges and a white trim that makes her hair and skin glow.

My jaw tightens. She looks so beautiful. I can't remember the last time I saw anyone as beautiful as her, even in her baggy sweaters and big, thick scarves. But this...

"So?" she asks, doing a little twirl, the fabric of the dress swirling around her legs. "What do you think?"

I rub my jaw, trying to clear the lump in my throat. She looks stunning, but the words get stuck somewhere between my chest and my mouth. "It's…" I clear my throat. "That's… good," I finally manage, though it sounds hollow.

Her face falls, a frown tugging at her lips. "Oh. This isn't the one, then."

Damn it. Why couldn't I have just told her the truth? Told her how the sight of her in that dress nearly knocked the breath out of me, told her she looked beautiful—no, more than beautiful. But instead, I tried to play it cool and unintentionally insulted her.

"What about this?" she asks, reaching into her closet and pulling out a top and a mini leather skirt that looks like it would barely cover her ass.

I will fucking die if she puts that on.

"Sure," I say, trying to keep my voice steady, even though all I want is to end this torture and take the coldest shower of my life. "That one looks good."

"Really?" Her eyebrows arch in surprise, and she gives me a curious look. "Huh."

"What?" I ask, suddenly feeling like I've missed something.

"Nothing," she replies with a smirk, her eyes twinkling mischievously. "It's just a little... risky, that's all."

I narrow my eyes at her. "You picked it out."

"And you chose it," she counters, lifting her shoulder in a shrug. "You said the other one was hideous."

I sigh, rubbing the back of my neck. "I definitely didn't say that."

"It's fine, Mark," she says, smoothing her hands down the dress still hugging her body, the fabric clinging to her curves in a way that's making my head spin. "It's just not your type." She pauses, her expression turning thoughtful. "But then again, I guess I'm not either," she adds with a laugh that doesn't quite reach her eyes.

My brows furrow at her words, something about them not sitting right.

"What is your type?" she asks suddenly, catching me off guard.

"In clothes?" I ask, trying to deflect, though I know that's not what she means.

"In women."

I shrug. "I don't think I have one."

"Oh, come on," she presses, sitting down on the bed beside me, her knee brushing against mine. "Everyone has a type."

"I don't," I insist.

She studies me for a moment, her eyes searching my face as if she's trying to read between the lines. "What was your ex like?" she asks, the question carrying more weight than it should. I turn to her with a dry look, my expression closing off at the mention of her. Holly seems to sense she's touched a nerve, and she lets out a small sigh. "Fine. I won't pry," she says. After a beat, she tilts her head, a playful glint returning to her eyes. "You want to know mine?"

"Not particularly, no."

"My type is kind," she says, ignoring my response as a small smile tugs at her lips.

"Wow." I shake my head, smirking at her. "The bar is in hell."

She nudges my shoulder playfully, letting out a laugh that's so sweet it almost makes me forget what we're talking about. "I'm serious," she says, her laughter fading. Her eyes lose some of their usual sparkle as she looks down at her hands. "I've met so many assholes before. All I want is someone to be kind to me. Gentle. Patient." She turns her head to meet my gaze, her expression open and vulnerable in a way I'm not used to seeing. "I want them to understand me, even though I know I'm a lot."

"Understatement," I mutter, trying to lighten the mood, but she just breathes out a small laugh, her eyes drifting away as she gets lost in thought.

"I want him to look at me and have his breath taken away," she says softly, almost like she's admitting a secret she's held onto for too long.

"You want to kill the guy?" I joke.

She laughs, the sound light as she meets my eyes. "Yes," she confirms with a grin. "I want him to be socked in the chest at the sight of me." She shrugs slightly, her expression softening. "It might be too much to ask for, right? I mean, I know I'm not a supermodel or anything special. But that's what I want."

Hearing her talk about herself like that makes something in me twist. Kinda hated hearing her say that.

Her eyes flick up to mine, filled with uncertainty. "Do you think it's too much to want?"

The look in her eyes kills me. I want to tell her that the odds of someone looking at her and falling head over heels might be impossible, and that life isn't a fairy tale where everything just clicks into place. But who the fuck am I to tell her she can't have what she wants? Who am I to crush that hope?

"No," I say, my voice firm. "It's not too much." I take a breath, meeting her gaze. "There's going to be some guy someday who won't know what hit him when he meets you."

Her pink lips curve into a smile, and she looks so genuinely happy that it makes something warm settle in my chest. I like that I can do this for her, even if it's just with a few words.

"Do you think Ryan will like me?" she asks, her eyes bright with hope.

I rub my jaw, the thought of Ryan making that warmth fade. Don't know why I hate hearing his name on her lips so much. "He'd be an idiot not to."

Her eyes widen slightly, shocked by admission, and my jaw tenses. The silence lingers between us until she tears her away, her fingers tracing the lines of the dress. "I hope I find it soon," she says, her smile fading slightly. "Henry looks at Olivia like that, even when they argue." Her voice drops a little. "My dad looked at my mom that way."

"Yeah?"

She nods slowly, her gaze fixed on the floor as if searching for something she's lost. "They were so in love. I've never seen anything like it. I didn't even mind seeing them kiss in front of me," she says, her lips lifting slightly as her voice cracks.

I see the tears well up in her eyes, her chest rising and falling unevenly, and I can tell she's fighting to keep it together.

Fuck.

I reach out and take her hand, giving it a gentle squeeze. The contact seems to break something inside her, and Holly collapses into tears. Her sobs are raw, each one pulling at my chest and twisting my heart.

I just hold her hand, providing whatever comfort I can as she lets it all out. "I'm sorry," she says between sniffles, her voice trembling as she tries to wipe her eyes with the back of her hand. "I haven't cried in a while."

"You don't need to apologize," I say softly as I keep holding her hand. "Cry all you need." She lifts her head, her glassy eyes meeting mine. "I'm right here," I reassure her. "I won't judge you."

Tears continue to fall from her face, mingling with her laughter as she shakes her head, trying to compose herself. "You really are a softie, aren't you?" she says.

"No," I reply, trying to sound firm, though I can't help but feel relief at the sound of her laugh.

A faint smile tugs at her lips as she shrugs. "Okay."

I narrow my eyes at her, trying to maintain some semblance of seriousness. "I'm not."

"Sure," she replies, her tone light and teasing as she shrugs once more. "Whatever you say."

"I'm…" I groan, blowing out a frustrated breath. "You know what? I give up. Can I go now?"

Her laugh eases something inside me, and she nods. "Yeah, you can go. Thank you for coming over and helping me choose an outfit."

I tip my chin. "You're welcome, Bambi."

She flashes me another smile, and I linger for a moment longer, feeling like there's so much more I want to say but not knowing how. So, instead, I nod once more and finally turn to leave.

My hand reaches out to grab the doorknob, but something stops me, and I pivot back around, catching her staring at her reflection in the mirror.

"Holly."

She looks up, her attention shifting from her own reflection to me. "Hmm?"

"Wear the dress."

Chapter Fifteen

Holly

After three hours of getting ready and an extra twenty minutes standing in front of the mirror—ensuring every detail of my outfit was perfect—I finally arrive at the restaurant Ryan reserved for our first date.

I take a moment to glance at my reflection in the restaurant's tinted window, smoothing my hands down the length of my long, black dress. My hair, freshly styled into soft waves by Olivia, is still holding its shape, and I quickly tuck a stray lock behind my ear. I know I've overthought every aspect of this night, but I want everything to be perfect.

With a deep breath, I reach out to grasp the door handle, my stomach fluttering as I push the door open. Tonight's the night I've been anxiously anticipating since I ran into Ryan. For the first time in a long time, I have a good feeling about this date.

I pause, taking in the warm, cozy glow of the restaurant, the soft hum of conversations, the gentle notes of a piano playing in the corner, and the clinking of glasses. My eyes scan the room, flitting between tables as I search for Ryan.

"Good evening, ma'am." A voice pulls me out of my thoughts, and I turn to see the host raising an eyebrow at me. "Do you have a reservation?"

Meeting her gaze, I offer a friendly smile. "Hi. Um, yes, I think so," I say with a nervous laugh.

She doesn't seem amused as she glances down at the reservation book. "Name?" she asks, her eyes still on the pages.

"Ryan," I reply, fidgeting with the strap of my purse.

Without lifting her head, she flicks her eyes up at me over the rim of her square, dark red glasses. "Ma'am, I'm going to need a last name."

My brows knit together. "Oh. Um, I actually don't know his last name."

She sighs, closing the book with a resigned expression. "Ma'am, I can't let you in without knowing the full name of the reservation."

Anxiety spikes within me, and suddenly, my dress feels too tight, too hot, and my bag threatens to slip from my sweaty fingers. "Right," I murmur, shaking my head slightly. "It's just… this is our first date and—"

"She's with me." My breath catches as I feel a hand on my waist, and I turn to see Ryan smiling down at me. "Hi, Holly."

"Hi, Ryan," I reply, trying to swallow down my nerves.

"Ready to head to our table?" he asks, an amused smirk playing on his lips. I nod, offering a quick smile to the host, who quickly returns her attention to the reservation book.

Ryan guides me to our table, his hand warm and reassuring on the small of my back. He pulls out a chair for me and waits until I'm seated before taking his own seat across from me.

"Thank you," I say, feeling a bit more at ease.

"I was starting to think you wouldn't show up," Ryan laughs softly as he slips off his coat, hanging it on the back of his chair.

A nervous laugh escapes me as I brush a stray lock of hair behind my ear. "I'm sorry. My friend was cooking dinner, and then her husband forgot to do the laundry, and I had to—you probably don't want to hear all of this."

Ryan leans in slightly. "Sure, I do."

"Really?"

He nods, flashing me a smile. "I wouldn't have asked you out if I didn't want to hear you talk."

"Wow," I say with a small scoff. "That's a first."

"I doubt that's true," he counters, tilting his head.

I shrug. "You have no idea how many people tell me to shut up."

"Idiots," he says with a warm smile. "All of them."

A genuine smile spreads across my face, and I begin to relax, comforted by his words. It's nice that he likes to hear me talk, just like Mark. Mark never once told me to shut up. He might roll his eyes and act like a big, broody bear, but he always listens, asks questions, and genuinely cares.

"Long story short, my roommates are hectic, and traffic was horrible. That's why I'm late," I sigh, offering Ryan an apologetic smile.

"I'm just glad you're here now," Ryan says, opening his menu and glancing over the options.

"Yeah, me too," I agree, flashing him a warm smile. I like Ryan. He seems kind, and that's all I've ever wanted. Though a nagging thought creeps into my mind. Is Mark right? Should I want more than just someone who's kind to me? I do want more. I want someone who makes me laugh, who makes me happy, who makes me feel comfortable.

Just like I do with—

I blink in the dimly lit room, glancing at the entrance when the door swings open, a brisk wind flooding inside. At first, I think my mind is playing tricks on me, but as I stare, it becomes clear. There, by the door of the restaurant, is—

"Mark?" I murmur to myself, my brows knitting in confusion.

What is he doing here? Why is he at this restaurant, of all places? And why does he look so good, his hair styled perfectly, dressed in a suit and tie that I've never seen him wear before?

Our eyes meet, and his gaze lingers on me, moving slowly down my body as if he's seeing me for the first time. He lifts a hand to rub his mouth, and I can't quite read his expression. There's something in his eyes that makes my heart skip a beat.

He tears his eyes away from me and heads toward the host, giving her a curt nod before he heads toward a table in the corner.

"It's Ryan, actually," Ryan's voice pulls me back to the present, snapping me out of my thoughts.

I blink, refocusing on my date. "Oh, sorry. I just—I thought I saw someone."

"Mark?" Ryan asks, a hint of curiosity in his voice.

I nod. "Yeah, he's… a friend," I reply, sneaking a glance past Ryan's shoulder to catch another glimpse of Mark, but the room is too dimly lit to see clearly.

"A close friend?" Ryan asks, his eyes searching mine for answers.

"Sort of?" I say with a shrug, trying to keep my voice casual. "I met him a few weeks ago," I explain, my fingers absently tracing the edge of the menu in front of me.

"Someone you're seeing?" Ryan asks, raising an eyebrow.

"No, no," I laugh, shaking my head firmly. "Mark would never date me."

"Why not?" Ryan asks, tilting his head.

I shake my head slightly, the idea seeming absurd. "I just don't think I'm his type. Mark is… moody and broody, and I'm…" I gesture to myself with a smile. "The complete opposite."

Ryan chuckles, nodding in agreement. "Well, that's good. I'd hate to have to compete with another guy."

"No competition," I assure him, smiling softly. "He's just a friend."

Ryan's lips curl into a satisfied grin. "So, Holly, besides shopping until you literally drop, what do you do?"

A laugh bubbles out of me at the reminder of our first meeting. "I work with foster kids," I reply.

His brows shoot up. "Oh yeah? That's so interesting," Ryan says, leaning in slightly. "My parents actually fostered a few kids when I was growing up."

"Really?" I ask, my eyes lighting up with intrigue. "That's amazing."

"Yeah, it was very rewarding being a safe place for them," Ryan says, his lips lifting into a smile.

A hint of sadness hits my stomach. I always wished I had a family that wanted me, but most of the time, it felt like I was just passing through, never meant to stay.

I nod, not wanting to delve into my past on a first date. Though, with Mark, I shared my story within days of meeting him, and he has been so supportive, so caring, and—

Why am I thinking about Mark? I'm on a date with Ryan, who's kind, handsome, and clearly successful.

So why can't I stop comparing them?

"And then a couple years later, I took over for my brother and now, I own the company," Ryan finishes, snapping me out of my thoughts.

I blink, trying to remember what he was saying, but I fall short. "You own the company?" I say, my eyes widening.

"Yeah," he chuckles, fixing his tie and signaling the waitress. "I'm the proud CEO of Towner's Marketing Firm."

My eyes threaten to pop out of my head, my mind spinning as I take in what he's telling me. "You're a CEO of a company?" I repeat slowly.

He laughs, shaking his head slightly. "You've never been on a date with a millionaire before, have you?"

"Millionaire?" I say, louder than necessary, as my lips part in surprise.

He clears his throat, glancing around the other tables. "Maybe keep your voice down so we don't get robbed," he jokes, laughing. "But yes."

"Good evening," the waitress greets us, but I'm still staring at my date, my mouth agape in shock. "What would you like to order?"

"I'll have the smoked salmon trout with the pinot grigio," Ryan says, handing over his menu before glancing at me.

"And you, ma'am?" the waitress asks, turning to me.

I blink, trying to focus. "Huh?"

"What would you like to order?" she repeats.

I shake my head, glancing down at my closed menu. "I don't... I haven't..."

"She'll have the same," Ryan says, handing the menus to the waitress. I watch as she walks away, my mind still trying to catch up with everything that's happened in the last few minutes.

Ryan sighs, adjusting his tie as he leans back in his chair. "Maybe I shouldn't have mentioned my job so soon," he says.

"No, no," I reply quickly, shaking my head. "It's not that. I just got a little..."

"Shocked?" he finishes for me, one eyebrow arching up in question.

I nod, feeling a bit sheepish. "Yeah, I guess I was." His smile is reassuring, and I feel my shoulders relax just a bit.

"I get it," he says, leaning forward slightly. "I don't usually lead with that, but there's something about you, Holly." He pauses, his blue eyes locking onto mine as he reaches across the table and takes my hand. "Something I like."

As Ryan's soft hand rests on mine, I can't help but think of Mark's rugged hands that always seem slightly calloused from working at the bar, his casual unbuttoned shirts that somehow suit him perfectly.

Everything about him is worlds apart from Ryan, but there's something about Mark that's comforting and easy. It has been since the very first day we met. With Ryan, on the other hand, I feel like I'm stepping into a world that's not quite mine. And I don't know what to make of it.

There's nothing more to make of it, really. I'm on a date with Ryan, who's clearly interested and wants to pursue something with me. Mark is just my friend—a reluctant dating coach, if I'm being honest. He's been trying to help me navigate the dating world, but once he's done, he won't have any reason to keep me in his life. The thought of him no longer being a part of my life makes my stomach drop, but I have to remind myself that his role is temporary. Right now, I'm here with Ryan, and that's where my focus needs to be.

But my attention is drawn past Ryan as I see Mark standing up from his table. He slips his coat on, and for a moment, he looks over at me. Our eyes lock, and it feels like time slows down. His gaze holds mine for what seems like an eternity before he finally turns and walks out of the restaurant.

"I'm having a great time with you, Holly," Ryan says, his voice breaking into my thoughts and pulling me back to the present.

I force myself to focus, giving him a warm smile. "Me too," I reply, but even as I say the words, I can't help but feel a twinge of guilt. My thoughts keep drifting back to Mark. What was he doing here? Why did he look at me like that?

And why can't I stop thinking about him?

Chapter Sixteen

Mark

I jolt awake to the sound of persistent banging on the door. My groggy brain struggles to piece together what's happening. The noise continues, louder this time, and I grumble in frustration when Murray starts to bark.

"Jesus Christ, woman," I mutter under my breath, already knowing who's knocking on my door as I reluctantly pull myself out of bed. I shuffle to the door and fling it open to find Holly standing at my door with an arched brow.

"Were you sleeping?" she asks.

"What do you think?" I reply, my voice gruff as I try to rub the sleep from my eyes.

"It's almost noon," she says, her brows shooting up. "I would have imagined you to wake up with the sound of chickens."

I give her a dry look. "I don't have any chickens, and I had a long night last night," I mumble, watching as she breezes past me, placing her purse on my couch before she crouches down to pet Murray. "I don't know how I feel about you being so comfortable in my house."

She lets out a small laugh as she rubs Murray's head. "Please. Don't pretend you don't love it," she teases.

I can't even muster a response because… fuck me, she's right. There's something undeniably soothing about her presence. I rub my jaw, watching her kick off her shoes and settle cross-legged on my couch.

"So, what are we watching?" she asks, flopping down on the couch.

"We?" I ask, lifting a brow, still half-dazed.

"I'm here now," she says with a shrug. "So, it's *we*."

"I was planning on sleeping in today."

"Oh." A frown coats her lips. "I should have asked first," she says, standing up as she pulls her coat tighter around herself. "I'm sorry. I'll just—"

"Don't." She freezes, eyes widened as she stares back at me, wondering what I want her to do. Fuck. I hated seeing that frown on her lips or her thinking I didn't want her here. "You came all this way anyway," I say, trying to act casual as I shrug. "You can stay."

Her shoulders drop in relief as she throws her coat back onto the arm of the couch. "Good," she says with a smile. "Because I *really* didn't want to leave."

She shuffles back against the cushions and kicks her shoes off. My jaw tightens looking over her. This fucking woman. Came into my life, took over everything, and now acts like she belongs here.

I sigh, dropping down on the couch beside her.

She'd be fucking right.

My body goes rigid for a moment, unsure how to react when she lies her head on my chest. "What are you doing?" I ask, my voice rough with confusion.

She lifts her head, a small smirk tugging at her lips as her big eyes meet mine. "It's called cuddling, Mark. Get used to it."

"I hate it," I mumble, but when she starts to lift her head, I wrap my arm around her shoulder, halting her. "I didn't tell you to move."

She smiles, snuggling in comfortably. "I'm so happy I met you," she says, her voice a quiet hum, a sound so comforting I don't know what I'll do when I eventually never hear it again.

Her words catch me off guard, and I look down at her. I don't know what the hell hit me the day I met this girl. Before that, my life was black and white, a dullness coating it, and now, she's made everything bright and colorful. "Yeah," I admit. "Me too, Holly."

She lets out a soft laugh, shaking her head, making me furrow my brows.

"Why are you laughing?" I ask her.

She lifts her head to meet my eyes and shrugs. "I thought you'd tell me that you regret talking to me when we first met," she says.

I blink, a frown forming on my lips. "Why would I ever say that?"

She shrugs again. "Because then I wouldn't be in your life, disturbing your sleep, or making you be my dating coach," she says, her throat moving as she swallows.

God help me, but I actually like that she's in my life. *A lot.*

"Is that what I am?" I ask instead, trying to bury the thoughts deep inside my brain where they belong. "Your dating coach?"

143

"Well, you're my friend too," she says with a smile.

"Yeah?"

She nods. "And my bartender," she continues. "And my cookie taste tester."

"That, I'm not complaining about," I tell her, feeling my chest jump when she lets out a soft laugh. Our eyes lock and I feel my lips twitching, seeing her infectious smile.

"Shit," she gasps, sitting up when her phone starts ringing before she reaches out to grab it and glances down at the screen with a frown on her face.

"What's wrong?" I ask.

She lifts her head. "Ryan texted."

Oh. Right.

My shoulders feel tense at the reminder of watching Holly and Ryan on their date yesterday. I wasn't even supposed to be there. I was supposed to be behind the bar, working, like I always do. But I just… couldn't. I had to see him for myself. I had to see *them*. And when I did… fuck, my stomach dropped. She looked so happy, and he looked perfect for her. And I felt like I had been kicked in the fucking nuts.

I rub my chin. "What did he say?"

"He wants to go out again," she says, her voice flat, and her brows knitted together.

Of course he does. Just fucking look at her.

The muscle in my jaw ticks, tightening as I raise an eyebrow at her expression. "Do you like this guy?" I ask her.

She keeps hold of my eyes for a beat, the seconds stretching and then she lifts her shoulder. "I think so."

I nod. Nod again. Keep fucking nodding like it's going to erase those words from my mind. "And the date went well, yeah?" I ask, trying to maintain some composure but feeling nothing but the tightness building in my chest.

"I mean…" She blinks, her eyes meeting mine. "You were there," she points out, making me remember the way she looked last night.

It was one thing seeing her the other day, but seeing her in her full outfit, hair freshly done, and makeup on in the dim lighting of the restaurant.

Fuck, she looked so beautiful.

"I only came to see if he didn't check someone else out like the other assholes," I tell her. "I left when I saw you two laughing." I shrug, trying to keep my expression neutral. "I assumed it was going well."

That's a lie. I don't lie to Holly. I like how honest she is, and I always try to be honest with her too, but I just lied straight to her face. The reason I rushed out of the restaurant was because I saw him reach out to hold her hand in his, and I didn't fucking like the sight of it at all. Or the way my stomach sank to my ass at the thought of them together.

"Yeah," she says with a slow nod. "I guess it did."

I nod, trying to mask the hurt banging against my chest. "Then what's the problem, Bambi?"

She sighs, tilting her head back. "He wants to go ice skating," she says, squeezing her eyes closed.

"Okay…" I say, feeling a flicker of confusion as to why she's freaking out about it if she likes this guy.

When she opens her eyes, they meet mine and she frowns, shaking her head. "I don't know how to skate," she admits, her voice tinged with distress.

My brows shoot up. "You're serious?" I ask, unable to hide my surprise. "I know I call you Bambi, but…"

"I'm serious, Mark," she says, rolling those adorable eyes. Wait. Hold the fuck up. Did I just say adorable? "Now is not the time for your jokes," she says, frustrated. "What do I do? I would cancel, but…" She tugs her bottom lip between her teeth, shaking her head. "He seems like a good guy and is interested in me, and…." She exhales. "I think I like him, too."

The cramping in my stomach intensifies at her admission, but my jaw ticks at the sight of her saddened expression. Those lips downturned, and her eyes dropped to the ground. Fuck, I hate seeing her like this.

Don't do it.

Don't fucking do it.

Just sit the fuck back and let her deal with it. Let her cancel the date, that way she won't see the guy ever again.

Just stay the fuck out of it.

But I can't stop myself when I sneak a glance at her again and see the frown on her face. With a sigh, I stand up and grab my coat from the hanger, picking up my keys on the console table.

"Come on," I tell her, pulling my coat on.

"What?" she says, lifting her head in confusion. "Where?"

"We're going ice skating."

Chapter Seventeen

Holly

The cold air stings my face as we walk toward the rink, and I shove my hands deeper into my pockets, trying to warm up my body. But it's not working. I'm wearing a T-shirt, a big fluffy sweater, a puffer coat, a scarf, a hat, and I'm still *really* fricking cold.

I tell myself that's the only reason why my bones are shaking right now, and not the nerves building up inside me. We head toward the rink, and the sound of laughter and music fills the air, the magical lights making my eyes light up as skates scrape across the ice. It looks so magical, it almost doesn't look real, and I should be loving this, but all I can focus on is the nervous knot forming in my stomach.

"I'm nervous," I admit, glancing over at Mark. My voice comes out smaller than I intended, but I keep my eyes on him.

He raises an eyebrow slightly as he pulls his gloves tighter. "You've got nothing to be nervous about," he says, his voice steady.

I sneak a glance at the slick, shiny ice in front of us. "What if I fall?" I blurt out, worry creeping into my voice.

"You probably will," he replies, his tone matter-of-fact as he sits on the bench and starts putting his skates on.

I shoot him a dry look. "Thanks." Of all the things he could say to make me feel better, that definitely wasn't it.

Mark shrugs. "Just being honest, Bambi," he says, tying the laces before he turns his eyes on me. "If you've never skated before, then you'll probably fall, but I'll be here," he says. "And I'll catch you."

I try to shake off the nerves that are making my hands a little shaky as I pull my boots off before placing the skates on. "I should have just canceled," I mutter, more to myself than him.

He catches my eye, his expression tightening. "If you like the guy, then I don't see why you'd want to cancel."

I frown, the thought of having to do this all over again without Mark this time, only fueling the anxiety brewing inside me. "What if I make a fool of myself?" I ask.

Mark lifts himself off the bench and stands in front of me before kneeling down to the ground, on one knee, while he places my foot on it and ties off the laces. "We're here so that won't happen," he says softly. "You can make a fool out of yourself in front of me all you like." He tightens the last lace and slowly drops my foot back to the ground. "I won't mind. I won't judge."

My lips widen as a smile breaks through, and my chest starts banging. "You never do."

He stares back at me for a while before he nods, lifting himself off the ground. "Let's go, Bambi," he says, gesturing toward the ice.

I let out a laugh. "Oh hey, that nickname finally works in this scenario," I say, fitting my arm underneath his to wrap it around his arm as we head toward the ice.

"It works everywhere," he teases, glancing down at me with an arched brow. "You have no balance."

I gasp. "I used to do gymnastics in school," I say defensively.

Mark looks at me with a raised eyebrow, clearly skeptical. "Really?" He shakes his head. "I have a hard time believing that."

"Have I ever lied to you?" I ask.

He shrugs. "I don't know. You could be a pro at skating and lied just to get me here."

I can't help but laugh, the tension in my shoulders easing a little. "That's way too smart. I'm not that smart."

Mark's face drops slightly. "I hate when you say that," he says, his brows knitting together.

"What?" I ask, a little confused.

"I'm not that smart, I'm not pretty, I'm not funny," he says, repeating my words. "Holly, you've got to stop with the self-depreciation. You're all of those things."

A warmth spreads through my chest at his words, and I shake my head slightly. "I am?"

A low groan escapes his throat. "Don't make me repeat it," he mutters.

But I want him to repeat it. I want to hear him say I'm pretty, smart, and funny over and over again until these butterflies stop in my stomach, though I doubt they ever will. "I just didn't hear you, with these earmuffs and all,"

149

I say, tugging at the fluffy white muffs that are probably way too big for my head.

A puff of air leaves his lips, his breath visible in the cold air as he shakes his head. "You look like a huge marshmallow."

I frown. "It's cold," I protest, pulling my scarf tighter around my neck. "It's not my fault you're made of ice."

He arches a brow. "I'm used to the cold," he says. "I used to play hockey."

My eyes widen, surprise taking over. "You did?"

He nods, pressing his lips flat. "In college."

Wow. I rake my eyes over him, taking in his burly frame. "Were you good?"

He shrugs. "Pretty good."

"So why did you quit?" I ask, furrowing my brows.

He shakes his head. "It wasn't my dream to be a pro hockey player. It was just something I enjoyed doing."

I nod in understanding. I mean, I love shopping, but I wouldn't give up my dream of working with foster children for anything in the world.

"So, is the bar your dream, then?"

He turns his head, his brows tugging together and he looks lost in thought. "I never thought it would be," he admits. "But when I met Charles…" He doesn't finish his sentence, and I reach out, placing my hand over his as our eyes lock together.

A tap on the railing of the skating rink snaps us out of the moment and we glance at the guy in the ticket office. "You guys are up next," he says.

Mark holds eye contact. "You ready?"

"No," I admit, staring at the smooth ice with wide eyes. I'm pretty sure my knees are going to give out the second I step onto that ice.

"Come on, you'll be fine. I've got you," he says, untangling our arms before he reaches for my hand.

Reluctantly, I take it, and we step out onto the ice together. My legs wobble immediately, and I can already feel the panic rising in my throat. "Oh, fuck," I blurt out as I stumble, my feet slipping out from under me.

"That's the first time I've ever heard you swear," I hear Mark saying, though I can't see him, because I'm too busy trying not to fall on my ass.

I breathe out a scoff. "Yeah, well, excuse me for swearing when I'm on a block of ice with blades on my feet." My feet slip again and I groan, squeezing my eyes closed. "This is so not natural."

Mark's hand tightens around mine, and in an instant, he's there, steadying me, his arm wrapping around my waist to keep me upright. "I've got you," he says, his voice close, warm against the cold air. "Hold my hand."

"I don't think that's going to help me right now," I cry, wanting to go back to my warm comfortable stable bed. "If I go down, I'll take you with me."

"Bambi, you're half my size," he says dryly. "Just hold on and look at me," he tells me, his voice softer than usual.

I groan before snapping my eyes open and lifting my head to look up at him.

"That's it," he says with a nod. "Just keep your eyes on me."

For a moment, I'm frozen, but not from the cold. I'm staring up at him, my heart racing for reasons that have nothing to do with fear. His face is inches from mine, and I can see every detail. The way his breath fogs in the air between us and his eyes, usually so guarded, soften as they meet mine.

"Your eyes," I murmur.

"What about them?" he asks.

I keep my attention on the warm chocolate pools with specks of gold scattered. "They're… like honey. I never noticed how beautiful they are."

The silence between us stretches, the music filling the air before he murmurs so quietly I almost miss it, "Right back at you, Holly."

A flush creeps onto my cheeks as we start skating slowly, Mark keeping a firm hold on my hand. It's almost as if he's afraid to let go, and honestly, I don't want him to. I focus on moving one foot in front of the other, the feeling of sliding across the ice becoming slightly less terrifying with each step.

Mark squeezes my hand, drawing my attention back to him. "You see, Bambi? You're skating," he says, a hint of pride in his voice.

I glance down at our feet moving over the ice, and my eyes widen before I lift my head, looking back at him. "I'm doing it," I repeat with a chuckle. I'm actually skating. Clumsily, sure, but I'm still doing it.

"I knew you could. You ready for me to let go, yet?" he asks.

"Don't you dare," I warn, my grip on his hand tightening.

A laugh escapes him as he shakes his head and tightens his hold on me. "Okay, I won't let you go."

I freeze, my lips dropping open as I'm stuck staring back at him.

I stop moving on the ice, lifting my hand to trace his lips with my fingers. "Do that again."

His brows lift a little. "What are you talking about?" he asks, his voice low, his breath warm against my fingertips.

I lift my eyes to his and shake my head. "You… smiled," I say, feeling a rush of fluttering in my chest. "You finally smiled." I breathe out a soft laugh. "I was starting to think it was physically impossible for you to do."

He chuckles again, softly this time and the sound vibrates through me, warm and comforting and I've quickly become addicted to the way he smiles. "You make it easy," he says, covering his hand over mine.

His hand is firm on my waist, holding me securely, and suddenly, the world seems to narrow down to just this—just him and me and the way he's looking at me like he might see something in me I've never even seen in myself. I feel a strange warmth spreading through me, starting at the spot where his hand rests against my waist.

For a heartbeat, neither of us moves. We're just… staring at each other, caught in a moment I don't fully understand. I'm hyper-aware of how close we are and how easy it would be to just lean in and close the gap between us. My eyes drop to his lips, and I wonder if he's thinking the same thing.

Then, just as quickly as it started, the moment breaks. I blink, and Mark shifts, his arm still around me but his gaze moving away, looking out over the ice instead of at me. "Let's go, Bambi," he says gruffly. "We've got a lot of practice before your date."

I swallow hard, the reminder of why we're here jolting me back to reality. "Right, my date."

"With Ryan," he adds, his eyes hardening as his previous smile is wiped clean.

But my mind wasn't on Ryan. For a moment, it was about nothing and nobody but *us*.

I turn my attention back to Mark, I can't help the nagging thought in my mind. My eyes drift over his face, searching for… I don't even know what.

Ryan is a great guy. And he's funny and likes me. And I did have a great time with him.

Then why can't I stop wishing Mark would have kissed me?

Chapter Eighteen

Holly

"Don't burn it," Olivia warns her husband, narrowing her eyes as she hands him her trusty wooden spoon.

The smell of rich, chocolatey goodness fills the kitchen, and I can practically taste the gooey center of the molten lava cakes she's been promising to make for weeks.

"I won't," he grumbles, heading into the kitchen.

Olivia rolls her eyes as she turns to me. "He will," she says.

"He better not," I add, narrowing my eyes. "I've been waiting for you to make it for way too long." My stomach rumbles in agreement.

"Well, I can't promise anything. We might just end up having a burnt dessert on our hands," she says, shaking her head.

"Great," I mutter. "Why the hell are you trusting him with this anyway?" I ask her.

She sighs, subconsciously rubbing her belly. "He said he wanted to learn so that when I'd be with the baby, he could help me out." She scrunches her nose, letting out a laugh. "He's so cheesy."

My eyes soften. "That's so sweet," I say, wishing someday someone would love me that much.

"Yeah," she admits with a smile on her face, before turning to me. "So, you're staying for dinner today?" she asks.

I blink, fidgeting with my sleeve. "Are you sick of me already?" I joke, but my chest tightens at the thought that she might be getting sick of having me around. "I know it's not easy having me living in your house."

"Are you kidding?" she says, her eyes wide with disbelief. "I love having you here. Who knows, maybe I would have already killed Henry if it wasn't for you," she jokes, her lips curling into a smirk.

A laugh bubbles out of me. "He should be thanking me for saving his life."

"Exactly, she says, laughing softly, but then her expression becomes serious. "You know this is your home as much as it's ours, Holly. You don't need to run off to Mark's."

"It's not that," I say. "I just… like hanging out with him," I admit.

She hums in acknowledgment. "Then why aren't you going over there tonight?"

I swallow, looking away. "I thought it was best if I gave him a break," I say with a nervous laugh.

"I bet he's devastated," she says with a laugh.

I scoff. "More like relieved," I say with a shake of my head.

"I don't know about that," she says, her tone thoughtful as she glances at me. "It seems like he likes having you around. You go over there a lot. Are you sure nothing else is going on?" she asks, wiggling her eyebrows.

"Like what?" I ask, feigning ignorance even though my heart thuds against my chest.

"Do I need to tell you a little story about the birds and the bees?" Olivia says, tilting her head. "It all started with a little bee—"

I roll my eyes, trying to laugh it off. "Are you crazy?"

"What?" she asks innocently, though I can see the mischievous glint in her eyes.

"No," I say with a shake of my head. "Nothing like that is happening between us."

"Are you sure?" she presses, narrowing her eyes.

Memories of the night he took me ice skating come flooding to my mind and I tug my bottom lip between my teeth to avoid spilling out everything. But if I can't tell her, then who can I tell? "Well…" I start.

"Well?" she echoes, leaning forward with widened eyes.

"There was this… thing," I begin, struggling to find the right words.

"Thing? What thing? His thing?" she asks, her eyebrows shooting up in mock horror.

"No," I affirm, my cheeks flushing. "There was… a kiss. Well, an almost kiss."

Olivia's eyes widen even more—if that's even physically possible. "You kissed him?" she yells, loud enough for our neighbors to hear. I already know she's going to tell Henry everything I tell her, so I don't mind him hearing it from his wife's yelling.

157

"No," I say quickly, shaking my head. "But I almost did."

She leans in closer, her interest fully captured. "An almost-kiss, huh? And was it you that started this almost-kiss?"

"I mean… I think it was both?" I say with a shrug, but my brows dip as I replay the memory in my mind. "But what if it was just me?"

"So, what happened exactly?" she asks eagerly.

"He took me ice skating because I have a date coming up with Ryan," I explain.

"Ryan?" she asks, frowning slightly.

"The guy I'm dating," I remind her.

Her eyes bug open. "Damn, woman. How many balls are you juggling?"

"None," I say, playfully slapping her arm. "I'm dating Ryan, and Mark is just helping me since I suck at the whole dating thing."

"And?" she prompts.

My chest flutters at the memory. "He took me skating, held onto my hand the whole time, and then he… smiled." My cheeks flush. It seems like such a small, silly, insignificant thing, but it's a big deal to me. Mark has never smiled. Ever. And the other night, he looked into my eyes and smiled. Twice.

"He… smiled?" Olivia repeats, blinking in disbelief.

"Exactly," I say, throwing my hands up. "It's the first time I've ever seen him smile, and I was just so… and then we… I…" I shake my head. "I swear he was leaning in, but I don't know if that's just what I wanted to happen."

"And then?" she asks, her voice low.

I swallow the disappointment down, just like I did that night. "He pulled away, and we continued to skate like nothing had happened." I shake my head. "Or maybe nothing happened and I was just reading into it." A wash of embarrassment coats me. "I don't think he wanted to kiss me," I admit, my voice barely a whisper.

Olivia sighs beside me, leaning against my shoulder. "I'm sorry, Bambi."

"Don't call me that," I say with narrowed eyes.

She shakes her head. "No can do. It's stuck now."

Damn you, Mark.

"What are you going to do?" she asks, nudging her shoulder against mine.

"I don't know," I admit, my shoulders slumping, my thoughts a jumbled mess. "I'm dating Ryan. He's smart, and successful, handsome, kind, everything I'm looking for." I swallow harshly. "But when we were at the skating rink, I just wished Mark had kissed me."

"Holy shit," she breathes, pulling back to look at me, her eyes wide with realization. "You really like Mark."

I nod. "I think I do," I admit, finally letting the truth come out.

"Shit," she says again. "I've never known you to have feelings for a guy."

Yeah. Me neither. I've been on date after date, but it never turned into much. Either they didn't like me, or I didn't like them. But with Mark, I wasn't even trying. He just fell into my life, and I fell for him.

"Yeah, well, it's not like anything's going to happen," I say. "He doesn't see me that way, clearly."

"You don't know that for sure," Olivia says.

"He pulled away, Olivia," I remind her. "If he wanted to kiss me, don't you think he would have?"

"Maybe," she says with a shrug. "With Henry, I had to make the first move."

"That was different," I argue, closing my eyes.

"Not really," she says, shaking her head. "He was shy and grumpy and wouldn't even look at me." She sighs dramatically. "But unfortunately, my heart decided he was the one I wanted." She shrugs casually. "So I went for it. And now look at me," she says, rubbing her swollen belly.

"I don't think I can do that," I tell her. Olivia might not think it's a different situation, but it's not. I'm not the kind of girl that can make the first move.

"Why not?" she asks.

"I really like Mark," I admit, my voice breaking slightly. "And if I just kissed him out of nowhere… if he doesn't feel the same for me, I can't even imagine what would happen between us." I shiver at the thought. Everything is so fun and easy between us. "I don't want to lose him over a mixed signal." Olivia nods in agreement. "I think I'll see how it goes with Ryan," I say, though the words feel heavy on my tongue. "At least I know he likes me."

"But do you like him?" she asks.

"Yeah… of course," I say, the hesitation in my voice betraying me. "He's great."

"That didn't sound too convincing," she says, her brow furrowing.

"I barely know the guy," I protest, trying to defend myself. "I don't think it's a fair comparison."

"You hardly knew Mark, and you didn't have these hesitations about him," Olivia points out.

"That's different," I argue, shaking my head. "Mark was just a friend, and I loved his company. I'm trying to date Ryan—it's a completely different ballpark."

"If you say so," Olivia says, though the doubt in her voice is clear.

I sniff the air, catching a whiff of something that makes my heart sink. "Do you smell that?"

Olivia's eyes widen, and she whirls around to face the oven. "Oh no," she groans, rushing out of the room to head into the kitchen.

"I knew it," I hear her yell. "I told you to keep an eye on the stove!"

"I'm fucking trying!" Henry shouts back, clearly flustered.

I try to keep the smile off my face, but it's impossible when I hear Olivia curse.

"Jesus Christ," she mutters loudly. "Men. Can't live with them. Can't live without them."

My head turns to my phone sitting on my nightstand and I think of Mark. After what happened at the rink, I've been keeping my distance, but all I want to do is hang out with him. Besides, it's not like there will be any lava cakes I'll miss out on.

I grab my phone and scroll to his messages, my fingers hovering over the buttons for a few seconds, before I finally type out a message.

Holly:

Hi.

I wait, the seconds ticking by, my anxiety making the wait feel longer than it is. Finally, my phone buzzes with his reply.

Mark:

Yes. You can come over, Bambi.

Chapter Nineteen

Mark

My ears perk up at the sound of footsteps climbing up the stairs, and I don't even need to check the peephole to know it's Holly. I don't know what the fact that I've memorized her footsteps says about me.

I shoo Murray off my lap with a gentle tap and lift off the couch with a grunt before making my way to my door. When I open it, I see Holly standing with her arm in the air, fist curled up, ready to knock.

"Beat you to it," I say, opening the door wider so she can come inside.

"How did you know it was me?" she asks, her brows knitting in confusion as she walks inside.

My brow raises. "Did you forget you texted me?"

"It could have been someone else," she replies, pulling her big, puffy coat off before throwing it over the arm of the couch. "There are a lot of murderers in New York, Mark. You need to be careful," she says, my eyes dipping to the ridiculous green and red sweater she has on. I feel my lips tugging at the sight.

"You worried about me, Bambi?" I tease, watching her cheeks flush with a soft pink.

She ignores me, turning around to greet Murray. "Hey, boy," she says, her voice soft and kind and everything that she is. "I got you something."

She reaches into her purse, pulling out a red Christmas hat before she carefully positions it on top of his head. My brows dip—It looks fucking ridiculous, barely fits him—but Holly's smiling so wide, I don't want to say anything that will take that smile away. Besides, Murray's practically vibrating with excitement, his tail wagging as she kisses the top of his head.

Same, buddy.

I feel the same exact way whenever I see her.

I don't know what kind of magic she did, but Holly went from being someone who interrupted my peace and quiet with endless questions and a joy that suffocated me, to someone I look forward to seeing. I crave her company, her questions, her texts, calls, practice dates. Whatever it is, I can't wait to see her.

Jesus. *I'm so fucked.*

I run my hand over my beard, watching as she giggles with Murray, and my brows furrow, remembering what happened between us a few days ago.

The way she looked at me and traced my lips with her soft fingers… I was two seconds away from cupping her face in my hands and kissing the hell out of those soft, puffy, red lips. But I stopped myself when I remembered we were on a practice date for her actual date. The guy she's seeing. *The guy she likes.*

I've been out of my mind, wrestling with these feelings inside of me. I'm too damn old for her. I'm not right for her. I don't deserve someone as amazing as her.

164

She's so bright and colorful and brings joy with her everywhere she goes. And I'm... nowhere near what she's looking for.

Holly lets out a loud gasp that breaks me out of a million and one thoughts of her roaming in my head. "You lit a fire," she says, her mouth dropping in awe as her eyes lock on the cracking flames in the fireplace.

I arch a brow. "It's cold."

"That's Christmassy," she counters with a teasing smile.

"It's winter," I say with an eye roll before dropping on the couch beside her. "Stop trying to make me join your cult."

"Your daddy's a liar, isn't he, baby?" she asks Murray, giving him a scratch behind his ears, the Christmas hat wobbling to one side.

"He's not a baby. He's a dog," I say, though my heart melts a little at the sight of them together.

"And he's also a big grump," she adds, lifting her head to flash me a smirk.

I give up on trying to win this argument and let out a sigh. "What do you want from me, Bambi?" I ask her. We hadn't talked since our ice skating practice date, and I didn't know whether she was trying to avoid me or not. But now that she's here, it eases my mind a little.

"The pleasure of your company," she says, flashing me a sweet smile as she cuddles up next to me, the heat of her body radiating through mine.

"First person to say that," I grunt back.

"I'm sure that's not true," she says, lifting her head to look up at me. "What about your ex-girlfriend?" she asks, making my brows furrow. "She must have loved your company."

Hate the thought of my ex being in Holly's head. She's not even in mine. Hasn't been for a long time. I raise an eyebrow, hating that I have to be reminded of everything that went down between us. "If she did, then she wouldn't have cheated on me, sweetheart."

Her brows raise a little, shocked by the fact before they knit together. "I'm sorry."

I shrug. "Not your fault."

"I shouldn't have brought it up," she says, tugging her plump bottom lip between her teeth. "I was just curious—I always get curious—and I was wondering about her and you, and well…" She sighs. "I'm sorry."

"It's fine, Bambi," I say, my voice coated in amusement at the sound of her rambling. "It was a long time ago, I'm fine, everything's fine. You don't need to be sorry."

She nods a few times, stealing a quick glance at Murray before she turns to face me again. "Is that why you haven't dated anyone since her?"

The question catches me off guard, and my brows lift on their own accord. "I don't know," I admit, shaking my head slightly. "I was hurt after I found her in our bed with someone else, but…" I breathe hard, keeping my eyes on Holly. "I guess after that, it made me stop believing that the kind of love Mia and Charles had, existed."

Her eyes widen, worry tugging at her features. "You seriously think that?"

I rub my jaw. "I don't know," I say honestly, feeling conflicted with the whole thing. "Sasha was…" I halt for a moment. "She was highly driven, and I think the life we had wasn't what she wanted." I swallow hard. "*I* wasn't what she wanted. So, she found it someplace else." I shake my head. "I was a fucking idiot for thinking that if you loved someone, it would be enough. That they would love you back, that they'd stay with you, that they wouldn't break your heart." I meet Holly's eyes and see the worry tinged in them. "While you might find that someday, Holly. I know it's just not for me."

"Never?" she asks, her voice a little quiet.

I glance at her, feeling my heart bang against my chest at the sight of her. My instinct is to say never, but I can't help but remember the way I almost kissed her just a few days ago. I haven't felt the desire to talk to a woman, let alone kiss one in five fucking years. And then she comes into my life and…

"Never," I say instead because I need to cut these notions out of my brain. Holly isn't an option. She never was. She'll find someone she likes, whether that's Ryan or someone else, and she'll have a beautiful life with him, and I'll forget about her.

Probably.

"Oh," she says, her brows knitting together. She doesn't say anything after that, and I note a pensive look in her eyes, making me confused.

"You're quiet," I say. "It's not like you."

She lifts her head, frowning slightly. "I can be quiet," she says, which makes me breathe out a scoff.

"You can? I've never seen it," I tease her.

167

"I can," she says, lifting her chin. "I can sit here and read my book and you won't hear a peep from me." Reaching into her bag, she takes her book out and opens it up, scanning the pages.

I arch a brow when her eyes don't lift from the pages. Is she serious? I wait a few seconds, but when she makes no move to talk, I sigh, hating the quiet whenever she's here and even when she's not. I like hearing her talk. I've grown accustomed to it. "I give up," I say, throwing my arms up. "I don't like when you're quiet."

She looks up at me, her gorgeous brown eyes swirling with a mix of caramel and uncertainty. "You don't?"

"No," I admit. "I like hearing you speak."

Her lips quirk at the corners and she folds the corner of the page before placing the book back in her bag. "I knew you did."

My eyes widen, not bothering to correct her because… "You *fold* the page?"

She glances at me. "Of course. How else will I know what page I was last on?"

I blink, wondering if she's joking. Doesn't look like it. "I don't know, maybe by using a bookmark?"

She shakes her head. "I don't have one. This is just easier."

Christ. She's a menace.

She looks around my apartment and a soft sigh leaves her lips making my brows dip. "You're still quiet," I point out.

"Just thinking," she murmurs, lifting her shoulders in a shrug.

"About?"

Our eyes meet and I get lost in them for a moment, my stomach feeling weird. "Sasha was an idiot," she blurs out, shaking her head slightly. "You're an amazing guy, Mark, and Sasha was a fucking idiot for letting you go." My brows shoot up, partly because Holly rarely ever swears and partly because I've never heard her say anything like that before, and I don't know what the fuck to do about it. "I was at home and all I wanted to do was to come see you," she admits. "I really missed you. And I can't imagine how someone would prefer being anywhere but with you."

She lets out a heavy breath after saying all that, which is good, considering the breath has been sucked straight out of my lungs. Jesus. This fucking woman. Why the hell did she come into my life? And why am I dreading the day she finally leaves?

"Missed you too, Bambi," I admit, my voice rough.

Her eyes light up, widening a little. "You did?"

"Sure," I say with a shrug. "Who else is going to pester me about Christmas any chance they get?"

Her eyebrows furrow, a frown coating her lips. "That's not all I do," she says, trying to defend herself.

"No," I agree with a nod. "You're right. You talk my ear off about anything and everything," I tease.

Her frown deepens and the sight doesn't sit well with me at fucking all. "Well if I annoy you that much—" She grabs her purse and her coat, and my brows dip.

"What are you doing?" I ask her.

"Leaving," she replies, leaning down to kiss Murray's head. "I don't want to *pester* you anymore, so—"

169

"Christ, Bambi. I was fucking kidding," I say, feeling my pulse go haywire as I watch her shuffle off the couch, ready to stand, and before I know what I'm doing, I'm tugging on her wrist, pulling her into me until she lands straight on my lap.

She lets out a loud gasp, her widened eyes meeting mine as we both realize her ass is on my lap, an inch away from my cock.

Christ. Don't fucking think about that right now, asshole.

My hands, resting on her hips, squeeze slightly and another gasp is pulled from her throat, making me clear my throat. "You don't pester me," I say, my voice low as I keep my eyes on hers, our faces less than three inches apart.

"No?" she replies, just as quietly.

I shake my head, wanting to grip her hips in my hand again, but blaring alarms ring in my head and I'm reminded she isn't mine. She never will be. She's Ryan's. At least for now. I quickly lift her up and place her on the couch beside me, running a hand through my hair as I remember the warmth of her body pressed against mine.

"Tell me about the date," I say, trying to remind myself why having notions about this girl is a really fucking bad idea.

"Date?"

I turn to face her, seeing a confused, hazy look in her eyes and I blink, my eyes drifting to her parted lips, wondering what she'd taste like. I don't have a doubt in my body that she'd taste sweet. Warm caramel, freshly

170

baked cookies, vanilla, candy. Everything about this woman screams *sweet.*

"Yeah," I say, clearing my throat again. "With Ryan?"

She blinks, snapping out of it, and nods. "Right. Ryan."

"So? How did it go?" I ask. Don't know why I do. Don't want to know about their date.

She blinks again, tilting her head slightly. "Are you sure you want to hear this?"

"Of course," I lie through my fucking teeth, feeling my fists curl up beside me. "I'm your dating coach, right?"

"Right," she replies with a few nods, glancing down at her lap before she takes a deep breath. "It went well, I guess," she says. "He was nice and funny, and your ice skating lessons helped a lot," she says with a shake of her head, a laugh bubbling out of her. "But I still ended up falling on my ass." She lifts her head, meeting my eyes. "He didn't seem to mind, though. He actually thought it was pretty funny."

I rub my jaw, feeling the stubble of my beard pricking my fingers. "Sounds... great," I say, trying to mask the disappointment coursing through my body. I force a casual tone, though my mind is racing with a million and one thoughts. Did he hold her hand like I did? Did they laugh? What did they talk about? *Did he kiss her?*

A flash of the image crosses my mind, and I clench my jaw so hard that I can feel my teeth grinding.

"It was," she says with a nod before she meets my eyes. "And then at the end we uh... we kissed."

Fuck.

My heart sinks. Jesus. Get it the fuck together. You knew what the deal was when you met her.

"And?" I ask, trying to steady my voice.

"It was… nice," she says, with a lift of her shoulder.

"Nice?" I repeat, arching a brow at her uninterested demeanor. "Sweetheart, a kiss shouldn't be described as *nice.*"

"No?" she says, knitting her brows in confusion.

My jaw tightens. "Hell fucking no." I keep my eyes on hers. "It should be passionate. He should have cupped your face and looked into your eyes, showing you how much he wanted you." Her lips part slightly, and I don't even know what the fuck I'm doing. I'm telling her everything I'd do if I ever got the chance that asshole had. "He should have leaned in, his lips an inch away from yours, your breaths mingling before he finally kissed you." Fuck. My body grows hot with the image of doing just that to her. "He should have kissed you with everything in him. It should have been hot, he should have made you moan, he should have left you feeling like you couldn't *breathe.*"

Her gulp is audible as pink tints her cheeks. "Oh," she says, the flush of color coating her skin. "I mean, it was pretty quick," she admits. "It was more like a peck."

Fucking idiot.

How he had her in his arms, wanting him, and he didn't kiss the living daylights out of her I will never know.

"He hasn't texted me since, so maybe he isn't interested anymore," she says.

172

"Not fucking possible."

Her eyes widen. "What?"

Fuck. What the hell am I going to say now? *Not possible because you can't fathom the idea of not wanting her? Because you've been picturing yourself with her?*

"I saw you guys on your date," I remind her, swallowing down the bullshit. "I could tell that he was into you."

"You think?"

"Yeah, Bambi," I reply, nodding. "He'd be an idiot not to be. I'm sure he'll call again if that's what you want." My eyes shift to hers. "That is what you want, right?"

She's quiet for a minute, blinking slowly before she nods. "Yeah." Her voice wavers and I'm stricken with confusion. I can't quite read her expression. She kissed the guy, wanted him to text her, and said she likes him, yet I can't help but wonder why she doesn't sound convincing.

She glances around my apartment. "I can't believe it's December already," she says. "I miss searching for the perfect tree and decorating it."

"You don't decorate your tree at home?" I ask.

She shakes her head. "Olivia takes care of that. Even Henry isn't allowed to mess with her tree." She roams my apartment again, letting out a loud sigh. "I can't help but notice your living room is *so* empty," she says, turning to face me and fluttering her lashes.

"No fucking way," I say, my eyes hardening.

173

"What?" she says, shrugging as she keeps fluttering those lashes at me. "I was just stating a fact," she says, feigning ignorance.

I give her a dry look. "I know what you're doing," I reply, catching her sly smile. "And the answer is no."

She chuckles lightly, her shoulders dropping when she realizes I've caught on. "Please?" she begs, interlocking her fingers together and pressing her hands to her chest.

"I'm not putting a fucking Christmas tree in my house," I say firmly, trying to avoid her eyes.

"But it will make this place look so pretty," she argues. "You won't even have to do anything. I'll take care of everything."

I meet her eyes, see the pleading look on her face, and shake my head, though my chest does a little blip at the sight. "Not fucking happening."

She drops her hands, and her shoulders drop alongside them. "Fine."

I feel my brows tug together at the frown on her face, tugging at my chest. Christ. What is it about this woman that seeing her frown makes my chest hurt? I told her no, and she isn't pushing. She isn't even arguing with me.

But I can't help it.

I know I'm going to regret saying this, but...

I sigh. "So when are we getting this tree?"

Chapter Twenty

— Holly —

The air is filled with the scent of pine, cinnamon, and roasting chestnuts as Mark and I stroll through the market.

It's my favorite scent of all time. Warm, soft, comforting. The twinkling fairy lights strung overhead, the small stalls selling handmade ornaments, woolen scarves and warm, delicious food making me feel like a kid again. I can't help but smile as I take it all in, a rush of excitement coursing through me.

Mark, however, is walking beside me, his hands shoved deep into his coat pockets, looking as if he'd rather be anywhere else. "How the hell did you rope me into this?" he mutters, his breath puffing out in a little cloud.

"Because you love me," I tease, grinning up at him.

He blows out a breath, shaking his head.

"Look how pretty everything is, Mark. You need to appreciate the beauty." I gesture around us at the glittering lights and festive decorations.

He turns his head to look at me and I catch a glimpse of something soft in his eyes as they meet mine. "I am appreciating the beauty."

I roll my eyes. "No, you're not. You're barely looking around. You're missing all the magic."

He clenches his jaw, then sighs heavily before glancing up. "It's just lights," he mutters.

"Pretty lights," I correct him. "I love Christmas markets. They make everything feel so festive and warm."

He makes a face, blowing out a breath. "I fucking hate them." I let out a laugh, and Mark looks over at me with a raised eyebrow. "What?"

"It's just funny," I say with a shrug. "How opposite we are. I love everything about Christmas, and you hate it."

Mark tilts his head slightly. "Does it bother you?"

I shake my head, noting how he seems genuinely curious about my answer. "No," I tell him. "I like a challenge."

He arches his brow, leaning a little closer. "Is that what I am, sweetheart? A challenge?"

The nickname on his lips makes my face flush with heat, but I nod, forcing my body to act normally as I meet his eyes. "I'm going to make you like Christmas, Mark. Just wait and see."

He chuckles a low, grumbly sound that makes my belly do flips. "Trust me, not even you can get me to like this holiday."

"Come on," I say, grabbing his hand and pulling him toward a stall selling hot drinks. His hand is warm in mine, and even though he grumbles, he doesn't pull away.

"Where are you taking me now?" he asks.

"I want a hot chocolate," I tell him, dragging him into the line at the stall.

Mark lets out a sigh, but doesn't say anything as we wait in line. By the time we finally get to the front, I can tell Mark is frustrated as his eyes widen at the menu. "This is ridiculous."

"Hot chocolate is never ridiculous," I tease with a smile.

He raises an eyebrow, turning to face me. "There's no reason milk and powder should cost ten bucks."

He might be right about that, but I shrug anyway. "I don't expect you to pay. You're my friend, not a date."

His jaw tightens, and something crosses his face that I can't quite read. "I'm paying."

My brows dip as he reaches into his pocket and pulls out his wallet. "You don't have to do that," I tell him.

"Don't fight me on this," he says, glancing at me for a second.

"But you just complained about the price," I point out.

"Yeah, well, you want one, so I'm going to get you one," he says, stepping up to the counter. "Two hot chocolates, please."

I smile to myself, knowing this is just a small victory in my plan to win him over to the holiday spirit. When we get our drinks, I take a sip, the warm, sweet liquid sliding down my throat. "Oh my God," I say, closing my eyes as my mouth fills with the sweet taste. "It's amazing."

Mark takes a sip from his own cup, lifting his shoulder a second later. "It's alright."

"Alright?" I repeat, my brows shooting up.

He shrugs. "I've had better."

"Really?" I ask, my brows raising in shock. "I didn't think you of all people would drink hot chocolate."

He looks at me like I've just asked the dumbest question. "I don't hate chocolate just because it's associated with major holidays. I'm logical, not a monster."

"Of course, my mistake," I say with a grin. "So, where did you have this better hot chocolate?"

His face softens, a hint of nostalgia creeping in. "Mia used to make it around the holidays," he admits. "She made it with real dark chocolate, not this powdered stuff."

I wrinkle my nose. "I hate dark chocolate."

"Of course you do," he says, shaking his head.

I tilt my head at his expression. "What does that mean?"

He gives me a look as he drags his eyes down my body. "You're sweet as sugar, Bambi. Of course, you'd love the sweet chocolate."

My brows shoot up and a hint of a smile tugs at my lips. "Did you just compliment me?"

"Did I?" he replies, playing dumb.

"I think so," I say, nudging him.

"I don't remember," he says as he takes another sip.

I roll my eyes but can't hide my smile. "You're not such a grump after all, are you?"

He gives me a dry look. "The sugar's getting to your head. Is it time to go home now?"

I smile at the way he says "home." Not "my house" or "our house," just "home." It makes my heart feel warm. I've never belonged anywhere. After my parents died, every place I ever stayed at was temporary, and even though Mark's place isn't mine, it feels like I belong. It feels like home when I'm there.

"Of course."

"Thank fuck."

"After we get the tree," I remind him.

He lets out a low groan but doesn't argue or tell me no, and I take that as a win.

"It'll be quick, I promise," I say, leading him toward the rows of Christmas trees. "You might even enjoy it."

He steals a glance at me and blows out a hard breath. "Somehow, I don't believe you," he mutters, letting me drag him along.

❄

We walk between the rows of trees, and I examine each one, running my hands over the needles and checking for the right shape. "What about this one?" I ask, pointing to a big, puffy tree.

Mark looks at it for a second, then shrugs. "They all look the same to me."

"They do not," I protest. "This one is spiky at the end," I say, pointing at one that's completely the wrong shape. "And this one over here is more round. There are differences."

"Sweetheart," he says. "We're talking about a tree."

179

I love when he calls me that. I don't know why. I've never been a big fan of nicknames, but there's something about Mark being grumpy and burly and calling me sweetheart with his low voice that makes me shiver.

"This will be your first one, so I want it to be perfect."

"It's not my first one," he corrects me. "My parents had one every year, and Charles and Mia decked out the whole place." He shrugs, his hands in his pockets. "I've just never wanted one in my own place before."

I note the way he says wanted. As in past tense. As in he wants one now. I don't know if I'm slowly wearing him down to the idea of Christmas or if he's just doing this to shut me up, but regardless, I'm so happy right now. I can't remember the last time I decorated a Christmas tree. I used to love decorating mine with my mom when I was younger, but after she was gone, so was that tradition.

"I think this one is better," I say, holding up the fuller tree.

"Great, then let's get this one," Mark says, clearly eager to get this over with.

"Wait," I say, hesitating. "But that one is fuller at the bottom." I point to yet another tree.

Mark groans loudly. "How much longer is this going to take, Bambi?" He pinches the bridge of his nose. "I'm starting to regret this whole trip."

My eyes widen a little. "You are?" I ask. I thought he was enjoying himself here, with me, but maybe I was just focused on how much fun I'm having with him that I didn't stop to think that maybe Mark isn't enjoying it like I am.

He looks at me quickly, his eyes softening. "No, Bambi." He sighs. "Fuck. I was just kidding," he says, his voice gentler. "I think that one looks great." He points to the tree in my hands.

"Are you sure?" I ask, wanting him to be part of the decision since it'll be in his house.

"Yes," he says firmly.

"100%?" I press.

"Yes," he repeats.

"Okay, great." I grin, turning to the vendor, who's in a sweater and a red Santa hat.

He walks over with a bright red tag in his hand. "Good choice," he says with a smile, reaching out to attach the tag to the tree's trunk. "You can head over to the payment booth whenever you're ready."

Mark and I walk over to the booth at the front of the lot and he pulls out his wallet, ready to pay when his eyes widen at the list of prices resting on the counter. "Holy shit," Mark mutters under his breath. "That much for a tree?"

I let out a laugh. "They're good quality," I tell him, trying to justify it. "And they smell incredible."

Mark shakes his head, running a hand through his hair. "I have a tree growing outside my house. Can't I just cut that one down?"

"No, it's not a Christmas tree," I say, rolling my eyes.

"It's just a tr—you know what? Fine, here," he says, pulling out his wallet and handing over the money.

"Alright, you're all set," the woman says, handing him back his card. "You can pick up your tree over there," she says, gesturing toward the workers.

We head outside, where they wrap the tree in a netting. "Do you need help carrying it to your car?"

Mark shakes his head. "I've got it," he says, reaching out to take the tree. He hefts it onto his shoulder, handling it with ease.

I watch him, my brows shooting in surprise. "Look at you, Mr. Lumberjack," I tease, falling into step beside him.

He rolls his eyes but there's a trace of a smile on his lips. "You happy, Bambi?"

I nod, ecstatic that he went through all of this just for me. "I can't wait to decorate it. It's going to look so nice next to your fireplace," I say, already imagining the warm lights filling his living room.

"It fucking better, after it cost me an arm and a leg," he mutters, grunting as he hoists the tree onto his shoulder. "Let's just get this home. The quicker we do, the quicker you can start decorating and I can get this over with."

I laugh, looping my arm through his as we head toward the parking lot. "Deal. But first, you have to admit that you're having just a little bit of fun."

Mark doesn't respond, but as we walk, I swear I catch the edges of his mouth turning up just slightly.

I have a fucking tree in my house.

I can't remember the last time I had a tree in my house. Maybe a plant here and there that Mia would shove into my hands in her poor attempt to brighten up the place, but never a tree.

But of course, that was before Holly came into my life. I've got a bad feeling I'd let her do just about anything, even *plant* a damn tree in the middle of my living room if she wanted to. Hell, I'd let her rearrange my furniture, paint the walls, and fill this space with fluffy pink pillows. Anything, as long as it made her happy. Hearing her laugh and seeing her smile is like music to my ears, sweeter than anything I've ever heard.

And there she goes again, that beautiful smile lighting up her face as she spins the huge tree she picked out, adjusting it, taking a step back, tilting her head, examining it from all angles.

"How about from this side?" she asks, twisting the tree once more

I lean against the wall, crossing my arms as my eyes squint at the tree. "Looks the same?" I say with a shrug.

She glances at me over her shoulder, looking at me like I'm crazy. "I think it's best if the professional takes care of this, actually," she says before turning back to face the tree.

I let out a scoff. "You're a professional tree decorator now?"

"Of course," she says with a grin as she steals a quick glance at me. My heart does that stupid fluttering thing that makes me think it was dead before I met her. God, I love that smile. "My mom always let me decorate our tree. I was the best at it," she says, her eyes twinkling at the memory. "Still am."

I shake my head, a smirk tugging at my lips as I take a seat on the couch, Murray jumping onto my lap a second later. "As long as you're humble about it," I tease, shooting her a dry look. Truth is, I love how happy she seems about everything. This girl came into my bar and twisted my whole world around. She brought joy into my life again, and I know I don't deserve any of it.

She's everything I never knew I needed. Everything I thought I would hate but can't get enough of. She's light and laughter, smiles and joy. And what the hell am I? A grumpy fucking bastard with nothing to offer her.

Sasha found someone else who could give her everything she wanted, and Holly will do the same. There's nothing I can give her. I can't be what she wants. But fuck, I wish I could. I wish I could be exactly what she was looking for, because she's exactly what I've been searching for without even knowing it. She's exactly what I want, and I can't do anything about it.

It's too fucking late. She's already met a guy she likes, even practiced ice skating for him, for fuck's sake. And yet, I can't stop thinking about that day, what It felt like to have her in my arms on that rink, our faces inches apart, her fingers brushing against my lips and her gorgeous eyes locked on mine. She was right fucking there. And I chickened out.

And now I can't stop thinking about when the last time I'll see her will be. I know I won't see her anymore once this guy falls for her and they spend all their time together. Why would she want to hang out with me once she finds her dream guy? *She won't.*

"Can you pass me those lights?" she asks, pointing at a massive box with colorful string lights sitting beside me on the couch.

Quickly moving Murray to my side, I grab the lights and lift off the couch, handing them to her.

"Actually." She glances down at the lights in the box. "I might need your help," she says, glancing at me with a hint of uncertainty.

"I knew you'd rope me into decorating," I admit, arching a brow. Stop talking, jackass. Just do it. Whatever it is, if Holly asks, you do it. If Holly asks you to kill someone for her, you just fucking do it.

She sighs. "You're tall. I need you. Help me wrap these around the tree," she says, fluttering her lashes at me. Little does she know, all she needs to do is ask, and she's got it.

"Is that my only qualification?" I ask, raising an eyebrow, trying to ignore the fact that she said she needs me.

"Yep," she says with a grin. "That, and you're the only other person here."

I roll my eyes but move closer, taking one end of the lights from her. We start at the bottom, wrapping the string around the tree and working our way up. Holly hands me more of the lights as we go.

"Not too tight," she says, leaning in to adjust a loop I'd pulled too snug. "We don't want to crush the branches."

"Of course. The poor branches," I mumble, rolling my eyes as I try to focus on the tree, but fully aware of her proximity. Her scent, a mix of vanilla and cookies, fills the air, making my head swim and a groan rumble in my throat. *So fucking sweet.*

"See?" she says, stepping back to admire our work once we're done. "Teamwork makes the dream work."

I snort. "You sound like a motivational poster."

"Well someone has to motivate you to stop being so grumpy all the time," she says, flashing me a quick wink before she flips the switch and the tree lights up, casting a warm, bright glow over the room, full of color.

I glance down at Holly seeing her eyes light up as she stares at the tree and my heartbeat gets louder and faster. I love seeing her happy.

"It's perfect," she murmurs quietly before breaking out into a grin and grabbing the bag filled with a million and one decorations she picked out. "Now for the fun part."

She reaches into the bag and pulls out an assortment of ornaments. There's so many in here that I can't even see the bottom of the bag anymore. Glass baubles, tiny wooden reindeer, bells, snowflakes, bows. You name it, she probably bought it.

"Here," she says, handing me a glass ornament. "You can place the first one."

I take it from her, hesitating for a moment, before I reach out and hang it on one of the branches, carefully stepping back to make sure it doesn't fall since it's glass and cost me a fucking fortune.

Holly watches me, a smile tugging at her lips. "Look at you," she says softly. "You're enjoying this, aren't you?"

I scoff, rolling my eyes. "I'm only doing it for you."

"Uh-huh," she says, grinning as she picks up a delicate glass angel and hangs it on a higher branch. "You can't fool me, Mark. I see that smile."

I shake my head, turning back to the tree to hide the faint smile pulling at my lips. "Whatever you say, Holly."

We continue decorating as I hand her ornaments, and she finds the perfect spots, stepping back to admire her work after each one, humming softly under her breath.

When we finish, she takes a step back, her eyes shining as she looks at the tree. "It's beautiful," she says softly before turning to face me with a hint of uncertainty on her face. "What do you think?"

I swallow hard, my chest thumping loudly. *I think you bring the light into my life.* "It looks good," I say instead.

"Good?" she echoes, raising an eyebrow. "It's beautiful. Best work I've ever done, hands down."

I nod, struggling to find the right words. "It's the most beautiful tree I've ever seen."

She chuckles. "Well, you don't have to go soft on me. I like your hard exterior."

That's not the only thing that's hard, sweetheart. I clear my throat. Now is not the fucking time. "You do?"

She nods enthusiastically, turning to face me. "Of course. You balance me out. I see everything as sunshine, you see everything as a cloud of grey and rain. Together, we're a rainbow." She grins. God, she's the cutest thing I've ever seen.

Her phone buzzes, lighting up her face, and her eyes widen. "It's Ryan."

Of course it is.

"He wants to go out again," she continues, lifting her eyes to meet mine.

Of course he does. Who the fuck wouldn't want to go out with someone as beautiful, amazing and sweet as Holly? "That's great," I say, forcing my mouth to move. "I told you he would."

"Yeah," she says with a smile that doesn't quite reach her eyes. "Ryan's a great guy. I really did have a great time with him."

Jesus. It's like a knife through my fucking heart. "You think he might be the one?"

She shrugs, looking down at her phone. "I don't know. How do you know? Did you ever have… the one?"

I think I might be looking right at her. "No," I say quietly, swallowing the words down my throat. "I haven't."

"Really?" she asks, her brows dipping. "Not even with Sasha?"

I arch a brow. "She cheated on me, sweetheart. I don't think that equates to being the one."

"Right. Of course," she says with a nervous chuckle. "But there was... no one else?"

I hold her eyes. "No," I tell her. "There was no one else."

She laughs again, this time a little lighter. "Well, maybe if you weren't so grumpy and kept everyone away, you could have found someone by now."

A frown tugs at my lips. "I thought you said you liked that I was grumpy."

"I do," she confirms with a nod. "But that's just me. Other girls..." She shakes her head. "Might not like it as much."

That's why you're perfect for me. "That's fine by me," I tell her. "I don't want any other girls."

Her laughter fills the room, fills my heart. "No?" she asks, arching a brow. "So, I'd be the only girl in your life, then?"

If I got my way. "Is that a bad thing?"

"No, no," she says with a shake of her head. "Of course not. It's just... you don't want to get married?" she asks, tilting her head at me.

I've never thought of marriage. I didn't even think of proposing to Sasha, and maybe that's why she left, but something about hearing Holly speak about marriage makes the image pop into my mind. Holly in a long white dress. Holly holding a bouquet while smiling. Holly pulling the veil back and smiling up at... me.

"Not really," I tell her instead.

Her eyes widen a little. "And you don't want kids?" she asks. "You don't want to see little Mark's running around?"

My expression darkens, the weight of my past pressing down on me. "Do you want kids?"

"Of course," she says with a laugh, her eyes lighting up. "I love children. I've always wanted them. I think I might want four, maybe even five."

"Five?" My eyes widen, a cough escaping my throat.

She laughs again, lifting her shoulder in a shrug. "It might sound crazy, but I have so much love to give and I just want to share it. I've always wanted to adopt a kid or two." Her eyes soften. "There are so many kids without parents that need love. I want to be that for them."

Fuck.

She's the purest soul I've ever met.

How the hell did I get so lucky to have her in my life?

"You don't want any?" she asks, her voice gentle as she turns to face me.

I hesitate for a second. "I, uh… I had a vasectomy."

Her brows furrow. "Oh." She nods, her throat moving as she swallows. "Well, I guess that's alright since you don't plan on getting married or having kids, right?" she asks with a small laugh that doesn't sound quite right.

Fuck.

Why the fuck did I say that?

I do want kids. I want kids if it's with her. I want everything if it's with her.

"Right."

Holly presses her lips together in a smile before she lifts off the couch. "Come on," she says. "We still need to set up the tree skirt."

I furrow my brows, glancing as she grabs a large cloth, pulling it out of the bag. "Why the fuck does a tree need a skirt?"

Chapter Twenty-Two

Holly

"I'm so glad you said yes," Ryan says, his voice warm as he glances down at me with a smile.

I smile back, tucking a strand of hair behind my ear as the wind blows on my face. "I'm glad you asked me out again." At least, I think I am. Ryan is nice. He's fun and kind and brought me to the Christmas market of all places. He's the perfect guy. And yet, I can't stop thinking about the last time I was here with Mark.

We continue walking through the market, the sound of our footsteps crunching over the thin layer of snow on the ground as the lights glow above us. "I always love coming here. It's so beautiful this time of year," he says, admiring the lights.

"Yeah. The lights make it look magical," I muse, glancing around at the stalls, remembering how Mark was groaning at the lines and crowds of people. My lips twitch at the memory, kind of wishing he was here with me right now.

We wander past a stall selling homemade gingerbread cookies, and Ryan reaches out and buys two, handing me one. When our fingers meet, I let out a nervous laugh, but he holds my eyes as his fingers brush against my gloved ones. "I had a great time with you last time, Holly," he says softly.

"Me too," I reply automatically, but my thoughts drift. I can't seem to stop thinking about Mark. I picture him with his serious expression, his dark eyes that always seem to see right through me, and his deep, steady voice. Why the hell am I thinking about him? I'm here with Ryan. I should be focusing on him.

I press my lips together in a smile as Ryan leads us to a stall where a woman is selling handcrafted candles, and immediately, my mind wanders to what Mark would do if we were here together. Would he chastise me for complaining about being cold but then let me snuggle up to him to share his warmth? Would he grumble about the commercialization of Christmas, only to secretly enjoy watching me light up over the decorations? I can almost see him standing next to me, his expression softening as I laugh at his gruffness.

"You want one?" Ryan's voice pulls me back to the present.

"Huh?" I blink, trying to remember what he asked me.

"A hot chocolate," Ryan says with a chuckle, nodding toward a nearby stall where steam curls up from cups of hot chocolate. It's the same stall where Mark and I were last time we were here.

"Oh." My cheeks flush slightly, and I let out a nervous laugh. This is a great date—the perfect date, and yet I'm distracted, letting my thoughts wander to someone I shouldn't be thinking about. "I'd love one," I say, trying to enjoy the moment with Ryan.

He grins, his eyes lighting up as he turns to order. When he hands me one with a warm smile, I take a sip, savoring the warm sweetness that spreads through me. Ryan takes his own sip and closes his eyes, tilting his head back. "Damn, that's good." I can't help but laugh, the sound bubbling up before I can even think about it. Ryan's eyes snap open, and he looks at me with raised eyebrows, clearly amused. "Something funny?"

"Sorry," I say, shaking my head as I try to suppress my smile. "I was just thinking of something."

Ryan tilts his head. "Care to share?"

I pause, my thoughts drifting back to the last time I was at this stall. "I was just thinking about what Mark said the last time we were here," I admit, taking another sip of my drink.

His brows knit together in confusion. "Mark?"

I nod. "Yeah, he's a friend of mine. I think I mentioned him on our first date?"

"Oh, right," Ryan says with a nod as he takes another sip of his hot chocolate. "So, you two came here together?"

I nod, letting a genuine smile slip onto my face. "We came here to pick up a Christmas tree for his place."

"Ah," Ryan says, finishing off his hot chocolate. "And what did he say that was so funny?"

I laugh softly, shaking my head as the memory runs through me. "He said it was just cheap powdered stuff. He loves the rich, dark chocolate mixed with milk. Apparently, it's ten times better."

I think about the last time we were here, how Mark grumbled about the price but still bought me hot chocolate, his eyes softening as he watched me savor every sip. How he always pretends to be annoyed, but I know he'd do just about anything to make me happy.

Ryan chuckles, his expression lightening. "Sounds like you two are pretty close."

"I guess we are," I say, managing a smile. "He's a really great friend."

Is that all he is?

The question hits me unexpectedly, making my eyes widen slightly. I try to push it away, but it lingers as Ryan continues to smile warmly at me. "He's lucky," he says, his hand gently drifting to my waist, the touch making my heart race. "Having someone like you in his life."

His touch is warm, and he cradles my cheek, our faces just inches apart. My breath catches, and a rush of panic courses through me. Ryan's breath mingles with mine, his closeness making everything feel a little too intimate.

I had a good time with Ryan. This date is… everything I've always wanted. He's funny, a really great guy, successful, and loves Christmas. He's everything I should want. But I can't seem to get Mark out of my head, no matter how hard I try. I think about his deep voice, furrowed brows, gruff exterior, how he's secretly soft, just for me, and how spending time with him makes me happy. How close we were to something more that night at the rink, and how disappointed I was when nothing happened.

How I wish he were here right now, sharing this moment with me instead of Ryan. How it would feel if it was his big hands on my waist, his touch on my face, his lips an inch away.

And I know, without a doubt, Ryan isn't the one I want.

"Ryan," I say, taking a deep breath as I step back, creating some space between us.

He closes his eyes, his hand falling to his side. When he opens his eyes again, there's a raw vulnerability in them. "It's not going to work out between us, is it?" he asks, his voice barely above a whisper.

I shake my head, feeling a weight of guilt for agreeing to come out tonight with Ryan when my thoughts are so consumed by someone else. But it wasn't until this moment that I realized how much I want to be with Mark. It doesn't matter where we are—whether it's at his apartment, a noisy bar, or even in the freezing cold. I just want to be with him, near him.

I just want… him.

The connection I have with Mark is something I have never been able to find with anyone else. He makes me feel happy, even when he scowls. He makes all of my dreams come true, even if it goes against everything he stands for. He does everything he can to put a smile on my face, and I can't keep pretending any longer that my heart doesn't race extra fast whenever we're together.

Every moment we've shared has been leading up to this, making me realize, clear as day, that I have feelings for Mark. Big, strong feelings that I never expected.

What the hell am I going to do about this?

Chapter Twenty-Three

Holly

"Have you packed yet?" Olivia asks, her voice cutting through the silence like a knife. I glance up from my book to see her standing at my bedroom door, arms crossed and eyes narrowed, looking every bit like a mom scolding her teenage daughter.

"Yep," I reply, shifting slightly as I cross my legs on the bed, still focused on the page in front of me.

"Are you sure?" she presses, moving away from the door to sit on the edge of my bed, making the mattress dip. "We're leaving tomorrow, and you always forget something. Remember the time you forgot your entire suitcase?"

"That was one time," I mumble, still pretending to read. "And no, I didn't forget anything this time. I've got everything."

Olivia goes quiet, which is suspicious. Olivia is never quiet unless she's plotting something. I finally look up to find her staring at me like a hawk. "Did you make a list?" she asks.

I roll my eyes. "I don't need a list."

"You always need a list."

"Oh my God," I groan, laughing. "You're so dramatic." I dog-ear the page of my book and close it. "I don't need a list. I've packed everything, including ten pairs of underwear, which is way more than I need for a three-day trip. Can I please get back to my book now?"

She tilts her head, her expression softening a bit. "Are you okay?"

"Yes," I lie, feeling my stomach twist with anxiety. "I just want to read."

Olivia isn't buying it. She scoots closer to me, concern etched on her face. "Are you sure?"

"Yes."

"Are you lying to me?"

I let out a heavy sigh. "Yes."

Her brows draw together as she scoots even closer to me. "What's wrong?"

"I broke it off with Ryan," I admit, my voice barely above a whisper.

Olivia's eyes widen in surprise, and then they soften with understanding. She reaches out and pulls me into a tight hug. "Oh, Holly, I'm so sorry. I didn't know you liked him that much. I thought you were into—"

"I am," I say quickly, cutting her off. "That's why I ended things with Ryan."

She lets out a thoughtful hum, stroking my hair like she's comforting a puppy. "I see."

I chuckle weakly. "You've really got the whole motherly thing down," I say, pulling away slightly to look at her.

She laughs, shrugging. "Years of practice with you," she teases. "So, have you told Mark yet?"

"No," I groan, flopping back onto my bed. "How am I supposed to tell him? He's the one who helped me with the whole dating thing in the first place. I'm pretty sure there's a rule against falling for your dating coach."

"You could invite him to the cabin," Olivia suggests, her eyes lighting up. "What better place to confess your undying love than in a cozy, secluded cabin in Vermont?"

I raise an eyebrow. "Is this a romantic comedy or a murder mystery? Because that sounds like the setup for both."

She laughs. "I'm serious. Does he have any plans for the holidays?"

I shrug. "I don't think so. He doesn't have any family around, and he's not big on anything Christmas-related. He might not even say yes."

Olivia looks at me knowingly. "But you want him to come, don't you?"

"I don't want him to be alone for Christmas," I admit.

"And because you're head over heels for him," she adds, a knowing smile tugging at her lips.

I roll my eyes, but I can't help smiling. "Maybe."

Olivia grins. "Then invite him. We all love Mark, and it's the perfect chance to tell him how you feel."

I bite my lip, doubt creeping in. "What if he doesn't feel the same? He's always said he doesn't want a relationship. He's not interested in marriage or kids, and I... I really want those things. I don't want to give up my dreams for a guy."

Olivia nods, her expression serious. "You should never give up what you want for someone else. But maybe he's just scared to admit what he really wants. You should at least find out. You don't want to be kicking yourself ten years from now because you never took the chance."

I am scared. Scared of his reaction, scared of losing him if things go south. But I know deep down that I've been falling for Mark since the day we met. He's the only one who makes my stomach flutter without making me feel like I'm about to throw up.

"Where the hell are my socks?" Henry's voice booms from the hallway, breaking the tension.

"I already packed them," Olivia shouts back.

"All of them?" he yells. "What the hell am I supposed to wear until we leave?"

Olivia sighs dramatically, standing up. "I better go deal with the overgrown toddler I'm married to." She heads for the door but stops, turning to look at me. "Tell him, Holly. You've got nothing to lose."

As she leaves, I grab my phone, my heart pounding. I scroll through my contacts until I find Mark's name and start typing.

Holly:

What are you doing right now?

His reply comes almost instantly.

Mark:

Talking to you.

Holly:

Can I call you?

Mark:

Always.

The word sends a rush of warmth through me, and I hit the call button before I can second-guess myself. I bring the phone to my ear, my heart racing.

"Hey," Mark answers, his voice warm and familiar, sending a wave of comfort over me.

"Hey," I reply, unable to stop the smile from spreading across my face.

"What's up, Bambi?" he asks, using the nickname that never fails to make me smile. "Got yourself into some kind of trouble again?"

"Nope, no trouble," I say with a laugh. "Not today, anyway."

"I'm not buying it," he says. "Did you burn down Funnel Cake's house?"

"No."

"Break something?"

"No," I repeat with a laugh. "God, you have such little faith in me."

"Just checking. So, what's up?"

I fidget with the hem of my duvet, nerves fluttering in my stomach, and take a deep breath.

"I wanted to ask you something."

"Shoot."

"Henry's family has a cabin in Vermont, but they never use it so we go there every Christmas. And I was wondering if maybe… I mean, I know you're not big on Christmas, and you kind of hate all things that bring joy, but… would you maybe… you know what? It's stupid, forget I said anything—"

"Yes," Mark says, cutting off my rambling.

"Yes?" I repeat slowly, my brows raising in surprise.

"Yeah, Bambi, I'd love to go," he says, and I feel a wave of relief wash over me.

"Really?" My heart races uncontrollably.

"Yes," he says with a low chuckle that makes my belly flip. "That's what you were going to ask, right?"

"Yeah," I confirm, my voice a little breathless. "I wanted to know if you'd spend Christmas with me."

"I'd love to," he replies softly.

"Even though you hate Christmas and everything about it?" I tease.

He's silent for a moment. "I don't hate it so much when I'm with you," he says, making my heart flutter.

"Stop flirting with me," I tease.

"I wouldn't dare," he replies, but I can hear a hint of amusement in his voice. "You're still dating Ryan, aren't you?"

I hesitate, my smile fading. "Right. Ryan," I say quietly.

Except I'm not. I ended it with Ryan. But I don't tell him that. Not yet.

"So, you're coming?" I ask again, needing to hear it one more time.

"Yeah, I'm coming," he says. "The bar's usually dead this time of year, and everyone's been telling me to take a break."

"That's because everyone's with their families," I say. "And this year, you will be too."

"You're my family now, Bambi?" he asks, his tone teasing, but there's something deeper beneath his words.

I bite my lip, my cheeks warming. "I could be," I say softly.

He chuckles. "Sounds about right," he murmurs. "When are you guys leaving? I need to figure something out for Mia."

"Tomorrow. It's a long drive, so…"

"Tomorrow?" he repeats, sounding surprised. "As in, less than twenty-four hours from now?"

I wince, laughing nervously. "Sorry for the short notice."

"That's okay," Mark says, his voice gentle. "I'm just glad you want me there with you."

I always want you with me. I bite back the words, swallowing them down. "Yeah, well, it's all part of my plan to make you love Christmas," I say with a grin.

I hear him exhale, a soft, heavy sound. "Guess I'd better start packing, then. Goodbye, Bambi."

"Wait," I blurt out before he can hang up. I don't want this moment to end. I know it's irrational—I'll see him tomorrow, but still, the thought of saying goodbye feels too final. "I could come over," I suggest hesitantly, twisting my fingers into the duvet. "To help you pack."

There's a long pause on the line, so long that I almost think he's hung up. But then I hear his steady breathing, the sound calming and familiar. "You know," he says finally, his voice low and warm, "I am a pretty terrible packer."

A smile spreads across my face, the last of my nerves easing. "I'll be right over."

"We're here," Holly announces as we pull up to the cabin.

I step out of the car, the crisp, cold air hitting my skin as soon as I do. I blow out a breath, taking in the sight around me. The cabin is fucking huge, nestled between tall pine trees, covered in snow. It looks like something straight out of a Christmas card. Strings of lights wrapped around the porch, wreath hanging on the door, and snow covering every inch of this place. It makes me realize why Holly was so excited about it.

"Who owns this place?" I ask, impressed by the sight in front of me.

"We do, baby," Olivia says, beaming as she links arms with her husband.

"And I'm a part contributor," Holly chimes in, lifting her chin proudly.

Henry smirks at me, arching his brow. "Technically it's my family's, but Holly pays for the electricity while we stay here."

"So, I guess that means I own it too," Holly says with a grin, leaning against the car.

I glance back at Henry, who just shrugs, looking amused.

"Did you bring the turkey, honey?" Olivia asks Henry, rubbing her swollen belly.

"Yes, and it was heavy as fuck. If the baby's anywhere near that size, I feel sorry for you," Henry replies with a groan as he lifts a cooler out of the trunk.

"Not helping," Olivia shoots back, rolling her eyes.

"I know," he says, grinning.

They walk ahead of us, and I stay back, helping Holly with her suitcase, my lips twitching at the sight of her buried under a thick coat, scarf, gloves, hat, and ear muffs. I don't think there's a single item of clothing that she hasn't got on.

"You got it?" I ask her, handing her the suitcase, trying to tug it on the snow, my brows dipping when it barely budges.

"Yes. I've got it. Give it."

I shake my head. "Don't worry. I'll take it inside."

"What?" she yells behind me as I carry on walking. "But I brought two suitcases."

"Trust me," I say with a grunt as I carry the two large suitcases, dragging them through the snow, my small duffle bag swung across my chest. "I know."

I hear a soft chuckle behind me and I have the urge to stop and turn around just to see that smile on her face. But I shake my head as I let out hard breath after hard breath and walk through the thick blanket of snow, following Henry and Olivia until we're finally at the cabin.

"Home sweet home," Holly says, a soft smile playing on her lips when the door opens, Henry and Olivia heading inside.

I let out a breath, a little winded from carrying the bags, and arch a brow down at Holly, or a small face that resembles Holly buried under clothes. "This is home to you?" I ask, watching her closely.

She shrugs, her smile fading a little. "When I was in foster care, I tried not to get attached to anything or anyone because I knew it wouldn't last. But this place... we come here every year, and it's always the same. Same tree—fake, by the way, ugh—same snow-covered roof. I like it. It's tradition."

"You love traditions, don't you?" I ask her, already knowing the answer.

"Yeah," she says with a chuckle that burns my insides despite the cold air hitting my face. "I hope my future husband likes them too because it'd be extremely hard to have to change." She heaves out a breath. "I like when things stay the same."

I could get into tradition. The thought pops into my head without any hesitation. I like when things stay the same. I like routine. I like not being surprised. The only big change in my life was... her, and I couldn't fucking be happier about it. But she's not talking about me. She's talking about Ryan. The thought makes my chest tighten, and I clear my throat, my lips settling into a thin line as I look down at her pretty face, flushed from the cold. "I'm sure Ryan likes tradition just fine."

Holly looks up at me, her expression uncertain. "Yeah," she sighs. "You want to go see your room?" she asks, changing the subject.

"I have a room?" I raise an eyebrow.

"Why? Did you want to sleep with me?" she asks, waggling her eyebrows playfully.

"That's not what I meant," I say quickly, feeling my face heat up.

She laughs. "I know. I know. You're repulsed by me."

"Not what I meant, either," I reply, narrowing my eyes down at her. Repulsed? Jesus. She should fucking read my mind.

"It's just an empty guest room we never use," she says. "But it's yours now."

My brows shoot up. "Is this trip going to be more than a one-time thing?" I ask.

"If you want," she says, her voice hopeful. "I'd like to think you'd come here next year with us as well."

Next year. She'll probably be dating that guy. And the idea of coming back here next year, only to watch her with Ryan, cuddling by the fire, kissing under the mistletoe. And he'll probably end up marrying her because… why wouldn't he want to marry her? She's fucking amazing. I don't think I could bear to watch them together.

"Maybe," I say, noncommittal. I don't plan on coming back next year. Who knows if she'll even remember me a month from now?

We head inside, the warmth of the place hitting me first as I follow Holly into what I assume will be my room for the next three days. I drop the suitcases on the ground as Holly rounds the bed and flops onto it, stretching out with a satisfied sigh. The bed is huge. Must be a king-size, and she looks so fucking tiny compared to it.

"You enjoying yourself?" I ask, leaning against the doorframe.

"Of course your bed would be better than mine," she grumbles, sitting up on her elbows.

I chuckle softly, watching her eyebrows knit together in an adorable frown. "You want to swap?"

"Or I could just stay here with you instead," she says with a teasing smile.

I narrow my eyes at her. "You kick in your sleep, don't you?" I ask trying to deflect the tension that's suddenly thick in the room.

"What?" she asks, confusion taking over her features.

"You're trying to punish me by kicking or screaming. Do you scream?" I ask, raising an eyebrow.

"No," she says, rolling her eyes. "I just want to stay here."

I hum, trying to ignore the way my heart thumps against my chest. I swear it wasn't working before I met her because it's never done that before, and yet she walks into my life and the bastard won't stop banging against my chest. "Don't think your boyfriend would like that," I tell her, my jaw clenching at the thought.

"He's not my boyfriend," she says quietly.

"Not yet," I murmur. "But he will be."

She watches me for a while and then sits up on the bed. "I'm only kidding," she says with a shrug, avoiding my gaze. "I don't want to sleep next to you. You probably snore anyway."

"I don't," I lie. I totally snore.

"Do you want to go sledding?" she asks suddenly, changing the subject.

"Now?" I ask, looking out the window at the dark sky.

She shakes her head. "Tomorrow," she says, lying back on my bed. "I'm too tired right now," she mumbles, closing her eyes.

I let out a scoff. No shit. She wouldn't shut up the whole drive here. Six hours in a car with three loud, lively people singing along to Christmas songs the whole drive and playing car games would have been unbearable if I wasn't itching to spend some time with Holly. Even if I had to listen to her awful singing.

I watch as she twists onto her side and places both of her palms together, propping them under her head. My lips twitch at the sight as I approach her.

"You sleeping in my bed, Bambi?" I ask, unable to help myself.

She curls up, closing her eyes, letting out a sweet, soft sound that makes a chill creep up my spine. "I love when you call me that," she murmurs sleepily.

I chuckle once again, not bothering to wake her up. This bed is big for the both of us, so I quickly pull my coat off and head toward Holly, lifting her up to get her under the covers.

I lie down beside her, letting out a contented sigh. My heart is thumping in my chest, and I don't know how much longer I can keep pretending I don't have feelings for her.

"Sleep well, sweetheart," I whisper, leaning over to kiss her forehead. Her skin is warm under my lips, and I break out into a smile as she mumbles something. I turn around, closing my eyes, knowing that there's no place I'd rather be than right here with her in this moment.

Chapter Twenty-Five

Holly

I wake up to the steady rise and fall of Mark's chest beneath my cheek. It's such a nice, comforting feeling that for a moment, I let myself enjoy it, keeping my eyes closed as I snuggle closer until a deep rumbling noise reaches my ears.

My brows furrow as I slowly open my eyes, realizing it's coming from Mark. So much for not snoring.

Half-awake, I prop myself up on one elbow to watch him. His lips are slightly parted, his hair tousled in every direction. He looks so different from his usual gruff self. He almost looks… adorable. I bite my lip to keep from laughing, but I must not do a very good job because the snoring stops abruptly as his eyes snap open, immediately glaring at me.

"You snore," I tell him with a smirk, unable to help myself.

"Excuse me?" His voice is deep and gravelly with sleep, sending a shiver up my spine. *God, that voice. That voice could make me do anything.*

I smirk, shaking my head. "You said you didn't snore," I remind him. "You were so loud, I thought there was a moose outside."

Mark groans, rubbing a hand over his face, trying to shake off the last remnants of sleep. "Funny," he mutters, closing his eyes again as if he might just drift back off.

"You're grumpy in the mornings," I tease, poking him in the arm.

He cracks one eye open to give me a half-hearted glare. "According to you, I'm always grumpy."

"I'm not so sure about that."

One eyebrow rises in a silent question. "No?"

"You tucked me in last night," I say, leaning closer. "And kissed my forehead. That's not very grumpy behavior."

His brows furrow in surprise. "You were awake?"

Yeah, I was still awake, even though his bed was so comfortable and I was so tired I didn't want to move. I heard him call me "sweetheart" in that soft, gentle voice that still echoes in my mind and felt the brush of his lips against my forehead. My heart had pounded so loudly, I was sure he'd hear it and know I was still awake, but he just slipped into bed beside me, turning away from me, and eventually, we both fell asleep.

I lift my shoulder in a shrug, my lips lifting slightly. "Would it change anything if I was?"

Mark's jaw tightens, and I notice the tension in his shoulders. My brows knit together, wondering if I've somehow crossed an invisible line between us. Maybe he didn't mean anything by it and I'm making it seem like it's something more than it is, and he doesn't know how to let me down gently.

I sit up, putting some distance between us. "Do you regret coming here with me yet?" I ask, trying to keep my tone light though my heart hammers in my chest.

He shakes his head, keeping his jaw tight. "No," he says earnestly.

"Really?" I ask, tilting my head and studying his face. "Not even the fact that I stole your bed?"

A small smile tugs at his lips, sending a flutter through my belly. "I don't mind," he says, his eyes softening in the morning light filtering through the curtains. "This bed's too big, anyway. It'd feel empty without you."

I laugh, but his words make my heart do a little flip. "And it doesn't, with me here?"

Mark's gaze meets mine, his expression softening further. "No," he says quietly. "Nowhere feels empty with you there."

His words hang between us, and for a moment, I forget to breathe. My heart pounds, and I open my mouth to say something, anything to break the silence, but my mind is blank.

"Do you want to go sledding today?" I blurt out the first thing that comes to mind.

Mark blinks, arching his brow. "Have you ever been sledding, Bambi?"

"Of course," I say with an eye roll. "I do this every year."

He gives me a knowing look. "You're not going to let me say no, are you?"

I can't help but laugh. "You act like I make you do things you don't want to. I'm not that powerful, Mark."

He shakes his head slightly, a light scoff escaping his lips as his eyes lock with mine. "You have no fucking idea, Holly."

His words make my heart pound and all the breath in my lungs gets caught in my throat. I swallow hard, trying to get my body working again. "So," I say, trying to shake it off. "Is that a no, then?"

He sighs, and before he even speaks, I know his answer. "It's a yes."

I squeal, a huge grin spreading across my face. "Thank you, thank you, thank you!" I lean forward impulsively and before I realize what I'm doing, I press my lips against his cheek, the roughness of his stubble prickling my lips in the best way.

I pull back quickly, my eyes wide, meeting his equally startled gaze. A moment of awkward silence hangs between us, and nerves wrack through me. Then Mark clears his throat and nods curtly. "You're welcome, Bambi."

I let out a laugh of relief, swinging my legs over the edge of the bed. "This is going to be so much fun."

He grunts, rising from the bed, and when I turn around, I catch a glimpse of his shirt riding up, exposing a trail of hair on his stomach. My cheeks flush at the sight, but when Mark lets out a sigh, I quickly avert my eyes and meet his. "You want coffee first, right?"

I laugh, feeling the butterflies in my stomach. "You know me so well," I say, smiling. "What would I do without you, Mark?"

His eyes never leave mine as the muscle in his jaw ticks as he mutters, "I feel the same fucking way, Bambi."

"I thought you said you do this every year," Mark says, his brow arched as she watches me struggle to climb up the hill. He, on the other hand, has his sled propped up on his shoulders as he climbs the hill effortlessly, barely breaking a sweat.

"I do," I huff, out of breath as I shoot him a glare. "Not well, but I still do," I admit, letting out a hard breath.

He laughs, a sound I've become addicted to that warms me even as the ice-chill weather hits my skin. "What the hell am I going to do with you?" he asks, shaking his head down at me.

I pause, giving him a teasing smile. "I'm sure you can think of something."

He raises an eyebrow, and for a moment, it feels like he can read all my unspoken, inappropriate thoughts about him.

A blush creeps up my neck. "Help me, please?" I request, wincing as my aching arms struggle to keep up.

His lips curl into a slight smile before he leans down, wrapping his hand around mine as he tugs me up the mountain with ease.

"You're wrong, you know," I tell him, a smile spreading across my face as I watch him turn around, his skin flushed from the cold and those big eyebrows of his furrowed once again.

"What do you mean?" he asks.

"You try to convince yourself you're grumpy and unapproachable and blah blah blah," I say, with an eye roll. "But you're so nice to me."

He holds my eyes for a second before looking to the side with a shake of his head. "I'm not sure other people would agree with you."

I take a step closer to him, a frown pulling at my lips. "Why not?"

He shrugs, focusing on the snow. "Because I'm an asshole," he says. "I snap at people, I don't socialize with anyone, and couldn't care less about their problems." Turning to face me, his jaw tightens. "I like peace and quiet and to be alone."

When I first met him, I might have thought the same, but for a very brief moment, because even back then, I could see something in him. Something warm and kind, and as we've gotten to know each other, he's shown me time and time again how much he cares.

"But I'm not quiet," I point out with a tilt of my head. "I always annoy you with my problems, and I never leave you alone."

He sighs, his breath turning into a puffy white cloud from the cold. He runs a hand through his hair, disheveling it as he looks at me, *really* looks at me, his eyes softening. "You're different."

You're different.

Two words.

Two simple words that make my body warm and my stomach flutter.

"I am?" I ask, my voice barely above a whisper.

"You know you are," he says, a hint of a smile playing on his lips. "You weaseled your way into my life, and... *fuck me*, I actually like having you around," he admits.

I laugh, my heart threatening to explode out of my chest. I love hearing Mark admit he likes my company. Sometimes, I wonder if he's just secretly wishing I'd leave him alone, but I'm so happy that's not the case.

"But you're not like this for anyone else?" I ask him.

He shakes his head, his dark brown eyes locking onto mine. "No."

"Just for me?" I ask, my heart doing that little flip again.

"Yeah, Bambi," he says softly, using the nickname that makes my heart melt. "Just for you."

Our eyes lock together for what feels like an eternity before Mark clears his throat and takes a step back, glancing behind me with furrowed brows. "Where the hell is your sled?" he asks.

My eyes widen when I turn around and glance downhill, seeing the red board deep in the snow. "I forgot to bring it up."

"You're joking," he says dryly. "Please tell me you're kidding."

I shake my head, slowly turning to face him. "I was thinking about climbing the hill for the third time in a row and was tired and..." I breathe out a sigh. "I'm sorry," I say with a wince. "Don't hate me."

Mark's brows lift a little. "I could never hate you." He glances down at his sled, hesitating for a second. "Are you sure we'll both fit on this?" he asks.

A smirk slides on my face. "I could always sit on your lap."

His face hardens, his shoulders tensing as he releases a heavy breath. "Don't think that's a good idea."

"Why not?"

Mark looks away, his jaw tightening. "Need I remind you, you have a boyfriend?"

I roll my eyes. "Not my boyfriend," I correct him.

"Whatever he is," Mark mutters with a shrug, turning back to me. "He wouldn't like this."

"It's just sledding," I say, tilting my head.

His eyes narrow slightly. "With your body pressed tightly against mine," he says, his words sending a rush through me. "My hands on your waist and your ass nestled on my lap."

The breath is knocked out of me, my pulse quickening as the weight of his words dawn on me. A shiver runs through my body, liking the sound of it way too much.

He breaks eye contact first, glancing down at the sled. "Besides, I'm too big."

I can't help but break out into a smirk, my eyes lighting up. "Yeah? How big?"

Mark narrows his eyes. "Behave."

"I didn't do anything," I say, feigning innocence.

He gives me a look, running a hand through his hair. "Sure you didn't."

I let out a laugh at his expression and shrug. "I don't think it'd be a problem," I tell him. "It would take us way too long to bring the other sled up here, so…"

He clenches his jaw, glancing back down at the sled on the snow before closing his eyes and whispering something under his breath. "Fine," he says as he drops down, settling himself on the sled before lifting his eyes to meet mine. "Get on."

I swallow hard at the sight of Mark seated on the sled, his legs stretched out with a space in front of him for… me.

Turning around, I climb into the space in front of him, shifting back slowly until I hear his low, deep groan and feel his body against mine, not a single inch of space between us. His hands instinctively find my hips as I settle in, lying back against his chest.

"Are you still sure this is okay?" he asks, his lips brushing against my ear, making me suck in a breath.

"Yes," I whisper back, licking my lips nervously as his hands slowly lift and wrap around my waist, pulling me back so my back is pressed against his chest, securing me in place. We stay like that for a while, just our bodies together, his arms wrapped around me, and neither of us moving or speaking, the sound of our breaths the only noise between us.

"Holly?" Mark says, his voice deep and low making my bones shake.

"Hmm?"

"You need to grab the reins."

I blink, focusing on the reins in front of me. "Right. Sorry."

I hear his soft chuckle as I lean forward slightly and grab the reins, clutching them tightly as I lean back against Mark.

Mark plants his feet firmly on either side of the sled before he gives us a strong push until we're hurtling down the mountain. I let out a yelp as the sled picks up speed, the wind rushing past my face and hitting my cheeks. It doesn't matter how often I do this, it's always just as fun as the first time.

Mark's arms tighten around me, sending a warmth through me despite the cold air. We're flying down the slope, the world around me completely blurred in a white, snowy blanket as we rush down the hill.

I grip the reins tightly, trying to steer us straight as the sled bounces and glides over the uneven snow. The wind roars in my ears until we finally reach the bottom of the hill, the sled coming to a stop.

I tip my head back and laugh, and glance behind my shoulder, spotting Mark smiling ever so slightly. "That was so much fun," I say with a laugh, still feeling the rush of adrenaline through me.

"I could tell Bambi. I think my ear drum burst with your screams," he jokes, his hand reaching out to brush my hair out of my face, tucking it behind my ear.

Our eyes lock and everything feels so warm, and comfortable, and… right. Like this is exactly where I'm meant to be. "I feel safe like this," I admit quietly.

"On the ice going a million miles an hour?" he jokes.

I shake my head, leaning in slightly. "With you," I whisper, staring deep into his eyes. "I always feel safe with you."

Mark is quiet for a moment, and I feel his breath warm against my cheek. Our faces are so close that I can see the specks of gold glistening in his eyes. I tilt my head slightly up to look at him. His eyes are dark, intense, and for a heartbeat, I think he's going to kiss me.

But he pulls back, and his arms loosen around me as he snaps his head to the side. "C'mon, Bambi. We'll miss dinner at this rate."

I nod, trying to hide my disappointment as he lifts out of the sled and holds his hand out to pull me up. He grabs both sleds, slinging them over his back as we start the climb back up. All I can think about is the moment that almost happened. How close we were to kissing, how much I wanted it.

And how much it hurt when he pulled away.

Chapter Twenty-Six

Mark

"God, I'm so full," Olivia murmurs, leaning back in her chair with a satisfied sigh, resting her hand on her round stomach.

"You ate half the turkey," Henry says, arching his brow at his wife. "I'd be surprised if you weren't."

"Don't judge me," Olivia retorts, narrowing her eyes at him. "I'm eating for two."

"Are you sure it's not five?" Henry teases.

Olivia twists in her chair, her eyes turning to slits. "Are you judging what I eat?" she asks, her tone menacing.

"Of course not," her husband replies, his eyes widening a little. "You want dessert?"

She leans back in her chair with a knowing smile, lifting her head in a nod before he heads toward the freezer, grabbing a tub of ice cream out of it.

I can't help but make a face. Who the hell eats ice cream in winter?

"And I want it in bed," she says simply, heading toward her room.

"Yes, dear," Henry mutters, grabbing a bowl and two spoons before joining her, leaving Holly and me alone out here.

"That man is whipped," I say with a shake of my head.

"He's in love," Holly replies as she tilts her head back. "I've witnessed it for years how in love those two are, and it sucks that I still don't have that."

"You will," I reassure her, watching as she turns her head, those caramel eyes locking onto mine.

"Yeah?" she asks, her voice tinged with doubt.

"Yeah, Bambi," I say, swallowing the rock lodged in my throat. "You have Ryan, right?"

Holly's eyes flicker away, her smile fading. "Yeah," she laughs softly. "Right."

My brows dip at her expression, and I lift myself out of the chair with a groan, completely stuffed from the turkey we just devoured, but if I know anything about this girl—and I like to think that I know quite a lot—she's going to want a sweet treat.

"You want me to make you some hot chocolate?" I ask her, glancing down at her smile, widening at my words.

"You'd do that for me?" she asks, her brows lifting in surprise.

I'd do anything to see you smile. I clear my throat, lifting my shoulder in a shrug. "Of course," I tell her. "I know how much you love sweet things."

"You gonna make the real stuff?" she asks, wagging her brows as she follows me into the kitchen.

I look over my shoulder, a smirk tugging at my lips. "With horrible, bitter dark chocolate and everything."

"I can't wait," she says, her voice dripping with warmth as she wraps her arm around mine, leaning into me. I glance down at her, and I can't help but laugh at the sight of the thick, green, and red Christmas sweater scattered with snowmen. How does she still look so effortlessly beautiful?

I think back to the day I met her. I had no fucking clue that she'd be this important to me, that she'd mean this much to me, make me this... happy. She's brought so much light into my life and made me feel things I never expected. Even if she leaves with Ryan and I never see her again, she'll always be etched in my memory and heart.

I really did not know what hit me the day my eyes landed on hers.

I tear my eyes away from her and open the cabinets to grab the saucepan and a bar of dark chocolate covered in a thin layer of dust. I shake my head with a smirk. It figures these people would prefer the cheap, sweet stuff.

"Make sure you put a lot of sugar in it," Holly tells me with a smile as she leans on the kitchen counter.

I glance down at her in fucking awe of how gorgeous this woman is.

Her smile.

Her eyes.

Her plump, pink lips.

Her cheeks flushed pink from the cold.

Christ.

This girl is so breathtakingly beautiful.

225

I busy myself with heating the milk, trying to get thoughts of Holly out of my mind. Won't work, though. Hasn't since she entered my life. I grab the chocolate, breaking it into chunks before adding it to the milk and stirring until it melts, then sweetening it with a generous amount of sugar.

Once I'm done, I pour the hot chocolate into a mug and hand it over to Holly. "Careful," I tell her. "It's still pretty hot."

She takes a tentative sip, closing her eyes and letting out a soft, satisfied moan.

"Good?" I ask, my lips tugging at the sides.

She nods, opening her eyes. "So good I'm considering kidnapping you just to make this for me forever."

I let out a laugh, noticing some hot chocolate lingering on the corner of her mouth, and gently wipe it with the pad of my thumb.

Her lips part, and our eyes lock, the distance between us shrinking. I swallow hard, my thumb lingering on her lips, and before I can talk myself out of it, I trace her plump bottom lip slowly. She sucks in a breath, making my head dizzy.

I should pull away.

I *need* to pull away.

But she's right fucking here, so close, so beautiful I'm losing my goddamn mind, and I can't find an inkling of willpower in my body to step away from her.

"Mark," Holly whispers, her voice barely more than a breath.

I trace my thumb lightly across her lips again, my heart pounding. "Yes, Holly?" I ask, hyper-aware of how close we are right now.

Her eyes flicker upwards quickly, then back to mine. "Look up," she says softly.

I manage to tear my eyes away from her and glance up, seeing the mistletoe hanging directly above us. My brows furrow. *When the hell did that get there?*

I glance back down at Holly, seeing her eyes hooded as she takes another small step closer to me, erasing any distance that was previously there as she places her hands flat against my chest. Fuck. "You know, they say it's bad luck not to kiss under the mistletoe," she says.

My body sings. I can't think. Can't breathe. Can't do anything but stare down at her. My heart races, her touch sending a jolt of warmth through me. I want to kiss her so fucking badly, but my mind is screaming all of the reasons I shouldn't.

And unfortunately, I choose to listen and take a step back, my hand dropping from her face.

"Holly, this is... no," I say, my voice strained as I shake my head, trying to steady my racing heart.

Her face falls, her cheeks flushing a deeper shade of pink. "Oh," she says, her voice trembling slightly, "I'm sorry. Of course you're not attracted to me. I don't know what I was—"

"Stop," I say firmly, her eyes snapping to mine, slightly widened at my sharp tone. "Don't ever insult yourself like that. You're beautiful."

"I am?" Holly asks, her brows knitting together.

227

I nod, letting out a hard breath. "So fucking stunning, sometimes I can't believe you're real," I admit, running a hand through my hair in frustration.

Her chest rises and falls with hard, heavy breaths. "But you still don't want to kiss me?"

I almost laugh. She has no fucking clue how much I want to kiss her. It's all I can think about. All I dream about.

"You have a boyfriend," I remind her and myself.

"Ryan is not my boyfriend," Holly says, stepping closer.

My jaw tightens. "He might not be your boyfriend right now, but you like him and—"

"I broke up with him."

Her confession catches me off guard, hitting me like a ton of bricks. "What?"

"I ended things with him," Holly says. "On our date."

My mind races, spins, flips. She's not with him. She's not with *anyone*. And here she is, standing right in front of me, looking up at me with a look that says she wants me.

"Why?" I ask her. She liked the guy. Went on multiple dates with him. Wanted him to text her. What the hell changed?

A slow smile spreads across Holly's face, and she rises onto her tiptoes, wrapping her arms around my neck. My hands instinctively move to her waist, pulling her closer, my heart pounding in my chest. "I guess I want my dating coach more than my date," she says, her voice teasing.

"Dating coach, huh?" I smirk, my fingers tightening on her waist as I draw her even closer. "Is that all I am?"

"Depends," she shrugs, her lips just inches from mine. "Do you want to be something else?"

I laugh softly, my heart racing. "So many things."

"Yeah?" she asks, her breath warm against my lips. "Like what?"

"I want to be the guy who kisses you," I confess, my voice trembling with desire. "I want to touch you, to know what you sound like when I'm buried deep inside you, I want to wake up next to you, to date you, to take care of you... I want *everything* with you. But a kiss is a good start."

Her eyes widen a little, struck by my confession and I get it. I did a really good fucking job at keeping my feelings for her buried deep inside. But fuck if I'm going to deny her anymore. Not when she's right here, looking at me with those gorgeous eyes of her, wanting me, and *finally* fucking single.

"We *are* under the mistletoe," she points out with a smile that makes my body burn.

"And you mentioned it would be bad luck not to kiss, right?" I ask, my voice dropping to a husky whisper.

"Extremely," she replies, her eyes shining.

The need to kiss her is overwhelming. My hands grip the hem of her sweater, my restraint hanging by a thread. "Tell me this is a bad idea," I beg.

Holly shakes her head, her gaze remaining on mine. "I think this is the best idea I've ever had."

That's all I need to hear. I cup her face with my hand, my thumb brushing gently against her skin. Leaning in slowly, I give her every chance to pull away if she wants to, but she doesn't. Her eyes flutter shut as our lips meet in a kiss that starts soft and tentative but quickly becomes heavy and charged.

Christ.

Her lips are warm and incredibly soft, moving with mine in a way in sync. The world outside seems to disappear as the kiss deepens, and I lose myself in her touch, in her sweet taste, feeling as if everything that came before led to this. To her.

She moans into my mouth, making my cock harden against my jeans.

Fuck. Is this what kissing feels like? I haven't kissed anyone in a long time. Haven't wanted to. But my god, there's no way a kiss has ever felt like this.

"This," Holly mumbles against my lips. "This is it." Her hands tangle in my hair as she pulls me toward her.

"What?"

She groans—actually groans—and tugs on my head, pressing me closer against her. "Just shut up and kiss me."

A laugh bubbles out of me and I lift her up, placing her on the counter and stepping in between her legs. "Bossy," I murmur, tugging on her bottom lip with my teeth. "You gonna be like this in bed?" I ask her, my lips making their way down her exposed neck, hot and smelling like a gingerbread cookie. "Ordering me around?"

She whimpers. *Fuck me.* Sweet, soft sounds leave her lips as she tips her head back, giving me better access. "Maybe."

I chuckle against her skin, my hands landing on her thighs, clad with thick jeans, wanting to feel her skin, wanting to *see* her. "Please, sweetheart. We both know you'll be happy to get on your knees if I ask you to."

She shivers.

Actually shivers at my words, and fuck me, I'm so hard it aches.

"Please," she begs so sweetly, so softly my head spins. "Take this off," she mumbles, lifting my sweater with desperation. Absolute pure fucking need.

I want that. Want to strip off my clothes and hers and spend hours mapping out her body with my fingers and tongue.

"We're in the kitchen, sweetheart," I remind her, arching a brow as she tries to remove my clothes.

"And?" she replies with a shrug.

"And your friends could walk in any minute," I tell her with little conviction, unable to resist her touch.

"They won't," she says, her hands landing flat on my stomach, running over my skin, making me suck in a hard breath.

"But what if—"

"Please, Mark," she says again, eyes locking with mine as she grabs my belt in her hand. *Oh fuck.* "I need you so bad."

My vision blurs, my head is dizzy. Never wanted anyone as much as I want her.

"I don't have anything," I say, my breath coming out choppy and heavy. "I never would have thought this would happen."

She shakes her head, and I begin to think she'll call this off. Smart. We probably shouldn't do anything if—

"I haven't been with anyone in so long."

Christ.

A thick groan escapes my throat as I clutch her thighs, spreading them wider. "Are you asking me to fuck you bare?" I whisper the words against her sensitive skin, warm and sweet and fucking delicious.

She chuckles, the vibrations tingling my lips on her neck. "Telling, kinda."

"Telling, huh?" I ask her with a smirk, slowly lifting her sweater up, up, up, until it's completely off. My eyes zone in on her pretty, perky tits bobbing free.

Oh fuck.

I didn't prepare for this.

Haven't been with a woman in over five years, and she just might be the death of me.

I groan at the sight, wanting to cup them, lick them, suck them. Sweetest tits I've ever seen. Prettiest fucking woman I've ever seen. Fuck, is this actually happening?

There's no going back now.

I run a hand through my hair, gripping her thigh. "You're too young for me," I mutter, knowing she deserves someone else, someone better, but wanting her all the same.

"Hardly," she replies with a shake of her head, her brown hair spilling over her bare chest.

I give her thigh another squeeze, slowly lifting my hand. "And too fucking good."

She parts her lips, heavy breaths leaving her as she spreads her legs a little wider. "I can be bad."

232

I let out a laugh, my heart hammering against my chest. "You're too fucking perfect," I tell her, shaking my head. "You shouldn't be with someone like me."

Holly lifts her hands from the kitchen counter and wraps them around my neck. "You're the only one I want."

God. Those words. They cave my chest in and make my heart pump to life. "Out of all the men in New York?"

She shakes her head, a smirk tugging at her lips. "Out of all the men in the world," she clarifies, her big eyes sparkling. "I'd choose you over anyone."

Fuck.

I lift my hands to wrap around her ass and lift her off the counter, and carry her toward the living room, dropping her onto the couch, and crowding her a second later. "I'd choose you too," I tell her, cupping her face and looking into those eyes that sucked me in since the day she entered my bar. "No doubt. First pick."

She smiles so brightly, makes me feel alive, butterflies fluttering around in my stomach and shit. All the fucking feelings, I feel them. Right here. With her.

"Even though I'm too young?" she teases, tilting her head.

Little shit. I chuckle, my eyes dropping to her sweet tits. "Might be fucked, but hell fucking yes."

"Even though I talk too much and never shut up?"

I shake my head. "I love your voice, Bambi. Never stop talking."

She grins. "Good, because—"

I arch a brow. "Maybe stop talking right now."

She lets out a laugh and I don't waste any more time, diving in to capture her lips once again. My hands run up her body until I *finally* cup her breast, rubbing the pad of my thumb over her hard nipples I can't fucking wait to put in my mouth.

"Fuck," she moans, tipping her head back, breaking apart from my mouth. "That feels so good."

"You feel perfect," I mutter, running my hands over her face, her hair, her lips, her tits. All of her. "You look so fucking perfect."

She lifts her hips, grinding on my cock, our jeans a thick barrier that does nothing to make my cock harden at the feel of her warmth.

A rough noise leaves my throat. "Stop grinding on my dick, or this will be over before it even begins."

She whimpers, rolling her hips to thrust against me again. "It aches."

Fucking ditto.

"Yeah, baby?" I ask her, pressing a kiss to her sweet lips. "How much?"

"So much," she whines, locking eyes with me. "Please touch me."

"Fucking gladly."

I lift onto my knees and tug her jeans and panties down, throwing them across the room, sucking in a breath when I finally see her.

Fuck.

The sight of her pretty pussy makes my head feel like it's going to explode. Or my cock. One of the two. Both, maybe.

She parts her thighs a little, and my nostrils flare when I see her gorgeous, dripping-wet pink center, practically screaming for my tongue.

Shuffling back, I grip her thighs in my hand and spread her wide open, staring at her for a second before I dive in and fucking *eat*.

Christ. I've been fucking starving my whole life and didn't even know it.

"Fuck," I mutter against her, parting her with a slow, languid flick of my tongue. "You're dripping all over my tongue, sweetheart."

Gripping her thighs, I wrap my mouth around her, sucking her into my mouth, flicking my tongue over her sweet, swollen clit until her body sings for me, hips moving out of control, her hands tightening on my hair, letting out soft moans that make my cock harden to the point of physical pain.

"I've thought about this so many times," she admits, catching me off guard. I lift my head, seeing her tits rise with each breath she takes.

"You have?"

She lifts her head, her cheeks flushing, which is funny, considering I have my head between her legs and the taste of her pussy all over my tongue.

She nods slowly. "I'd... touch myself, imagining it was you."

Fuck me.

The visual of this girl circling her pretty little clit to thoughts of me makes me groan, wanting, needing to be inside her.

"Like this?" I ask her, circling her clit with two fingers so slowly her hips rock, wanting more,

"Mmmm, yes," she whimpers.

"Christ, I want you," I murmur, eyes fixed on the way her hips roll and thrust against my fingers.

"Then have me."

A chuckle rolls out of me, and I pull my hand away, taking off the rest of my clothes, her eyes widening at the sight of my cock in my fist as I stroke it to the sight of her.

My sweet, innocent Holly widens her legs even more, playing with her nipples as she makes room for me, craving me inside her body.

It's been way too fucking long, and I have no doubt this won't last long when I lean forward and position my cock at her entrance, slowly rubbing the tip over her wetness.

Oh fuuuuck.

I underestimated how fucking good this would feel.

I'm not even inside her and I have to grind my teeth and clench my fists to keep from exploding right fucking here.

"Put it in me," she murmurs, shuffling down on the couch so she brushes against the tip of my cock.

Seeing how needy she is makes my body shake, and I finally thrust the tip in.

A moan escapes her when a couple of inches enter her, and fuck, fuck, *fuck*, this feels so fucking good.

I thrust slowly into her, heavy, labored breaths leaving my throat with every inch I push inside her, feeling her wrapped so fucking tightly around me, hot and wet and fucking perfection.

"God," she moans, tipping her head back when I thrust to the hilt. "You're so big. I can practically feel you in my throat."

Squeezing my eyes closed, I beg myself to have some control and restraint before I come from her words alone. "I love when you talk," I tell her. "But you seriously need to stop before I come."

She chuckles, running her tongue over her lips. "I kinda want to see that."

I thrust into her, groaning at the feel. "Rather fuck you first."

She moans, her tits bouncing with every thrust. "Yeah," she pants. "That."

"Fuck yourself on my cock," I tell her, gripping her hips. "Move your body. Take what you need from me."

She wraps her arms around my neck and pulls me closer, bringing her lips to mine, moaning into my mouth when she grinds her clit against the base of my pelvis.

"God, you taste so fucking sweet," I murmur against her lips, pumping my cock into her. "You taste like my own version of heaven."

She pulls back and smirks. "Your version?" she asks, breathlessly.

I nod, bringing our foreheads together. "Where only you and I exist."

Another sweet moan leaves her. "I want to go there."

"We're right here, baby," I say, grabbing her hips before flipping us over so she's straddling me now, my cock driving into her. "It's you and me."

She lifts off my cock, dropping back down, her tits bouncing in my face with her movement. "Just for tonight?"

"For as long as you'll have me," I correct her, clutching her face in my hand.

She smiles at my words, slowing the movement of her hips as she wraps her arms around my neck, leaning in until our lips are stacked. "Forever?"

I smile back, finally having everything I've ever wanted in my arms. "I love the sound of that."

Chapter Twenty-Seven

— Holly —

It's Christmas morning.

I've been waiting for this day since January 1st, and yet, here I am, not making any effort to move as the light spills in through the sheer curtain while I watch the rise and fall of Mark's chest as he sleeps, low rumbly snores coming from him.

I can't help but feel disbelief that this is actually happening, that he's real, that he's actually lying on this bed naked. My heart races a little as I reach out slowly, poking him in his cheek, making sure he's not just a figment of my imagination.

He stirs, a low, growly noise leaving his throat as his eyes flutter open with a drowsy frown before a smirk tugs at the corner of his mouth.

"Are you poking me?" he asks, his voice rough and gravelly, making my body shiver at the sound.

"I wanted to see if you were real," I reply, unable to resist the urge to poke him again.

"What else would I be?" He arches an eyebrow.

"A dream," I sigh. My heart clenches slightly at the thought that this could all be too good to be true, that he'll disappear if I close my eyes.

He chuckles softly, the sound deep and warm. "No one would dream of me."

"I would," I tell him as our eyes meet.

He pauses, his lips tugging into a small smile. "Yeah. I dreamed of you a lot, too," he admits quietly.

"You did?" I ask, my heart beating faster with each second his eyes are on mine.

"You still doubt that after last night?" he teases, raising an eyebrow as a playful grin spreads across his face.

A warm flush spread across my cheeks at the reminder of last night. "I just thought you wanted me for my hot bod," I joke with a grin.

He scoffs, shaking his head as laughter bubbles up from deep within him. "Jesus, I can't believe I just slept with you."

"Was it great?" I ask, waggling my eyebrows at him. He laughs again.

"Better than anything you ever imagined?" I tease, running my hand up his chest, the soft hair beneath my palms as I feel the steady beat of his heart.

"Bambi—"

"Heaven on earth?" I continue, a teasing grin spreading across my face.

He lets out a sigh, but his lips are curved, unable to stop smiling. "I should have known you'd be like this," he says with a low chuckle.

"You told me never to change," I point out, my eyes never leaving his as I remind him of the words he's said to me before, the ones that have always made me feel like I could truly be myself around him.

He nods, reaching up to cup my face. "And I mean it," he says without an ounce of hesitation. "Don't ever change. I want you just as you are."

His words hit me, making my chest pound.

"Loud and messy?" I ask, trying to keep my voice playful but wanting to know the truth.

He nods again. "All of the above and much more to come," he says before he leans in to kiss me, his lips soft and lingering on mine. The kiss is gentle but filled with so much emotion that it takes my breath away.

I pull back slightly, my heart pounding as I look into his eyes. "You've made a mistake, Mark," I tell him.

"Yeah, what's that?" he asks, his brow furrowing slightly as he searches my face for an answer.

"I'm afraid I'm never letting you go now," I say as I cling to him, my arms wrapping tightly around his neck, wishing I could keep him close forever.

His face settles, shaking his head slightly. "That's fine by me," he whispers, his breath warm against my neck as he presses soft kisses along my jaw and down to my neck, each touch sending shivers through me.

God, is this a dream? Please let it be real. This is everything I've wanted. Everything I've craved to have for years. And now I finally have it. I don't want it to get ripped away from me. My eyes snap open when I remember everything we've talked about. How different we are. How we want completely different things.

"What about… everything?" I ask, a little breathless from his kisses. There's so much that I want in my life, and I need to know if he's on the same page.

"Like what?" Mark asks, pressing his lips to the hollow of my collarbone, making me lightheaded.

"Everything I want," I say.

He pauses and lifts his head, his expression serious as he shrugs. "I'm willing to give you anything you want," he replies, making my heart race.

"Anything?" I repeat, hoping he means what I think he means.

He nods in confirmation, leaning down to kiss my lips. "Everything," he murmurs. "You want a house? Then I'll sell my loft and buy one tomorrow."

The way he says that with so much certainty makes my brows raise. "Are you somehow rich and I didn't know it?" I ask, a small laugh escaping me.

"No," he says, his lips twitching. "But I do have a good bit of money saved up, which we'll need, especially if our kids want to go to college." A smile plays on his lips as he watches my reaction.

"Kids?" My brows shoot up in surprise, my heart skipping a beat at the thought.

"You want kids, don't you?" he asks, his voice gentle as he studies my face.

"Of course I do, but—"

"Then we'll have kids," he says simply, leaning down to kiss me again.

I want to get lost in him, to close my eyes and feel and kiss him until I can't breathe, but the weight of his words hit me, and I moan into his mouth as I pull back, my brows knitted together and my mind spinning. "Wait a second, you can't just decide."

"I didn't *just* decide."

"What?" I ask, my confusion deepening.

Mark lets out a sigh, softly grazing my cheek. "I decided the night you told me you wanted kids that if I ever got the chance to be the guy for you, I'd give you anything you wanted. Marriage, kids, Christmas, dressing up as Santa—"

"You'd dress up as Santa?" I ask, a smile tugging at my lips at the image.

"For our kids? For you?" he asks, his smile genuine and warm, making me feel like the center of his world. "Yeah."

I secretly pinch myself, unable to believe this is real. This is too good to be true.

Mark's eyes narrow as I pinch my forearm and he chuckles, shaking his head. "You don't need to pinch yourself. This isn't a dream, Bambi," he says, his voice full of conviction. "I'm in this for the long haul. Growing old with you, spending the rest of my life with you."

"That's a long time," I whisper, my heart hammering against my chest.

"Not long enough when it comes to you," he says before kissing me again, the kiss filled with so much love that it makes my heart ache.

He rolls on top of me, and I part my legs, making room for him. I get lost in his kiss and scent, smiling against his lips, when a loud bang hits our door, making us jolt apart.

"Get out of my best friend," Olivia shouts from the other side of the door. "We have presents to open."

Mark turns to face me, his brows furrowing. "How the hell did she find out?"

I shake my head, a laugh bubbling out of me. "I have no idea."

"I walked in on you guys," Olivia replies. "Gross, by the way. There were two empty bedrooms available."

Mark shakes his head, a grin spreading across his face. "I told you they would walk in on us," he says. "We've traumatized your friends."

I laugh, rolling my eyes. "Trust me, I've been traumatized enough by them. It was time for a little payback."

Mark chuckles, leaning in to press one more kiss to my lips. "Let's go," he says, pulling me close for a moment before sliding out of bed. "Let's celebrate Christmas."

Chapter Twenty-Eight

Holly

"Finally," Olivia says as Mark and I make our way down the stairs, his hand intertwined with mine. "We've been waiting forever," he says, throwing her hands in the air. "What the hell took so long? You're usually the first one down here."

I shrug when we finally step into the living room, sheepishly glancing up at Mark. "We were a little distracted," I tell her, seeing his lips twitch as his eyes meet mine.

Olivia's rolls her eyes, a knowing smirk creeping onto her face, knowing she can't be mad at me when I'm this happy. After all, she had been rooting for Mark since the very first day I met him.

She takes a seat on the couch, and we join. Mark settles into the corner and I lean against him. I look up and see the Christmas tree, fully decorated, with twinkling warm white lights covering the branches and presents stacked underneath.

The cold air hits my skin and a shiver runs through my body as I nestle into Mark, trying to warm my body up, which he takes notice of as he grabs a knitted blanket hanging over the edge of the couch and wraps it around my shoulders, pressing a light, gentle kiss to my cheek. God, he's so soft and warm and kind, and he knows me so well. Knows exactly what I need.

I smile up at him, warmth coating my body with the way he looks at me, and I hear Olivia's laugh.

"I knew this would happen," she says, glancing between the both of us before she turns to Henry and taps his shoulder. "Didn't I?"

Henry lets out a sigh, grinning back at her. "Yes, you did." He glances at us, lifting his brows. "Wouldn't stop talking about it."

"I just have a strong intuition when it comes to things like this," she says. "Plus, you left your sweater in the kitchen," she finishes, her eyes twinkling with mischief.

My cheeks flush with embarrassment. I completely forgot about that. It was the last thing on my mind at the time.

"Okay," Olivia says, clapping her hands. "I'm opening my present first since I'm pregnant and all," she says, dramatically rubbing her pregnant belly.

I arch my brow. "And that gives you priority for opening gifts?" I joke.

She blinks, her face remaining blank. "Duh." She turns to the tree, humming as she glances around at the presents. "I want the big one," she says, turning to Henry.

He heads toward the tree and grabs the large box at the back, handing it to her. She eagerly tears off the wrapping paper, grinning as she unwraps her gift. But when the paper is finally off, her eyes widen in surprise and fill with tears.

"You got us a new toaster?" she asks, her voice breaking as tears spill over.

"Why is she crying?" Mark asks, a puzzled look crossing his face.

"We got our toaster when we first moved in together," Henry explains with a smile as he glances at Olivia. "And now we're about to have a baby. I thought it would be a nice, fresh start. The toaster for our family."

Tears spill down my best friend's face as she leaps into Henry's arms. "Jesus, woman," he grunts, laughing as he wraps his arms around his wife.

"I love you," she murmurs, kissing his face. "I love you. I love you."

I chuckle, watching them both. I've known Olivia for what feels like my whole life and Henry for a good chunk of it, and I couldn't agree more that they're completely perfect for each other.

Mark clears his throat, and I glance up at him. "I still don't understand why she's crying," he says, making a laugh bubble out of me.

"Hormones," I explain with a shrug. "I'm pretty sure she'd cry over fluffy socks. She loves gifts. No matter what they are."

"Do you want your gift now?" Olivia asks her husband, still tackling him to the ground.

He laughs, brushing her hair out of his face. "Yeah. I'd like it if I could also breathe."

She shuffles off him and heads toward the tree to grab his gift, and I lean into Mark, glancing up at him with a smile.

I hope we're like that someday. I've only known Mark for a short amount of time, but he makes me feel like no one ever has. He listens to me, likes it when I speak, and does everything to make me happy. He's exactly what I've been looking for, and I've never been so grateful for a failed date than I have been for the asshole who stood me up because if not, I never would have met him.

Mark presses a gentle kiss to my forehead. "You having fun?" he asks, his voice full of tenderness.

"Of course," I say, lifting my eyes to meet his with a smile. "I love Christmas."

"I know," he teases, rolling his eyes playfully. "You're just a little quiet. I kind of expected you to be bouncing off the walls, kind of like…" He gestures towards Olivia, who's now squealing with delight over the lawn mower she gave Henry. Henry looks both bewildered and amused.

"You're going to be a hot suburban dad," she tells him with a grin. "I can't wait to see it."

Mark and I laugh at their antics. "Kind of expected that to be you," he says, his lips twitching into a smirk.

"I'm just soaking in this moment," I admit, leaning into him. "This is the best Christmas I've ever had."

"Yeah," Mark says as he meets my eyes. "Mine too, sweetheart."

I glance around the room, taking in the snow-covered world outside the frosted windows and the sparkling Christmas tree. My stomach sinks a little. "I wish my parents were here," I admit quietly. "I wish you could have met them."

Mark's gaze softens as he looks at me. "I would have loved them," he says. "It would be impossible not to love the people who created you." His hand clutches my face, smoothing his thumb over my skin. "You want your present now?"

"You got me a present?" I ask, blinking in surprise. "Mark Lawson bought me a *Christmas* gift?"

"Stop trying to make me join your Christmas cult," he says dryly. "It's just a gift."

"A Christmas cult?" I muse with a playful grin. "That would be so fun."

"Of course you'd think that," Mark says, leaning forward to grab a rectangle box. "Here, open it."

I study the box, noting the folded edges of the wrapping paper slightly misaligned and my lips twitch. Mark did this himself. He bought and wrapped a Christmas gift for me. I quickly tug at the paper before lifting the lid of the box, finding a light blue knitted pouch I assume is to keep my books, given that it's accompanied by a Christmas tree-shaped bookmark.

"To protect your books," Mark says with a teasing smirk. "Since you're a menace who folds the pages."

"Did you get this gift for me or for you?" I ask, raising an eyebrow.

"Both," he replies with a mischievous twinkle in his eye.

I close the box and lean in to kiss him. "Thank you," I say softly. "I love it."

"I actually got you something else," he says, making my brows knit together as he reaches over and grabs a larger gift, bulky and lumpy, underneath the wrapping paper.

"Another one?" I ask. "Mark, I only got you one gift."

He shakes his head. "I don't care about gifts, Bambi. I just wanted you to have this."

My curiosity takes the best of me as my brows knit together, wondering what the hell this is, and I quickly unwrap the gift, tearing at the paper.

I freeze, my smile slipping when I see what it is, and my jaw drops open, unable to believe what I'm looking at.

"What—" I glance up at Mark, shaking my head. "How?"

He shrugs. "I couldn't stop thinking about how you told me the last thing you got from your parents was a pink Barbie backpack and how you lost it," he starts, my eyes filling with tears. "So I got you one, so you can always have a piece of them."

My lip wobbles as tears fall down my cheeks and I shake my head. "I can't believe you found it."

"It was hard to find," he admits with a chuckle. "But I knew I had to get it for you. Whether we never spoke again once you and Ryan started dating or not," he says, the muscle in his jaw ticking. "I just wanted you to be happy."

Dropping the bag, I lift my arms and wrap them around him, practically climbing onto his lap as I kiss him, wiping my tears as I let out a laugh, pure joy and happiness bubbling inside me. "Thank you. Thank you. Thank you," I tell him, kissing his cheeks. "I love it so much."

He hums against my lips, pulling back with a soft smile as he wipes my tears. "You're welcome, sweetheart."

"I got you something, too," I say, reaching for his gift.

"Yeah?" Mark asks.

"Duh," I reply with a grin, sniffing as I wipe my eyes. "Christmas gift shopping is my favorite thing ever."

Mark laughs, shaking his head in amusement. "Why doesn't that surprise me? You're so giving, so caring of others."

"Stop flirting with me," I tease, playfully swatting at him.

"Now that I can?" Mark says with a smile. "Don't think I ever will."

I blush, handing him the wrapped gift. He carefully unwraps it, pulling out a sweater and a smaller, matching one in an ugly, loud green Christmas pattern.

"I'm afraid to ask what this is," he says, his brows furrowing in confusion as he examines the items.

I let out a laugh. "It's a matching sweater for you and Murray."

He arches his brow, dropping the gift back into the box. "Is this gift for me or for you?" he asks, echoing my earlier question.

"Both," I reply with a playful wink.

Mark chuckles and pulls me close, his hands gently cupping my face. "I love it."

"Really?" I ask, a little surprised. "I got it mostly as a joke."

Mark shakes his head, his expression softening. "I love that you thought of me, that you got something for me. It doesn't matter what it is."

"I can get you a better Christmas gift," I offer. "One you actually want."

"You're the only thing I wanted," Mark says, his eyes locking with mine. "And now I finally have that. I don't need anything else."

I get lost in his warm eyes, and I can't help but let out a heavy sigh. "Are you sure this isn't a dream?"

Mark chuckles softly. "Not a dream," he promises. "I told you I'd get you your Christmas boyfriend, didn't I? Turns out it was me all along. We just didn't know it."

I laugh, my heart swelling. "I guess I was your Christmas angel after all, making you believe in the magic of Christmas again."

He scoffs playfully. "I believe in *you*. You're the magic in my life."

I glance around at the snow-covered world outside, the ice frosting the windows, and the Christmas tree glowing with lights. "You've got to admit, this is a beautiful time."

"Any time with you is beautiful," Mark replies, making my heart pound.

"Oh, Mark," I say, smiling up at him. "I always knew you were a big softie."

He laughs, shaking his head. "Only for you, Bambi."

Chapter Twenty-Nine

Mark

I've spent most of my life in the city. Never been anywhere else. So, it's a little weird being back after experiencing the peace and quiet out in the cabin. I thought I was used to this, the noise, the hustle, and the constant buzz of traffic, but I kind of miss being back at the cabin, covered in snow, with Christmas music constantly playing around the house.

The good thing about being back is getting to see Murray and Mia. They had a great time over at Johnson's place for Christmas. She seemed so happy, so joyful, my heart ached. It's been a long time since I've seen Mia that happy.

And the other good thing… I'm looking right at her. My lips curve into a smile as I glance down at my—can't believe I'm going to say this—girlfriend, and watch as she skips down the street, my hand swaying in hers with every step she takes.

I raise my brows in amusement. "Why the hell are you skipping, Bambi?" I ask with a grunt. "It's seven in the morning."

My girl wanted her coffee fix before we went back to my place. I should be working, I'm always working. I had nothing better to do before her. Nothing I looked forward to. Nothing expecting me. So I put my all into work, trying to busy my time, but now that Christmas is over, I just want to spend all my time with her before I have to go back to work.

Christ. What the hell has she turned me into?

You know what? I don't even care. I haven't been this fucking happy in years. Whatever it is, I hope it never stops. Hope she never leaves.

She looks back at me with a huge grin on her pretty little lips I want to kiss so bad. "I'm happy."

Love hearing that. Love that I'm the one making her happy. Love her.

What the fuck.

I pause, my feet halting as the thought comes out of nowhere, hitting me right in the chest, a blaring admission I hadn't thought about until now.

Holly stops, seeing I'm not moving, and turns to face me, her brows knitting together. "What's wrong?" she asks.

The last time I was in love was years ago, and my heart was shattered, but even with Sasha, it never felt like this. I cared about her, but with Holly... my chest feels like it's being cracked open whenever she merely glances my way. Whenever she smiles, I feel my belly fluttering like fucking crazy. Whenever I hear her laugh, my body breaks out into a shiver, wanting to hear it again and again and again. I have never been truly in love before. Not like this. Not like I am with Holly.

I shake my head, tugging on her hand to pull her into me, lifting her chin with my thumb, her lips parting slightly as our eyes lock together. "I'm really fucking happy, too."

Her shoulders settle as a smirk tugs at her lips. "That's not possible."

My brows furrow. "Why not?"

"Robots don't have feelings," she teases, breaking out into a grin that eases my chest.

I shake my head with a scoff. "You're funny," I say dryly.

She laughs, poking at my cheek. "We need to return you to the manufacturer."

I smile as I clutch her face in my hands. "You've always made me happy, Holly."

Her eyes warm, glistening as she looks at me, but then she lets out a sigh. "I thought you were grumpy," she says. "I liked you grumpy. What happened?"

I look into the eyes of the most beautiful girl in the world and tell her the honest to god truth. "I met you."

Her smile widens, a small laugh bubbling out of her. "I think I like that even more," she admits.

I lean forward to press my lips to hers, loving the feel of her face in my hands, her warm, soft lips on mine, and the way my heart feels like it's going to burst.

When we pull apart, the hazy look in her eyes makes me groan, knowing all kinds of dirty thoughts are roaming around in that head of hers, and I tighten my hand around her waist. "Wanna go home?" I ask, pressing a feather-light kiss to her jaw.

She chuckles. "You don't even have to ask."

Fuck yes.

I grab hold of her hand in mine and we start walking down the street, ready to get to my house so I can peel every inch of clothing off her beautiful body and worship her, make her feel as good as she makes me, hear her beautiful moans.

But Holly's pace slows down as she glances at a shop window, tilting her head at the plush light grey round armchair-looking thing.

I pause, and she snaps her head to mine. "What are you doing?"

"Seeing what you're looking at," I tell her, heading closer toward the window.

Holly shakes her head. "It's nothing. Just looking."

I squint at the sign, reading the description, seeing it's a reading chair. "You should get it," I tell her. "Looks like something you'd like."

She lets out a sigh. "I love it, but…" She hesitates a little. "I don't have the space in my room."

"We've got space in my room," I say without thinking, the words just stumbling out of my mouth.

She blinks, taken by surprise. "*Your* room?"

I nod, not an ounce of hesitation within me. "Yeah. My room." I smirk, turning away from the window to face her. "I already told you I'm all in, Holly. I'm in it for the long haul. I want you over at my place as often as you can be, so if having a reading chair over there is going to incentivize you to come over, then get it. Redecorate the place, paint the walls, buy five hundred plants, whatever you want, you can have it." I take a breather, watching as her eyes widen, her lips parted in shock. "What do you say?"

256

She shakes her head slightly. "I… are you sure?"

My lips widen into a smile and I nod, tucking a strand of her hair flowing in the wind behind her ear. "About you? A thousand percent." Our lips meet in a soft kiss, and she clings to me, her hands clutching my sweater.

I was looking forward to getting her naked and in my bed, but seeing her smile is my favorite thing ever, and if this reading chair is going to do that, I'm getting it for her.

❄

"Fuck," I mutter, my body breaking out in a sweat as I climb the final step, hauling the massive reading chair before I finally set it down on the ground.

"I know you're tired and sweating," Holly says as I wipe the sweat off my forehead, glancing up at her and seeing her press her lips together in an amused smile. "But you look so hot right now."

I let out a laugh, my shoulders shaking. "You like a man who does hard labor?" I ask, arching a brow as I approach her, my hands resting on her waist.

"Mmm." She hums, wrapping her arms around my neck. "I like you."

Christ. Love hearing that.

I lift her into my arms, and she squeals as I kiss her, pushing open the door, barely caring where we end up— bed, couch, whatever's closer. Dropping her onto the couch, I follow her down, her legs spreading to make room for me.

Murray barks, wanting to jump onto Holly, but I shoo him off, wanting to have some time with Holly without my damn dog interrupting us. But Holly moans into my mouth and pulls back, her brows knitted together.

She starts to sniff the air. "Why does your place smell like caramel?"

"It's called a candle, Bambi," I say with an arched brow. "Kinda thought you'd be familiar with them."

She rolls her eyes. "You know what I mean. Since when do you have candles?"

I shrug. "Since I found one that smells like you."

Her eyes soften. "You bought a candle that smells like me?" she asks, her lips widening into a smile.

I nod, sitting on the couch as I pull her up to sit beside me. "Wanted my house to smell like you," I admit. "It feels like home whenever you're here."

Her eyes widen slightly, searching my face. "It does?"

My hand reaches out to cup her face, holding her gaze. "Has done since the very first day you pushed your way inside," I tease with a smirk.

She doesn't laugh, though. Her eyes stare up at me, blinking rapidly as her bottom lip wobbles slightly.

It fucking kills me that she's never experienced this kind of love before. "Holly, you *are* my home," I tell her. "This guy," I say, gesturing to Murray, "and Mia were the only important people in my life. I only cared about them. I didn't think there was any space left in me for anyone else." I keep my eyes on her soft ones. "But then you stumbled into my life and everything fucking changed." She inhales a sharp breath. "My whole world opened up and it turns out, there was room. An empty, hollow space… waiting for you."

Her lips part in shock and fuck. I love her so much. And I want the whole world to know it. The thought pops into my head. "I want you to meet Mia."

Her eyes widen. "Mia?" she repeats. "Are you sure?"

So fucking sure. I didn't want Mia to know about Holly when we were… whatever we were. I knew she'd cling to the idea of matchmaking, and I was convinced Holly was just a friend. But I was so fucking wrong, and now that we're finally together, I want Mia to meet her.

I nod. "Mia is the closest thing I have to a parent and she means a lot to me, as do you," I tell her. "I'd really like to introduce you to her and tell her we're together." The thought makes my lips lift into a smile. I think back to what Mia told me about Charles, how he was grumpy until he met her. How she changed him. Kinda think Holly did the same for me.

Holly tugs her lip between her teeth, her expression filling with nerves. "I've never met anyone's parents before," she admits.

I chuckle at her nervousness, and I pull her closer. "You have nothing to be nervous about, Holly," I assure her. "Mia is going to love you." I look into her gorgeous eyes that sucked me in from day one and shake my head. "You're perfect."

She raises an eyebrow, a teasing look in her eyes. "Perfect, huh?"

I let out a scoff. "So perfect, I'm starting to wonder how I didn't find you in the manufacturer's warehouse."

She narrows her eyes at me, smirking. "Funny."

I hold her gaze. "You're the only one who thinks so, sweetheart." I sigh. "So, what do you say?"

She twists her lips but then breaks out into a grin and nods. "I'd love to."

"Yeah?" I ask, feeling my heart race. "Then let's go." I lift off the couch, holding her hand.

"Wait." Holly's eyes widen as we make our way toward the door. "Right now?"

I arch a brow. "When exactly were you thinking?"

She shakes her head. "I just… I don't know what to say. I'm not prepared." She glances down at her outfit. "This is the wrong outfit and—"

"Calm down, Bambi," I cut her off, letting out a laugh. "What you're wearing is beautiful, you look amazing and you don't need to be prepared. Just be yourself and she'll love you." *I sure fucking do*. I swallow the words down, watching as Holly drops her shoulders.

"Okay," she says, letting out a hard breath. "Okay, let's go."

We head over to Mia's, knocking a couple of times before I open the door. Murray heads inside, and a moment later, I hear Mia's laugh.

She loves that dog. So I tend to bring him around as often as I can, loving when she smiles and laughs when she sees him.

"I was thinking you'd forgotten about me," she calls out, and I turn the corner, seeing her petting Murray as he lies beside her on the couch.

I was supposed to come here an hour ago, but seeing as I was out with Holly, I'm a little late. I think Mia will forgive me when she sees her, though.

"Never," I confirm with a smile. "I just wanted to surprise you."

"Surprise me with what?" She turns her head, the wrinkles around her eyes deepening when she frowns, but then when she sees Holly standing beside me, our hands intertwined, her eyes widen as she lets out a loud gasp.

Holly and I make our way beside her and she looks at Holly, her lips lifting into a grin. "Well, this is a surprise," she says. "You brought a girl with you?" She tuts slightly. "I was starting to think the day would never come."

I let out a laugh. *Yeah. Me too.* "Worth the wait, though, right?" I say, glancing down at Holly, feeling her hand squeezing mine.

Mia smiles. "Good thing it happened while I was still alive," she jokes as she lifts off the couch and reaches out to cup Holly's face in her hands. "Look at you." Her eyes flick to mine. "You did good, Mark. She's beautiful."

Holly laughs, her eyes sparkling as Mia still has her captured between her hands. "Thank you. It's so nice to finally meet you. Mark talks about you all the time."

"Does he now?" She tuts, her hands dropping from Holly's face. "All good things, I hope. He hasn't told me a peep about you. That boy is always full of surprises."

I arch my brow. "I can hear you, you know?"

She waves me off, tugging Holly's hand and dragging her toward the kitchen. "If I'd known you were coming, I would have baked some cookies or a lemon tart. Do you like lemon?"

"I love it," Holly replies.

"Good." Mia grabs hold of the apron hanging on the oven door and hands it over to Holly with a warm smile. Jesus. I haven't seen her this happy in so long. "You're on lemon squeezing duty."

Crossing my arms, I watch as Holly grabs hold of the lemons and the bowl and starts cutting the lemons. I clear my throat, garnering the attention of the two women. "Did you just steal my girlfriend?"

Holly's smile widens at that word. I guess I haven't said it since we've gotten together, at least not out loud, and *fuck*, I love the way it feels coming out of my lips.

"We have baking to do," Mia replies. "Besides, I still need to hear about everything that happened between you two, and you sure as hell won't tell me." She glances at Holly. "How did you two meet? And more importantly, how has he managed not to scare you off yet?"

Holly laughs, stealing a quick glance at me. "It came close a few times, but he managed to redeem himself," she teases.

Mia laughs, tapping her cheek as she turns to face me. "I like her already. You better hold on tight, Mark."

I swallow hard, watching the two most important women in my life. "I plan on it."

Chapter Thirty

— Mark —

I haven't been on a date in a really fucking long time.

And now I remember why.

Women take forever to get ready.

Lifting my arm, I check my watch for what feels like the millionth time tonight, seeing that we're now five minutes late. Feels like I've been waiting here, sitting on her couch, for an eternity.

So long in fact, that Funnel Cakes and her husband are leaving.

She glances at me with a tilted head, amusement crossing her features. "She's still not ready?"

I reply with a sigh.

Olivia lets out a laugh, sharing a look with Henry. "She's always like this so… good luck, I guess."

"Thanks," I say with a shake of my head. "Think I'll need it."

She laughs again, grabbing her keys from the console table. "When you guys finally get ready, make sure you lock the door," she tells me, shaking her head slightly. "She tends to forget."

I blink. "She forgets to lock the door?" I repeat, hoping I heard wrong.

Olivia shrugs, a smile tugging at her lips. "She's so forgiving, I don't think she realizes there aren't good people out there."

A smile creeps onto my face at the thought. Yeah. Sounds like her. I love how she always sees the best in people. She saw the best in me and wanted me. Still can't fucking believe it.

"Can I tell you something?" Olivia says, approaching me.

"Sure," I say with a shrug.

She smirks, pressing her lips together. "I was rooting for you."

I blink, not understanding what she's saying.

"When she was dating…" She waves her hand around, glancing up, trying to remember the name.

"Ryan," I fill in for her.

Clicking her fingers, she points at me. "Ryan, yes." She sighs. "When she was dating Ryan, and everything was brewing between you two," she says, her shoulders dropping as she smiles at me. "I was always rooting for you."

Really like hearing that. Holly's friends are practically her family, so the fact that they like me and were rooting for us to be together means a lot. "Thanks."

She nods in acknowledgment. "You're good for her," she says. "You're very patient with her and kind and…" Her eyes narrow. "You won't hurt her right?"

"Never," I say without an ounce of hesitation.

She smiles at my answer. "She deserves someone to love her," she tells me, her tone a little more serious than before. "She's spent so many years without anyone to love her, well, except for me."

"I'm ready to give her the kind of love she's always been looking for," I tell Olivia, seeing her eyes widen a little at my confession. Kinda wish I had told Holly before anyone else, but I want them both to know I will do anything it takes to keep her in my life. Whatever she wants, I'm willing to give her. I'll be at the ready to do whatever she needs.

Her smile widens a little, as does Henry's. "I'm happy to hear that," she says, turning to fix her husband's tie.

"Ready to go?" he asks her.

She nods, shrugging her coat on, and they both head toward the door. "Have fun," she calls out before heading out the door.

"You too."

"But not too much fun," she says with a laugh, rubbing her pregnant belly.

I let out a scoff as they head out and close the door behind them, leaving me alone in an empty living room... still waiting.

"Holly," I call out. "Are you almost done?"

"Almost," she calls back, her voice a little muffled since she's behind her bedroom door. "I just want to look perfect," she says. "It's our first date."

First date.

My lips twitch. God, I love the sound of that. First of fucking many dates to come.

"You already look perfect, sweetheart," I call back.

I hear her laugh from the other side of the door. "You're sweet, but you're a man. Men don't know anything."

A scoff leaves my lips. "Fine," I mutter because she's right. Don't know shit about clothes and makeup and all that shit. I just know she looks stunning in anything she wears.

Might just be her, though.

I lean back on the couch, breathing out a sigh. My eyes catch on the book lying face down on the coffee table, the green Christmas tree-shaped bookmark poking out of it. I laugh to myself. She finally used it.

Reaching out, I grab the book and flip it open to where the bookmark is when my eyes catch on a word.

Cock.

The fuck?

Scanning the page, my eyes widen in seconds when I read the explicit sexual scene on the page.

"Holy shit," I murmur to myself, running a hand over my mouth as I read the words on the page, feeling my heart pick up as I imagine Holly tucked under the covers, reading this.

"Okay, I'm ready. We can..." I lift my head, seeing Holly standing in the middle of the living room, looking like she came straight out of a fucking magazine.

"*Holy shit*," I say again, this time louder, my jaw dropping as I trace my eyes down her figure, the tight red dress clinging to her body, the dress reaching mid-thigh, paired with boots that go right up to her knees.

My head spins, unable to believe I'm about to go on a date with her. That this is the girl I get to kiss and make love to.

"Holy shit."

"You said that already," she says with a chuckle. Her eyes drift to the book in my hands. "What are you doing with my book?"

I'm reminded of what I was reading a few minutes ago—what my Holly reads, and a smirk creeps onto my lips as I lift myself off the couch, placing the book back on the coffee table.

"*This* is what you read?" I ask, arching a brow as I approach her, a groan building in my throat when I finally touch her, holding her hips in my hands, feeling the soft material of her dress under my touch.

She parts her lips on a shaky breath, her eyes narrowing slightly. "How far did you get?"

"Enough to know it's a dirty book," I reply with a chuckle, seeing her cheeks flush a deep shade of pink.

"Oh," she says, her voice hushed as she pulls her lip between her teeth. "Yeah."

A low rumble leaves me as my hands shift, grabbing her ass and giving it a squeeze. "I thought you were sweet," I say, leaning down to press my lips against her jaw. "Innocent. And yet here you are reading these dirty little books." My teeth graze at her earlobe, my cock rock hard when she lets out a sweet, little moan.

"It's... romance," she gasps out, tipping her head back to give me better access.

I chuckle against her skin. "I'm sure."

"It is."

267

"Mhmm," I hum, kissing her slender throat, feeling it bob under my lips. "Do you get turned on when you read them?"

A heavy breath escapes her. "Sometimes."

Fuck.

"Are you turned on thinking about it?" she asks me, catching me off guard.

This woman. "Already was when I saw you in this dress, knowing you're mine to touch, and kiss, and fuck," I tell her, hearing her soft whimper when I clutch her ass tight in my hands, wanting to rip this dress off. "But now that I know you read this… I'm rock fucking hard."

"Mark," she says with a gasp when I twist her around.

"Lift your arms, sweetheart," I whisper against her ear, feeling her back her ass onto me, slowly grinding against my aching cock.

"I should be angry," she says with no conviction at all. "I worked so hard on this makeup and outfit."

"But you're not."

She shakes her head, glancing at me over her shoulder with a look in her eyes that makes me groan. "No," she says, pressing harder against me. "I don't care if you mess it up."

I chuckle, thrusting against her. "Oh, I'll mess it up."

"Promises, promises."

"I keep my promises, sweetheart," I tell her, slowly lifting the dress up her smooth, tight body until it's completely off, leaving her completely braless, only a pair of flimsy red panties covering her. "So fucking perfect," I murmur, smoothing my hand over her cute little butt, teasing me as she sways her hips subtly.

"Bend over the couch," I tell her, my voice thick.

Without any hesitation, she bends her pretty ass over the couch, folding in half, perfectly positioned for me. I groan at the sight, growing harder with each second my eyes are on her.

Shedding my jacket off, I quickly make work of my buttons, tugging my shirt off until it hits the ground.

Holly twists her head, letting out a whine. "I want to see you."

My body grows hot, seeing my dream woman bent over, almost completely naked, whining for me with her gorgeous ass in the air.

"Don't worry, baby," I murmur, tugging my pants off until I'm buck-naked behind her. "You'll feel me instead."

Grabbing my cock, I give it a sharp stroke, sucking air into my nose when the pleasure curls up my spine. Fuck. My head is spinning. I want to do so many things to her, I can't even think. Can't breathe. Can't function without feeling her right this second.

Without taking off her panties, I thrust my cock against her, earning a loud moan from her as I push my cock against the curve of her ass, unable to think as I dry fuck her.

"Mark," she gasps. "Oh god."

"You're getting so wet for me, sweetheart," I grunt, tugging her panties tighter so the material of her panties molds her pussy perfectly.

"You don't want to take them off?" she asks, her panting breaths making me fuck against her harder, her panties getting wet from her arousal, coating my cock.

Fuck. I breathe in through my nose, fighting the urge to just plunge into her, wanting to take my time to feel her, every part of her.

"Not yet," I reply gruffly.

Reaching for her, I grab her waist and flip her over, staring down at her gorgeous tits, pink pebbled nipples begging to be sucked, licked, teased.

Lifting her legs, I spread them open. My eyes zone in on the dark patch on her underwear, clinging to her pussy. A groan builds in my throat when I grip my cock and thrust it against her, sliding my cock between her folds, still covered by the underwear.

Precum spills out of my cock, dribbling out onto her panties, and I quickly rub my cock through it, using it as lube to thrust against her, feeling her wet and hot and so fucking needy with each soft moan leaving her lips.

Her noises are something made of my dreams, designed just for me, made to drive me to insanity. Hard breaths leave my lips, unable to keep the pleasure inside of me as I push my cock hard against her clit, her panties serving as a delicious, torturous barrier.

Her hips move, grinding uncontrollably against the length of my cock and I can't fucking take it anymore. Sliding her panties to the side, I run my cock through her juices, feeling how fucking wet she is, and her eyes drop to where we're connected, watching me tease her, please her, and rub her sweet little clit with the tip of my dick.

270

"Put it in me," she begs so sweetly, so fucking addicting.

A zing of pleasure curls up in my balls at the sound of her begging me. *Fuck*. I pull away from her quickly, trying to regain some control. Can't fucking look away, though. The sight of her completely disheveled for me, her panties pushed aside and her bare pussy on display, dripping wet makes me lose my goddamn mind.

Kneeling down, I grab her thighs with my hands, spreading them wider as I slowly trace the tip of my tongue over her pussy, unable to carry on without tasting her, without feeling her on my tongue.

"Fuck, you're so sweet, baby," I grunt, pressing featherlight kisses to her pussy. "So fucking sweet, I could just drink you up."

"Please," she pants, tipping her head back when I French kiss her clit, making love to her pussy with my mouth. "Fuck me, lick me, just make me *come*."

I chuckle against her. "So demanding, sweetheart." Spreading her pussy open, I groan at the sight of her pink, wet center and lick her, savoring the taste as I flick my tongue over her swollen clit.

"Mark," she warns, bucking her hips.

I let out another laugh, done with teasing both her and myself, and press my lips against her thigh, kissing up until I reach the hem of her panties. Tugging them between my teeth, I pull them down her legs until they're completely off.

"Yes," she gasps when I lift onto my feet.

Wrapping one hand around my cock, I give it a slow stroke, bringing it to her entrance, and start to push in slowly.

"God, yes," she moans when she swallows the first inch inside of her.

"Fuck, you feel good," I murmur, my head feeling dizzy as fuck as I watch my cock tunnel into her. She throws her head back when she finally takes all of me, her tight pussy gripping my cock inside of her, coating it with her wetness.

Pulling out of her a few inches, I thrust into her, hard and demanding as I grip her waist in my hands, lifting her off the couch to fuck her onto my cock. Fuck. She looks so perfect right now, completely succumbing to the pleasure coursing through her as I take control of her body.

"You fit so well in my hands, sweetheart," I murmur, my voice raspy as my own pleasure takes over me, curling up my spine every time I push into her tight heat.

Gripping her tighter, I lift her up, keeping my cock deep inside of her as I turn around and lean her against the dark wood bookshelf, placing her ass on the shelf as I pull out and push back in.

"Oh fuck," Holly gasps, wrapping her arms around my neck as I fuck her, dropping her onto my cock, meeting every thrust. "I'm so close. I'm gonna—"

"Come, sweetheart," I grunt, driving my cock deeper into her, feeling her muscles clenching tight around me. "I've got you."

Her pussy flutters around me, making me groan. I fuck her harder, deeper, the bookshelf rattling with every thrust of my hips. Her moans get louder and louder until she tips her head back and closes her eyes, her nails clawing at my back, her body shaking as the orgasm crashes through her.

"That's my girl," I grunt with a smile, loving the sight of her falling apart in my arms. Her pussy continues to clench around me with every drive of my cock and it doesn't take long until I'm right behind her, my balls getting tighter and heavier and… "*Oh fuck.*"

Heavy grunts leave my lips as I spill inside her, thrusting lazily until I'm completely empty.

My chest rises and falls with every heavy breath leaving my lips, Holly's breath matching mine and I place my forehead against hers, still deep inside her body, trying to keep the memory of this preserved, not wanting to let it go.

Fuck. I don't ever remember sex being this good.

"You okay?" I ask her.

She nods, a soft noise leaving her. "So good."

I chuckle, knowing exactly how she feels. Pressing a kiss to her lips, I pull my cock out of her and lower her to the ground.

"You ready to go on our date now?" I ask her, with an amused look on my face.

"Yeah," she says with a sigh, attempting to smooth out her hair, which looks unruly. "You'll need to wait until I get ready again, though." Her eyes narrow. "It is your fault."

My lips twitch. I guess it is. Don't regret it, though. If I had the option, I'd do it again. And again, and again. I might have been in a rush before, but I was a fucking idiot. I've been waiting all my life for her. I can wait a few minutes more. "Take your time," I tell her. "I'll wait for however long you need."

She smiles and leans on her tiptoes to wrap her arms around my neck as she kisses me deep and hard, smiling against my mouth.

When she pulls back, she has a soft, lazy smile on her face which makes my body grow hot. Fucking love making her smile. Love making her happy.

She starts to pick up her clothes, ready to head back to her bedroom, but before she can leave, I stop her.

"Holly."

She glances at me over her shoulder, giving me a delicious view of her ass. "Hmm?"

"Are you sure you're okay?" I ask, my brows knitting together. I've never been that rough with her before, I love taking her slowly, wanting to feel her, to look at her when we make love, but when I saw her in that dress, all I wanted to do was *fuck* her.

She flashes me a smirk and nods. "I'm sure," she says, her eyes flicking to the length of my body, my cock twitching at her ogling. "You weren't bad… for an old man."

A growl leaves my lips as she chuckles and heads into her bedroom.

Can't wait to get back here and make her take back those words.

Chapter Thirty-One

Holly

"I look like a mess," I groan, glancing at my reflection in the shop window.

Mark chuckles. "You look like you just got fucked."

I shoot him a glare. "That's not a good thing."

He presses his lips together, attempting to stop the laughing as he shrugs. "Is to me," he says. "Tells other guys you're all fucking mine."

I roll my eyes, pretending like I don't like hearing that from him. I've never belonged anywhere, let alone to anyone, but the idea of belonging to him sends a rush of warmth through me.

I turn back to the window, attempting to fix my makeup and hair again. Mark had kissed me so hard after I finished getting ready that I didn't even realize the mess it made until I saw myself in the reflection.

"You look beautiful, sweetheart," Mark murmurs, wrapping his hands around my waist and kissing the top of my head. "You always do."

I glance over my shoulder, catching the soft smile on his lips. It makes my heart race, just like the very first time I saw him smile. I love that I'm the one who puts that happiness on his face. He deserves it.

"C'mon," he says, gently turning me away from the window. "We're going to be late."

"What are we doing?" I ask, for what must be the hundredth time tonight. We missed our restaurant reservation, seeing as we were late, and Mark mentioned that he had a surprise for me. And while I love surprises, I'm too curious to wait.

He chuckles, glancing down at me with a twitch of his lips. "Something Christmassy and awful."

My brows shoot up, shocked at him finally answering me, but then the realization of what he said dawns on me, making my brows knit together. "What?"

His smile widens slightly as he glances at the other side of the street, and my eyes follow his, noticing the big red sleigh parked on the side of the road, being pulled by two horses.

My heart bangs against my chest as my jaw drops open. "You're joking."

He sighs. "Unfortunately, I'm not."

"We're going on a sleigh ride?" I ask, still unable to believe this is happening.

Mark's eyes soften as mine widen and he smiles. "Yeah."

"But…" I shake my head. "You hate that sort of thing."

He nods. "But I don't hate you."

I shoot him a look. "You know what I mean."

He holds my face in his hand, softly smoothing his thumb over my cheek. "I meant it when I told you I would give you everything you wanted no matter what. I would do anything and everything to make you happy,

276

Holly." Tears prick my eyes as his shine down at me. "I wouldn't have booked it if I didn't want to go. I want to see you smile. I want to make you happy. I want to treat you right and love you right."

I suck in a breath. "*Love*?"

He smiles warmly. "I think it's pretty obvious how I feel about you."

"You…" I shake my head, feeling dizzy and weak, and… did I just hear him right? "You what?"

"Speechless?" Mark jokes, letting out a soft laugh. "I never thought I'd see the day."

My mouth is still dropped open, my heart banging uncontrollably against my chest, hoping I heard him correctly. Hoping this isn't one of my dreams. That this is actually happening.

"Can… Can you say it again?"

His brow quirks. "Speechless?"

"No." I shake my head. "No. The… the other thing."

His smile widens. "That I love you?"

My chest rises with a hard breath, his words running through me, swirling around my stomach. "Yeah."

Both of his hands cup my face now, looking deeply into my eyes. "I love you, Holly. I never thought I'd end up loving someone, let alone this fucking much. But you walked into that bar, and my world fucking flipped on its head. I loved being your friend since the moment I met you, and it just deepened into something more every second I spent with you." He rubs his thumb over my cheek, holding me in his hands like I'm something precious he can't bear to lose. "I fucking love you. And I'll love you 'till the day I die."

277

My heart is beating so fast, so hard I'm worried I'll pass out right now, and silence stretches between us, my ears muffled as I hear nothing but the sound of my heart pounding. I finally suck in a deep breath and shake my head. "Wow."

"Sweetheart," Mark murmurs, rubbing his thumb back and forth. "Now would be a good time to say whatever you're thinking."

My hand reaches up and I tap his cheek twice. "You're okay, I guess."

A low growl escapes his lips, his grip on my waist tightening as he steps closer. "Woman," he warns, his voice deep and rough.

I chuckle, loving how desperate he is to hear me say it back, and I wrap my arms around his neck, leaning on my tip-toes until our lips are stacked. "I love you, too, Mark," I tell him, my smile slipping as seriousness takes over and our eyes meet. "So fucking much."

He inhales sharply, his grip on me tightening. "Say it again."

I grin. "I love you."

"Again."

I chuckle. "I love—"

My words are cut off when Mark presses his lips to mine, making me yelp. He pulls me against him, a groan leaving his lips when mine part open and his tongue swipes against mine, kissing me so heated it leaves me dizzy.

"God, baby, you taste so damn *sweet*," Mark murmurs against my lips, kissing me again, his hand curling around my neck, his thumb resting on my cheek.

A throat clears beside us, and we pull apart, blinking in surprise. My eyes widen when I see who interrupted us.

"Ryan."

He quirks an eyebrow at me, his hand intertwined with a blonde woman's. "Holly," he replies before his eyes travel to Mark standing beside me. "And I assume this is Mark."

"Yeah," I reply as Mark's hand intertwines around mine, squeezing slightly.

Ryan nods again. "I thought he was just a friend?" he asks, seeming a little hurt.

"He was," I affirm.

He lets out a laugh. "I can see that."

I don't owe him an explanation. We only went on a few dates, but he was a nice guy and I don't want him to think I was being sleazy. "Ryan," I sigh. "When we went on a date, Mark was just a friend. He was actually helping me, well… date you."

He lets out a scoff. "He did a fantastic job."

Mark's hand tightens on mine and I shake my head. "I ended up catching feelings for him instead," I tell Ryan. "That's why I ended things with you. You were great, but…" I lift my head, glancing up at Mark, seeing his lips lift a little in the corners. "You weren't him." I look at Ryan again, lifting my shoulder. "For what it's worth, I'm sorry."

"Don't be," he says, his eyes flicking between Mark and I. "You seem really happy."

My shoulders drop, a smile curling my lips. "Yeah. I am."

He nods. "And I started dating too," he says, glancing at his date. "This is Freya. Freya, this is Holly."

"Nice to meet you," I say, flashing her a smile.

"Nice to meet you, too," she replies.

Ryan swallows, nodding at me. "It was nice to see you," he says.

"You too."

Pressing his lips together, he glances at Mark and then at me and sighs, giving me a warm smile. "I hope you have a good life, Holly."

He tips his chin before walking ahead, my eyes fixed on the back of his head. He was a great guy, but Mark is the only one I want. The only man I thought of whenever we were on a date. The only one I can imagine spending the rest of my life with.

"I hate that guy," Mark murmurs beside me, making me laugh.

"He's a nice guy, Mark."

"Don't care," he says with a shrug. "He wants what's mine."

I arch a brow, pressing my lips together to hide how much I like the fact that he's jealous. I've never had a guy want me this badly before. "Wanted," I correct him. "He's dating someone else."

He sighs, knowing I'm right. "Still hated seeing you two on a date," he says, the muscles in his jaw clenching.

My lips lift, remembering that very first date, how Mark stole my attention when he walked into the restaurant, and how he told me he just came to 'check on me' and how it might not have been the whole truth.

I tilt my head. "You liked me back then?"

He shrugs. "Think so," he says. "I can't remember a time when I didn't. It just sort of melted into each other. There was a time in my life before you, and it was empty and gray and miserable." He pauses, staring into my eyes. "And then there was a time after you walked into my bar, and everything became light, easy and so much fucking better." He shakes his head. "I can barely remember my life before you came into it."

I've never meant this much to someone before, and I don't know what to do about it. I've never loved anyone, but I know without a fact that this... this feeling in my chest, the way I feel whenever his eyes meet mine, that this is love. This is what was missing from my life. And I couldn't be happier that I found it.

Mark's hand squeezes mine, pulling me from my thoughts. "Let's go, Bambi."

We cross the street, and the sight of the sleigh makes my heart thud with every step we take. I still can't believe he did this for me. I don't know how he pulled it off, since Christmas has passed, but I don't care about the logistics. I just care that he loves me enough to do this for me, even if he hates everything to do with Christmas.

Mark opens the door for me, helping me onto the sleigh before he climbs in after me, my head resting on his shoulder as we start to trot on the street. The lights shine as we make our way, and I glance up at Mark, feeling my heart so full.

"I can't believe you did this for me."

He laughs, his eyes meeting mine. "Dear god, neither can I."

I smirk. "You know you're going to have to do this every year now, right?" I tease.

His laugh dies down as his gaze meets mine, his voice low and serious. "As long as I get to keep you… I can't fucking wait."

Epilogue

— Mark —

"Santa came! Santa came!"

"And daddy didn't." With a groan, I roll off my wife, my dick shriveling up at the sound of my five-year-old daughter running up the stairs.

She still doesn't understand the concept of don't wake mommy and daddy when they're sleeping. And knocking? She doesn't even acknowledge it.

Which is why I pull my boxers on and pull the sheets up as quickly as I can before the door is pushed open.

Her little excited breaths come out choppy as she jumps up on the bed, almost crushing my balls in the process. "Daddy, Mommy, Santa came while we were sleeping," she says, panting just like Murray does. It's kinda funny how she imitates him sometimes. "And he left *so* many presents," she says, opening her arms as wide as they can go.

My brows furrow. "Why does that fat bastard keep breaking into our house?"

My daughter gasps. "Daddy," she chastises, a small frown appearing on her lips. "Don't call him that."

I chuckle, shaking my head. "Sorry, princess."

Holly smiles at our daughter, opening her arms to hold her. "How many presents?" she says in that adorable excited voice I love so much.

"So many," our daughter repeats with a sigh, replicating her mother's. It's crazy how much they're alike, given that she's not biologically ours. Holly's dream was to adopt, to give a child the opportunity that she never got to have, and two years ago, this little girl came into our life.

She might not be biologically ours, but she's ours in every other way. Knew it as soon as I looked into her eyes, knew it when I first heard her little laugh, knew it as soon as she wrapped her little fingers around mine. She's our daughter. And she acts just like her mother. She has Holly's spirit, big brown eyes, and the same ridiculous love for Christmas as my wife.

"Really?" Holly gasps. "Are there any for us?"

"I don't know," Emma says with a shrug from her little shoulders. "I wanted to wait for you."

God, I love this little girl. She's as sweet as her mother, so kind and nice and I'm so fucking lucky. Can't help but smile as I watch my two favorite girls interacting, smiling, happy, excited. This is everything I didn't know I wanted. Christ, I can't believe this is my life.

It wasn't long ago that I thought I would end up alone. And if I'm honest, I was fine with it. All I thought I needed was the bar, my dog, and Mia. But I was so fucking wrong. I didn't know how much my life would change in the span of a few years.

And I'm so fucking lucky this girl walked into my bar six years ago.

"Should we go and open them?" my beautiful wife asks, tickling my daughter's side.

Her little giggles are like sunlight, lighting up the dark room. "Yes," she says, kicking her feet when the tickles get too much.

"Careful with mommy's belly, princess," I tell her, placing a hand over Holly's swollen belly. We weren't expecting to get pregnant so soon, but it just happened, and honestly, I couldn't be happier about it. Two kids is going to be a ton of work, but I know it'll be worth it.

"Oh yeah," she chuckles. "My baby sister is in there." Her little finger pokes at Holly's belly.

"That's right," I say, leaning down to press a kiss to her soft belly. "Your sister is so excited to meet you, Charlotte."

Holly smiles down at me, the name still bringing an ache to my chest. When Mia found out we were naming our daughter after Charles, she cried. Tears were streaming down her face as she clutched my face in her hands and kissed my forehead, thanking me. I nodded, unable to say anything, wishing he were here, wishing he could have met my daughters.

"Have you woken up Grandma yet?" I ask Emma, tapping on her nose.

She chuckles, wiping her nose and nodding. "She said she was tired."

I nod, pressing my lips together. She's tired a lot recently, and it pains me to think she might not stick around for long. My eyes sting and I blink, trying to handle my emotions.

Fuck.

"Okay, let's go," I say, lifting out of bed, watching as Emma and Holly rush out of the room, holding hands before they head downstairs. Pulling my pajama pants on, I leave my room, knocking on Mia's door twice before opening it slightly.

She's awake, propped up in bed watching TV, and her lips curve into a smile when she sees me.

"Merry Christmas, Mia," I say with a smile as I approach her.

She taps my cheek, smiling up at me. "There was a time where you'd rather die than say that."

I chuckle, agreeing with her. "That was a long time ago," I affirm, knowing ever since Holly has been in my life, I don't despise the holiday as I once did. "We're opening presents," I tell her. "You want to come down?"

Her face lights up. "I'd love to. Watching that little girl open presents is the best feeling in the world."

Couldn't agree more.

"Then we better hurry before she opens them all without us," I say with a laugh as I help Mia out of bed, wrapping her arm around mine as we both make our way down the stairs, seeing Emma sitting on Holly's lap as they laugh together, Murray's tail wagging as he sits beside them, wearing a red Christmas hat.

"Kinda thought she would have opened them all by now," I admit with a smirk, helping Mia sit down on the couch.

"She wanted to wait for Mia," Holly says with a smile. Our daughter has the biggest heart. Breaks mine how someone could have abandoned her when she's everything we've wanted.

"Gosh, there's so many presents," Mia says with a laugh, poking at Emma's cheek. "Santa must be rich, huh?"

I hum, crossing my arms as I see the mass amount of gifts under the tree. "Or his wife stole his credit card," I say with a smirk as I sit down beside Holly, leaning down to kiss her.

"Just look how happy she is," my wife says, her eyes shining with admiration as we watch our daughter fawn over the gifts, running back and forth to grab everyone's gifts, placing them in a pile in front of us.

Yeah, it's hard to feel anything but joy watching her adorable smile.

Holly glances up at me with tears in her eyes. "Thank you."

My brows knit together. "For what, sweetheart?"

She shakes her head, her glassy eyes meeting mine. "For being my family when I had none. For loving me the way I have always wanted to be loved. For giving me her," she says, glancing at Emma, who's still collecting everyone's gifts. "And her," my wife says, rubbing her belly. "For making me happy every single day of our lives."

Christ. Seeing my wife cry has never been easy, and my chest aches, cracking open as I hear her words of gratitude over what is the easiest thing in the world to do. I clutch her face in my hands, looking into her eyes

287

as I say, "It's my honor to love you, Holly. You came into my life and made every aspect of it ten times better. I would have never had any of this if it wasn't for you. You don't need to thank me. I will love you for the rest of our days and beyond," I say, her eyes fluttering closed when I lean down to kiss her. "Merry Christmas, Bambi," I whisper against her lips.

"Merry Christmas, Grinch."

My lips twitch at the nickname she gave me way back when we met. "Thank you for my family, sweetheart."

"You're welcome," she says with the sweetest smile.

And to think none of this would have happened if she hadn't walked into my bar, been stood up, and gotten drunk off her ass.

"I'm so fucking happy you suck at dating."

She arches a brow. "Excuse me?"

A laugh bubbles out of me as I shake my head. "Nothing, baby. Just kiss me."

Her face settles into a smile and she wraps her arms around my neck. "Gladly."

The End

Acknowledgements

First of all, I would like to thank you, reader, for taking a chance on me and picking up *Holly's Jolly Christmas*. Whether this is the first book of mine you've picked up or you've been with me since the beginning, I'm endlessly grateful for your support. Every like, comment and message keep me motivated to write the stories I love for you guys.

To my Patreon members, who have been there for every behind-the-scenes moment, from early teasers to sneak peeks, I can't thank you enough. Your feedback, enthusiasm, and support make a huge difference, and I'm incredibly lucky to have such an amazing community backing me.

A big thank you to Cassidy for editing this book and making it truly that much better.

And finally, I hope you loved Holly's Jolly Christmas and that you continue to stick with me through all the new books to come. Your support allows me to keep doing what I love, and for that, I'll always be thankful.

About the Author

Stephanie Alves is an avid reader and writer of smutty, contemporary romance books. She was born in England, but was raised by her loud Portuguese parents. She can speak both languages fluently, though she tends to mix both languages when speaking. She loves to write romantic comedies with happy endings, witty banter and sizzling chemistry that will make you blush. When she's not writing, she can be found either reading, or watching rom coms with her two adorable dogs cuddled up beside her.

You can find her here:
Instagram.com/Stephanie.alves_author
Stephaniealvesauthor.com

Printed in Dunstable, United Kingdom

71512811R10170